BLOOD AND SECRETS

THE FREELANCE VAMPIRE™
BOOK SIX

MICHAEL ANDERLE

LMBPN® Publishing
2375 E. Tropicana Avenue, Suite 8-305
Las Vegas, Nevada 89119 USA

Version 1.00, February 2026
ebook ISBN: 979-8-89354-876-1
Print ISBN: 979-8-89354-877-8

THE BLOOD AND SECRETS TEAM

Thanks to the JIT Readers
Christopher Gilliard
Wendy L Bonell
Diane L. Smith
Zacc Pelter
Dorothy Lloyd
Peter Manis
Jeff Goode
Jan Hunnicutt

Editor
The SkyFyre Editing Team

CHAPTER ONE

TATIANA

I checked my watch. The private business dinner would not finish for another hour. Already, it took every ounce of my willpower not to yawn as I stood at the door to the event room.

I peeked into the lobby of the Swan Hotel, where a chandelier reflected the warm glow of lamps. The space had a colonial feel with modern flourishes. Only one person occupied the lobby, a woman behind the front desk. Who *was* yawning.

I looked away to avoid doing the same. Too late. I caught the yawn and hid it behind my hand, hoping my client and her friends at the table on the other side of the room didn't notice.

Adeline Pike, forty-four years old and the well-established CEO of a high-end fashion magazine, sat at the table's head, surrounded by colleagues and connections. During my research earlier in the week, I'd flipped through several issues of her magazine. Pike was known for targeting New England residents with padded wallets, promoting classic, timeless styles with a touch of flair.

The magazine subscription cost more than I spent on coffee in a week, which was a good sign for me. She could pay me well to stand here and wait for something to happen, hoping that nothing did. Either way, she'd already advanced half the contracted fee upfront. I'd have the other half in an hour.

My client suspected a former business partner of hers might show up and try to make a scene. Hence, my presence at her otherwise private dinner. I wouldn't have usually taken a small job like this myself, but in recent months, I'd had so many clients that my entire staff, including my two new part-time guys, were busy tonight with other jobs.

I spent my time glancing into the hotel lobby and back at Ms. Pike and her guests. They spoke in low voices, laughing occasionally. All were well-dressed, expressing themselves in a variety of textures and colors that brightened the room.

I wore all black, my hair pulled back into my usual ponytail. I was armed only with a small handgun in my purse. The situation probably wouldn't require it, and I had my military training and honed instincts to kick in if things got gnarly.

Ms. Pike wore a pleasant smile as she conversed with clients and employees. Her skin was so smooth, I had almost asked about her skin care routine the first time we met a week ago. Her soft brown hair curled against her jaw as she lifted a glass of wine to her lips.

A glass of wine sounded nice.

In an hour, I reminded myself.

The glasses were close to empty and the plates nearly cleared when a tall man sailed into the room, red-faced and grumbling, "There you are! Meeting with everyone behind my back, are you? You know the magazine is still mine. I don't care if you're icing me out!"

The guests at the table started, shooting glances at one another and Ms. Pike. My client remained still, her expression unreadable.

I tapped the man's shoulder and cleared my throat. "Mr. Spencer, is it?"

He turned and demanded, "What do you want?"

I smiled. "I'm here to escort you out. Please come with me."

His face flushed redder. "I'm staying right here until Adeline explains herself!" He whirled, wagging an accusatory finger. He was about to go on when I interrupted.

"I'm afraid not. You weren't invited, and it's my job to see that you don't interrupt further. You can come with me, or we can do this the hard way."

His eyes flashed, and he turned his finger to my face. "Try it, missy!"

I needed no further encouragement. I locked a hand around his arm. My grip was tighter and my hold stronger than he expected. I was used to being underestimated, both physically and in other qualities.

"Hold on now, wait!" he yelped as I hauled him from the room. I closed the door behind us and flashed the woman behind the desk a smile as if to say, *I have everything handled.*

The younger woman watched, wide-eyed and unblinking, like a cat. She didn't say anything as I escorted Mr. Spencer through the lobby and out the front door. I released him outside, under the hotel's awning, and it felt like taking the trash out.

Mr. Spencer brushed himself off, shaking with ire. "You don't know what you're interfering with! She owes me a lot of money!"

"Maybe she does, but she hired me to ensure that you don't make a scene. Be on your way, Mr. Spencer, if you know what's good for you."

My curiosity about the drama between Mr. Spencer and Adeline Pike was piqued, but that wasn't part of my job. He blustered incoherently before turning on his heel and stomping down the street. He hailed a cab, then snapped the address of his destination at the driver.

I remained on the sidewalk, arms crossed, breathing in the cool night air. The task had been so simple that I wanted to yawn. I couldn't help but miss the bigger cases I used to work with JD, or Marcus Smith, as others knew him. Even though this job had been easy as pie, I wished he were here.

I had not heard from Jackson—or Jordan, as his real name turned out to be—since December, when the letter he left me in his abandoned house declared he'd gone somewhere to lay low for a while. He had given no indication of how long that would be or where he had gone.

I couldn't blame him after the incident with Victor Hume, a tech scientist who'd been secretly experimenting on enhanced humans like JD. It was now the middle of May, and JD had not sent word, not even a hint as to where he was or how he was faring. I had to admit it got under my skin. My curiosity itched. A voice in the back of my mind had been whispering for weeks and was now shouting, *It's time to move on!*

I wanted to know more about who and *what* he was. I wanted his full story, but mostly, I wanted my friend and colleague back. I missed the complicated cases, following a string of clues until I found a culprit hiding behind a curtain. In one case, the curtain had been literal. I'd had a few cases since December that had almost been as much fun, but working them without JD had not been the same.

Despite my job not having the same flavor as before, it was nice to have a social life again. I had more time to myself and my friends. I got a massage every week and went to boxing classes with Margo.

I had dinner with my mother more often, and I'd made a new friend at the gym, a fitness influencer named Valerie. I took my employees out to dinner every quarter, and hanging with our office cat, Linda's pet Whiskers, had almost convinced me to get a cat of my own.

Getting a cat was not the best idea for me, though, since I stayed out of my apartment as much as possible. JD had only spent one night with me there, but he still haunted one side of the bed, and the kitchen where he had cooked me an amazing Italian dinner. Without him, the place felt empty and quiet.

It didn't help that I went to the same office every day without him showing up, a basket of fresh-baked goods on his arm. I drank the same caramel lattes and wished he were the one bringing them to me. I made excuses to my staff regarding his whereabouts. Those excuses could only go on for so long, but I couldn't tell them the truth. Especially when I knew so little of it myself.

I banished all thoughts of JD and returned inside, where the dinner guests were disbanding. Ms. Pike approached me with soft eyes and a tentative smile. "Thank you, Miss Sterling. I knew you were the right person for the job. You may be hearing from me again."

I smiled back. "Of course, Ms. Pike. It was a pleasure." Escorting a douchebag to the street was always a pleasure, a spark of satisfaction that never grew old.

"I have a few friends who could use your services at their events. I will pass your information along. I'll have the rest of your payment wired immediately. Goodnight, Miss Sterling."

I echoed her goodnight and waited until she left the hotel in a chauffeured car. Mr. Spencer had not returned to make trouble for her, so my job was finished.

My car was parked down the street. I was up for the stroll, since the night air was pleasant and the streetlights gave a warm, inviting glow. As I passed a row of shop windows, my phone buzzed in my back pocket. The message was from my mother.

What do you want to do for your birthday next weekend?

I nearly groaned. I wasn't a big fan of birthdays, especially my own. However, my mother's vast, generous heart could not let a single birthday of mine pass without fuss. When I was a child, every birthday party had a theme. Six, cowgirls in the Old West. Seven, Wizard of Oz. Eight, cowgirls again—I had a horse phase.

I knew I was lucky to have parents who celebrated me so well, but this year, I wanted something simple. My mom wouldn't like it, but it was not her birthday.

Let's order something in. Watch TV.

I almost added, *and let's not remind anyone it's my birthday*, but that would only inspire her to do the opposite. My mother would probably sigh on her sofa while reading this text, then go to her favorite bakery's website to order a customized cake. If a cute man was working at the bakery when she picked it up, she would probably give him my number. "You're not getting any younger, Tati!"

My mid-thirties were looming, with a "Your biological clock is counting down" message blaring in red. I wasn't even sure I wanted children, and I sure as hell wasn't going to marry below my standards to do so.

I would let my mom order cake and give my number to the men she thought were attractive, as long as Thai food was on the menu and we re-watched one of the Audrey Hepburn movies we'd loved when I was a kid.

I shook my head, smiling, as I dug in my pocket for the key to the Mercedes I'd driven here.

I still couldn't quite call it my car, though I'd been driving it for five months now. I didn't like the constant reminder of JD, but his car was much nicer than my Nissan. My mother's car broke down last week, and it helped that I'd been able to lend her mine. So, JD's Mercedes it was.

"Excuse me, Miss Sterling."

I turned from the driver's side door toward the husky female voice. A tall, slim woman left the sidewalk and crossed the street toward me. Her chestnut hair was pulled back into a tight knot, her angular features pristine and unblemished. She wore a dark green jacket and black slacks. A string of pearls adorned her neck.

She was beautiful, not only in her appearance but in her easy stride. She almost seemed to *glide* toward me.

"Yes?" I asked, wondering how this woman knew me. I would have remembered her if we'd met before.

"We have been trying to get in touch with your office for weeks."

Who was "we?" It sounded like a job.

"Are you looking for security?" I asked, wondering if she had gotten the wrong person.

A small smile parted her lips. "Something like that." She extended a hand. "My name is Jessamine Lane." The woman wore thin, black gloves, which I thought was odd in May. Even through the glove, her touch was cold. Maybe she had bad circulation.

"Tatiana," I responded, not recognizing her name.

Her dark eyes glinted. "I know."

I couldn't decide how I felt about the woman. I was used to reading people within seconds of meeting them. Sometimes I was wrong, but generally, I was a good judge of character.

The glint in Jessamine's dark eyes was almost predatory. Despite my military training and the fact that I owned a security firm, I suddenly felt as if *I* was prey being cornered. The feeling did not sit well with me, yet I did not have the instinct to either run or fight. Rather, I wanted to draw closer to her. I wanted to shake her hand again, feel the cold press of her fingers against mine.

Jessamine drew her hand back, a knowing look in her eyes.

"I am not working now, but you are welcome to come by my office on Monday. We can discuss whatever your needs are then." I wasn't a fan of being approached on the street about a job. I was further perplexed that she had not contacted me through Linda.

My secretary wasn't the most organized person in the world, but she didn't like me missing out on jobs. More money in my pockets meant more in hers. Linda had also been busier than usual with bookings, so maybe she had missed one.

It was odd that the woman found me here. Had she been

following me, or was it a coincidence that she'd seen me walking down the street and, having been trying to contact me, took her chance?

"Very well. Better to have the conversation indoors, anyway," the woman drawled. She reached into a small purse dangling from one shoulder and withdrew a slim card.

I peered at the contact card, angling it so I could see it under a streetlamp. The card was dark green with gold lettering that read "Rose Conclave" beneath a simple, elegant logo of a rose. On the other side of the card was a phone number.

I didn't recognize the card or number. Usually, when I received new clients, I had at least heard of them or the organization they represented. They ranged from fashion magazine CEOs like Ms. Pike to senators and news anchors.

"We understand that you know Jordan Davenport. Perhaps you will be able to tell us where he has disappeared to."

Jessamine said these words as I was still examining the card. Shock rattled through me at hearing JD's name. However, when I looked up to respond with my jaw hanging open, the woman had vanished.

CHAPTER TWO

TATIANA

I was the first into the office Monday morning, as usual, and headed straight for the bathroom to change from my workout clothes into something professional. The sun was cresting the horizon when I settled behind my desk, basking in the silence before the others arrived.

I'd spent my Sunday cleaning my apartment and running errands, then joining my new friend Valerie for dinner. I'd also thought a lot about Jessamine Lane and worried more than I liked to admit about JD.

Few people in the world knew Jackson's real name was Jordan, as far as I could tell. Jessamine, whoever she was, had tracked me down, hoping to find him through me. She would be disappointed when she learned I hadn't heard a peep from my business partner since Christmas. That is, if she showed up today.

While waiting for Linda to arrive so I could ask if Ms. Lane had been trying to contact us over the last few weeks, I got to the admin work. The payment from Ms. Pike had come through, and I had other clients to follow up with. Two of my employees had finished security jobs over the weekend and would come in today to report.

I kept glancing at the Rose Conclave business card on my desk. I'd spent last night researching them online but had come up with nothing substantial. It was time I called in another favor to my old friend Jake Molina, who I'd met during my deployment days.

Jake had been a godsend on several occasions since I'd opened my security firm and was now basically another part-time employee. However, the only times I saw him were the nights I treated him to sliders at our favorite Brazilian place.

I sent a message asking if he could look into the Rose Conclave and included photos of the business card. After I finished, the office door opened, and Linda bustled in, with Whiskers in a bright pink harness at her heels.

"Good morning," I called through my office into the main room.

Linda replied with a cheery good morning. I responded to a few emails, then went to ask her if Jessamine Lane had been trying to contact us.

"I don't think so. I don't recognize the name," Linda replied, brow furrowing.

"What about a group called the Rose Conclave?"

"Let me check."

Linda scrolled through her inbox and work phone call log, but came up with nothing. "We had several spam calls over the last few weeks, though. Every time I answered, they asked for the boss. When I told them you were busy and asked if they would like to leave a message, they hung up."

Weird. I couldn't be expected to pick up every call, especially when I'd hired someone to do it for me. "What's the number?"

Linda told me, and sure enough, it matched the number on the card.

"Well, a woman from this Rose Conclave might show up

today," I told her. "If she does, have her meet me in the conference room."

Linda nodded, then a sparkle of amusement and scheming entered her eyes. "So...are you looking forward to your date tonight?"

I was halfway across the room when I turned, frowning. "How do you know about that?"

Linda opened her top desk drawer and drew out a nail file. "Your mother told me."

Of course. As Amy Sterling's only child, I was her favorite thing to talk about. I loved my mother more than anyone else on the planet, but sometimes I wished my whole life wasn't an open book for her friends.

"It's nothing. Only dinner."

"He's cute."

I wasn't surprised my mother had shown Linda a photo. If not for Linda mentioning it, I might have forgotten I had a date.

My mom had been trying to set me up for weeks with Landon Greene, a nephew of a family friend. I had finally agreed, if only to get her off my back. We had texted some, and he seemed pleasant enough. When he had asked me out to my favorite Brazilian place, probably a tip from my mom, I couldn't turn it down.

I supposed it would be nice to get back out there.

He *was* cute, too. Tall with wavy brown hair and pleasant hazel eyes. Or so he had looked in the photos my mom had sent me. Who needed dating apps when they had Amy Sterling? He was no JD, though.

I pushed the thought from my mind. I didn't have to continue the conversation with Linda, because the door opened again, and two men entered.

"I didn't think you were coming in until the afternoon. If I'd known you would be here early, I would have brought sandwiches!" Linda greeted them.

The taller of the two leaned against the doorframe, crossing his arms and smiling fiendishly. "Shucks, Linda, I know you missed me. Have you broken up with Harry yet? I'm still dying to take you on a real date. Somewhere fancy, where I can show you the whole city."

Linda swatted him. "Oh, quiet, Brando. You know you're far too young for me."

Brandon Swale would flirt with a pole if he could. He was a few years older than me, and Linda was right. Far too young for her. Besides, she and the landlord, Harry, had been dating for months. Linda had a history of growing bored with her suitors after the honeymoon phase ended, but she and Harry didn't seem to be getting close to that.

Gross. Last weekend, she'd sent me photos from their vacation at Harry's timeshare in Hawaii, and she'd happened to catch her boyfriend wearing a Speedo in the background. It was an image I wanted to scrub from my brain.

Brandon was considerably younger and hotter, though not to my taste. I'd made it clear from the moment I hired him as a part-time security guard that there would be no funny business. I'd had enough flirting from JD when we worked together.

Miraculously, Brandon had listened and turned all his flirtations onto Linda. It worked, because she often brought him and our other part-time guy breakfast sandwiches.

The other arrival was an old buddy of his, Marc Bradford. They called each other Brando and Marco. They'd come as a package deal and couldn't be more opposite.

Marco stood closer to me, subdued and quiet. He turned to hand me a report inside a manila envelope. "Sheftel job finished this weekend. Went off without a hitch." He was old-school like that, always typing up and printing everything.

"Thank you, Marco," I told him, accepting the envelope. I would look over the report later, then assign them to new jobs when they came up.

Brandon looked like he wanted to keep his conversation with Linda going, but Marc interrupted. "Time we got out of here, Brando. How's brunch sound?"

"Are you paying?" Brandon replied, laughing as they went for the door. They were hardly into the hallway when Brandon whistled. "Well, hello there." He stuck out his hand to someone I couldn't see. "Brandon Swale, at your service. Whatever security you need, I'm your man. I've been running this place like a well-oiled machine for years."

A crisp, cool voice replied, "I'm here to see your boss."

Jessamine Lane. She did not shake Brandon's hand. I felt an ounce of admiration toward her for not succumbing to Brandon's charm.

Brandon leaned against the wall. "You're in luck. I am the boss. Why don't we take this meeting inside, and you can tell me more about yourself?"

Marc stepped between Brandon and the woman. "Please excuse my friend's behavior. Our boss is through here."

"Thank you," Jessamine replied coolly.

Marc squeezed Brandon's shoulders from behind. "Let's go before you make an idiot of yourself and embarrass our boss."

After the part-time guys left, muttering about where they would go for brunch, Jessamine's lithe form filled the doorway. She looked much the same as she had Saturday night when we first met, though her clothes were different. That same dark, sharp gaze swept the front room, lingering longest on Whiskers.

"Good morning," Linda chirped. "You must be the lady Tatiana says has been trying to contact us. I apologize, but you didn't want to speak to me and wouldn't leave a message, so—"

"That's quite all right, Linda," I cut in, offering Jessamine a smile. Her gaze slid to me and stayed. Though she wasn't acting rude, nothing friendly showed in her face. I nodded toward the meeting room. "Shall we?"

Jessamine nodded and followed me. Before I closed the

meeting room door, I asked Linda, "Would you mind running out and getting us coffee? My treat."

Linda beamed. "Of course!"

I preferred the office empty if Jessamine and I were going to talk about Jordan.

"Wise move," she remarked after Linda left, and our only listener was her cat. Jessamine set a small purse on the table, then smoothed her skirt as she sat. "You have interesting employees here."

"Linda is a family friend, and those men you met are part-time." I didn't know why I was explaining. Something about Jessamine's presence made me want to. She reminded me of high school and college, when I'd come across women who were much cooler than me and felt the need to explain my every decision.

I reminded myself that she had come to me and wanted my help. She didn't know yet that I couldn't help her. "Anything to drink? Coffee? Water?"

"No, thank you. This won't take long."

I knew then that Jessamine wasn't here to hire me for anything. She only wanted to know about JD. I sat opposite her and braced myself.

Jessamine folded her hands and rested them on the table. Her sharp, almond-shaped nails were painted deep red, like blood. "I am a member of a council called the Rose Conclave. We exist to protect and preserve the right and ability to exist without harm for people like Jordan Davenport. Unfortunately, part of this mission means keeping the same people in line."

I raised an eyebrow, uncertain where she was going.

"Mr. Davenport has caused us a lot of trouble, you see. He's been too flashy, and we have had to cover up one too many of his messes. We understand you were part of the last."

I bristled. Was she talking about the ordeal with Victor Hume? That mess had hardly been JD's. In fact, he and I finding out the truth of the case stopped Hume from further experimenting on innocent anomalies, as he called them. I preferred to call them "enhanced humans."

I stumbled, not knowing what to say, and Jessamine continued. "Let me make myself quite clear, Miss Sterling, so that there is no room for misunderstanding. I am like JD, and the Conclave is made up of our kind. We take care of vampire affairs."

The blood drained from my face.

I'd known JD was enhanced but had no idea what, exactly, he was. Vampires weren't *real*. This woman had been hired to prank me. Was Dan O'Shay, my former business rival, behind this?

Then, I reminded myself of the transformation I'd seen in Lola Park. Enhanced individuals who could shift into other forms were real, so who was to say vampires weren't, too?

"Of course, we don't prefer the term 'vampire.' It is a human-given term, though I suppose it is better than 'bloodsucker' or 'nightwalker.'"

I swallowed. "What would you like to be called, then?"

Jessamine waved off the thought. "That doesn't matter, as hopefully, you won't be using any terms."

I reeled. A vampire had approached me in the night, and I'd felt like prey cornered by a predator. Perhaps I had not been far off.

"I see this is a lot for you to take in," Jessamine observed. "Would you like me to prove it?"

It took me a heartbeat or two to realize she was joking. I laughed nervously. "That's all right. I believe you. I'm just… processing."

"I'm afraid there isn't much time for that."

Because my secretary would be back with coffee soon? I heard the phone ringing in the front room but ignored it. "If you look after vampire affairs, does that mean…"

"That Jordan Davenport is a vampire? Yes." Jessamine seemed to be growing impatient.

Suddenly, dozens of oddities I'd noticed about Jordan began

to make sense. His surprising strength and speed, the way his eyes grew wide with hunger, the flask he carried around and drank from. It wasn't alcohol on the job. It was *blood*.

My gut stirred. I didn't blame him for not telling me. It was a crazy thing to say, and some aspects of his reality weren't pretty.

He didn't want me thinking he was a monster.

His acting gigs made more sense, too. If he'd been alive since the early 1700s, as his real name suggests, he had probably grown restless and bored. Hiring himself out for short jobs meant he could have human and, yes, sometimes sexual, connections, then cut them off.

He could live as Marcus Smith in one way and Jackson Dale Shade in another, all while really being Jordan Davenport. But he'd made mistakes. Working for me longer than he had intended. Taking me as a lover. Worst of all, becoming my friend.

I put him in this danger, I realized, feeling sick.

Jessamine watched me from across the table with deep intent. She unfolded her hands and tapped her long nails on the table. "The Conclave got in touch with Jordan through a former member of ours back in December. He was laying low at one of his safe houses. He has since disappeared, and we are hoping he is not causing trouble. We figured you might know something, so here I am. I'm quite busy, Miss Sterling, so I hope you can help me quickly."

"If you haven't heard from him, wouldn't that mean he's not causing trouble?" I asked.

Jessamine's eyes narrowed, but she said nothing.

I had a feeling something more was going on. They wanted to find JD not only to keep him in check, but for another reason. Finally, I answered, "I also haven't seen or heard from JD since December. I could have told you as much Saturday night."

Jessamine had wasted her time coming here to speak to me. Or maybe this wasn't about information. She'd wanted to meet me, maybe threaten me into not telling anyone about JD's true nature. All in the name of protecting and preserving.

I leaned back, considering. "I have no doubt part of your job is keeping you and your kind a secret. You don't like JD's theatrics because it risks exposing everyone."

Jessamine's face was tight and focused. She didn't reply.

"So if it is vital that you stay a secret, why have you come here to tell me all this?"

"You already know too much," Jessamine replied simply. "Jordan made a mistake getting involved with you. He never should have gotten so close. He knew the risks and the consequences, and he did it anyway."

I knew Jessamine was serious, but I couldn't help but feel special. JD knew he shouldn't have gotten close enough for me to learn the truth, but he had done it anyway.

"We will be acting accordingly," Jessamine added, rising.

"How so?" I countered, irritated at her vagueness.

Jessamine fixed me with a look similar to the one outside the Swan Hotel. Something predatory lurked beneath those eyes. I wondered how old she was. She appeared to be around my age, as JD did, but no telling how many decades or centuries she had walked the earth. "We can't force you to keep our secrets, but we can make your life very difficult if you were to share them."

She did not give me time to respond. She disappeared at a speed I could hardly register. I stood there bewildered as Linda bustled in, carrying two paper cups of coffee. "She's gone already? That was a quick meeting."

I nodded. "She got straight to the point."

And left me with about a dozen new questions.

CHAPTER THREE

TATIANA

Nothing helped me blow off steam better than a boxing session with Margo. During our shadowboxing warm-up, she noted, "You're wound tighter than a pissed-off rattlesnake. Anything you wanna talk about?"

"Nope," I replied, pounding my gloved fist into the flat of her hand.

"Punching it is, then," she mumbled back.

We had arrived at the boxing club fifteen minutes before the class started so the two of us could warm up. The instructor and a dozen other students soon joined. Margo and I remained silent during the class. By the end, I was drenched in sweat and beginning to feel better.

"Is it about your birthday?" Margo asked after chugging half her water bottle.

I did the same, wiping water from my mouth with the back of my hand. "How do you know about that?"

"Your mom texted everyone at the office, asking what we were planning. If I were you, I'd keep that locked up tight. No one needs to know such personal information."

I groaned. "Agree with you there, Margo. I'm glad you get it, but I'm sure Linda is already buying decorations for the office."

Margo cringed.

"She is, isn't she?" I asked.

A nod.

I groaned again.

Margo grinned. "Hey, it's a good thing to have people care about you that much. Though I'd feel more cared about if everyone pretended I was still in my twenties and knew I didn't like cake." She nudged me with her elbow. "If it's not your birthday, what is it?"

Aside from Jake, Margo was the most likely person I knew to take a secret to her grave. I was tempted to tell her about my conversation with Jessamine Lane, still unable to believe a vampire had been sitting in my office this morning.

More unbelievably, Jessamine wasn't the first vampire to do so. Many of my encounters with JD in the office made more sense now, and I recalled the strange friends he had kept. Were they all like him?

Despite wanting to fill Margo in, I decided against it. Instead, I told her, "I have a date tonight."

Margo laughed. "How awful for you, Tati."

"My mom set it up. He's a nice enough guy as far as I can tell, but..." I let the thought trail off.

Margo gave me a look but didn't say anything. She knew as well as everyone else that something had been growing between JD and me. However, I hadn't shared with the class that we had begun a relationship, only to have it dashed by the truth.

She winked as she stood to leave. "You were in the military, and now you own a security firm. You've put your life on the line more times than I can count since meeting you. I think you can handle a first date."

"It's the first date in the same week as my birthday double-whammy I can't handle." I smiled, getting up to leave with her. "See you at the office later?" I asked.

She nodded. "Aye-aye, boss." One of her jobs would finish up this week, then she would be in to report.

Outside the boxing club, we went our separate ways. The late afternoon sun poured across the street, reflecting on the building fronts. The air was warm enough to make my tank top and leggings comfortable, and a breeze relieved my flushed cheeks.

I headed to my car while checking my phone. Jake had responded to my request to look into the Rose Conclave.

Only thing I found was an old monastery in England. Once belonged to a Rose family, dating back to the 1600s.

He'd sent a photo of an aged stone building against an over-cast landscape. The function of the place was currently unknown.

I almost followed up with a request to look into Jessamine Lane, but decided against it. Jake already knew about shifters, but I would wait to reveal more, considering the vampire's warning. I wasn't afraid of her, but I didn't know what she wanted with JD yet. Until I knew more, I would keep this buttoned up tight.

I texted Jake back.

Thank you. This helps.

I would bank the information and hope something came of it later.

I opened the Mercedes and slid in, tossing my phone onto the passenger seat. As I turned on the radio, I decided to put all thoughts of vampires out of my mind.

It was time to get ready for my date.

***

The restaurant Landon Greene chose would normally be out of my budget, but the firm was doing well, and this was a date. *You deserve a nice night,* I kept telling myself as I did my makeup and hair, then got dressed. I wore my go-to date outfit—a black pencil skirt with tights and a simple black top. I brought a jacket in case it grew chilly. *The guy doesn't need to be your soulmate. Just have fun.*

The place couldn't have been more romantic, with moody lighting and tables set with a single rose in a vase. When I arrived, Landon was already seated. He rose to greet me, smiling pleasantly. He looked the same in person as he had in his photos. Nicer, even. Before JD, I might have thought him a very attractive man.

"Tatiana, good to meet you." He moved to hug me as I went for a handshake, and we did an awkward dance that ended with him holding my hand and patting my back. "I ordered a bottle already. If you don't like it, I'll be happy to order something different," he mentioned as he drew back and released my hand.

I smiled while he pulled out my chair. A waiter brought me a glass of water, then asked if we would like an appetizer. Landon ordered something while I said I still needed to look at the menu. I was feeling rusty. I hadn't been on a proper date in years. The "date" JD insisted we'd had before either of us had admitted our feelings didn't count.

Landon seemed to have already decided on what he was eating. He relaxed across from me. "So, Tatiana, I've heard you work for a security firm. You must see some exciting stuff."

I made myself smile over the menu. "I *own* a security firm, actually." I wasn't surprised my mother had told Landon's parents that I simply worked for one. Whatever made me seem impressive but not too intimidating.

Landon's eyes brightened. "Is that so? What led you into that area of expertise?"

I had expected small talk and was ready to answer mundane questions. Reminding myself of Margo's words earlier that day, I told Landon about my time in the military, then the few security jobs I'd had after.

"And why start your own firm? What about it gives you purpose?"

I leaned back, considering. "I suppose I've always wanted a job that helps people, but working security at the mall is a bit too dull, you know? I wanted to put my military training to use but be able to stay in one place. Near my mom. After my dad died a few years ago, I knew I wanted to spend as much time with her as possible."

Landon nodded. "I'm the same way. That's why I stayed in the D.C. area."

I asked him about his job. He was in his mid-thirties, never married, but was a divorce lawyer. "Not the most appealing part of law to go into, but there is no shortage of clientele."

"You must get some interesting clients," I mused.

He raised a wine glass and sipped. "Perhaps not as interesting as the ones you get."

He was right about that. Jessamine Lane's face flashed through my head. I glanced around the restaurant at the staff and several other couples. How many people like Jessamine existed in plain sight, adjusting their lives to blend in as well as possible?

The waiter brought our food, and as we began eating, Landon asked, "Hey, weren't you the one who found the stolen Washington sword from the National Gallery?"

I solved most of my cases under the radar, with no media attention. However, the case he mentioned was my last with JD before his disappearance, and the press had managed a snapshot of the two of us together. Some had speculated we were a power couple.

I banished the image from my mind and nodded. "That's me."

"And you have a partner at your company, right? Your mom said Sterling and Smith. I should have put together that Sterling was you. I guess I thought it was a coincidence."

I sipped my wine to keep my expression from faltering. "I started the company. My partner, Marcus Smith, came on last year." I didn't bother explaining that my mother had suggested I hire an actor, who typically made his money as an escort, to pretend he was my partner. Unfortunately, it was the best way to land clients who otherwise wouldn't give me, a woman, a second glance.

We spoke a bit longer about work and family. Landon told me where he went to school and his favorite travel destinations. Eventually, he stated, "This may seem too forward to ask, but we're not getting any younger, so I'll ask it anyway. Why did your last relationship end?"

We were moving past small talk quicker than I liked, which meant Landon was more serious about dating than I was. I hesitated, trying to figure out how best to answer. "Some things in his past came to light, and he decided it was better that we weren't together anymore."

I hoped Landon couldn't tell how hard it was for me to get those words out.

He gave me a soft smile. "I see. It isn't always easy moving on, is it?"

I was sure as hell trying. "How about yours?" I asked, if only to avoid talking more about JD.

"We were engaged, actually. For years, we had talked about having a family. After I proposed, though, she told me she didn't want to have kids anymore. It was a deal-breaker, so we separated. That was difficult at the time."

Proposals. Kids. All things people my age and far younger were focused on. Things my mother wished I prioritized more.

It was hard to do with everything going on. My job was no longer merely a purposeful way to earn money. I had a damn vampire showing up and warning me about spilling the secrets of a magical world I'd only learned about six months ago. My partner, friend, and one-time lover had vanished with no sign of when he might come back.

Landon Greene and I were living very different realities.

We finished our meals, and Landon quickly gave his card when the waiter came with the bill. "It was nice meeting you, Tatiana," he remarked after the bill was paid and we were free to go our separate ways. We stood on the sidewalk outside the downtown restaurant.

"Good to meet you too, Landon. Thank you for dinner."

He told me goodnight and went on his way. He was nice enough, but I couldn't stop thinking of JD. As I walked to my car, I realized Landon had said nothing about hoping to meet again. Was he not feeling it, either?

When I reached my car, I already had messages from my mother and Linda, asking how it was going. I would disappoint them both when I told them I probably wouldn't see Landon again. *No offense to the guy, but there was no spark.*

I slid into the car and closed the door behind me. It was only 7:30, and a big part of me wasn't ready to sit in my empty apartment. I turned in the opposite direction of home. If I couldn't get JD off my mind, I would do some digging. Jessamine and her Conclave could look into his disappearance all they wanted—and so could I.

CHAPTER FOUR

TATIANA

As expected, JD's mansion outside the city was dark when I pulled up the drive. It was set back from the street, and the moonlight illuminated the manicured grounds. It seemed he still had someone take care of the space. Maybe not inside, but certainly outside.

I killed the engine and got out. All the curtains were drawn across the windows as I approached the porch. I still had an extra key and used it to unlock the front door.

What am I doing here? I asked myself, closing the door behind me and slipping the key into my pocket. I hadn't been here since the day I learned JD was "lying low" for a while. I had seen no point in doing so and wasn't sure what the point was now.

JD was careful. If he didn't want to be found, he wouldn't be. I wasn't likely to find a clue in this house unless he had left one intentionally. Half of me hoped that when I arrived, I would find warm lights in the windows and JD in the kitchen, wearing a ridiculous apron and baking a competition-winning pastry.

No lights were on. No sweet scents drifted from the kitchen.

Where to start? Sheets covered the furniture. The books in his library had been removed. I remembered my first visit here and how I'd snooped through his office. I doubted he'd left anything important in there, and if he did, what were the chances I could access it now? He'd probably locked anything of value away.

I reached for a table lamp in the entryway, glad to find the electricity still on. The light made the place look less forlorn and eerie. My phone kept buzzing in my back pocket, and I was certain my mom and Linda had started a group chat about my date. I turned my text notifications off before heading through the house.

I went into the empty library first. The furniture was still covered, and the shelves were still empty. Dust covered both shelves and sheets. I walked across the room and opened the curtains, revealing the back portion of JD's property. From here, I could see the garage where he kept his prized collection of high-end sports cars.

I started at a sound and turned, then cried out and dove to the left as a fire poker barreled toward my head. It clanged against the windowsill, making me cringe. The figure wielding the poker whirled and swatted at me again. I evaded the blow, moving behind the arched back of the sofa. The fire poker swung and hit the furniture. Dust puffed up.

The room was too dark to see my attacker's face, but damn, he'd been sneaky. I lunged toward him, catching the poker as he swung again. I twisted it, along with his arm, and he cried out.

He staggered as I wrenched the poker from him, but I did not move to strike him. He put his hands up anyway. "Don't! Please don't hit me!"

"Who are you?" I demanded. I was sure I'd heard the voice before.

The man stepped back far enough that the moonlight coming through the window made him visible.

"Vinny?"

I recognized the man as JD's manager, though he was a lot more haggard than the last time I'd seen him. He wore a button-down shirt smudged with what looked like soot stains. The sleeves were rolled to his elbows, and the back of his shirt was untucked from his pants.

"Tatiana!" His eyes widened. "What are you doing here?"

I tossed the poker aside, certain he would not attempt to attack me again. "I could ask you the same. A 'hello' would have been a nicer greeting."

Vinny hesitated. "I came to pick something up. I doubt you were sent on the same errand as me." He flushed, realizing he'd said too much.

"Who sent you on an errand here?"

Vinny stammered, and I stepped toward him, locking my arms across my chest. "You've heard from JD."

"I… Well…" His face drained of color. "So what if I have?"

"Is he still in hiding?"

Vinny held my stare as if terrified of answering.

To help him along, I added, "Look, I only want to know that he's safe. I've had an extra-weird week, and JD seems to be coming up more than usual. Just tell me you've heard he's okay."

Vinny pulled a hand through his hair and nodded. "He's okay."

I sighed in relief, then turned and approached the sofa. I removed the sheet, balled it up, and tossed it into a corner. As I sat, Vinny added, "I've been coming here about once a month to make sure everything's still in order. That the place is secure and the grounds are being maintained."

JD wouldn't want overgrown grounds to signal to neighbors that no one was living here. He already had a strange enough presence as it was.

"And to pick something up," I reminded him.

"Yes, that's right. Some important paperwork, in case the wrong sort of people come and get it first." His look suggested that he thought I was the "wrong sort of people."

Well, it wasn't a lie to say I'd come to snoop through JD's

things, hoping for a clue to his whereabouts. Better I find it than Jessamine.

I frowned at Vinny. "Were you looking for important papers in the fireplace?"

"The fireplace?"

"Your shirt. Looks like you have soot on it."

"Oh, yes. Well, that was from the poker. I was upstairs in JD's office when I heard the front door open. I was sure someone had figured out the place was empty and was breaking in. Lots of valuable things to take from here, you know?"

Priceless paintings still hung on the walls. JD's cutlery was probably expensive, and he had a few nice pieces of glassware. "I had a key, and I wasn't planning on robbing the place." I leaned forward. "You said 'the wrong sort of people.' Have you heard from Jessamine, too?"

Vinny blinked. "I don't know who that is. A woman came by here the other night, though."

"Really?"

"I wasn't here, but she left a note." Vinny pulled a folded piece of paper from his back pocket and handed it to me.

I smoothed it on my lap. The words were written in elegant script. Vinny moved to an end table and switched on a lamp. Under the light, I noticed it wasn't black ink, but dark red.

This isn't ink.

My stomach turned as I read the message.

Game's over. Come out of your den, Fox.

A warning for JD to stop hiding. Or what? I wondered. What would Jessamine and the Conclave do to him? That is, if she'd left this message. It wasn't signed. "Wait, how do you know it was a woman if you weren't here?" I asked, looking up.

"I saw her on the camera footage," Vinny answered, as if it was obvious.

I stood. "Show me."

I wasn't surprised JD had hidden cameras, but I was

surprised to see how extensive his surveillance system was as Vinny pulled out his phone and opened an app. "JD has access to this, too. I bet he's been watching the place when he has a chance."

My heart skipped a beat. Was he watching Vinny and me now? Had he laughed at Vinny's poor attempt to knock me out with a fireplace poker? "He's asked me to occasionally look at the cameras to make sure the groundskeeper doesn't try to steal one of his cars."

On Vinny's phone, several videos played from different angles of the house. The date on the footage was Friday night. *The night before Jessamine came to me*, I realized.

A woman appeared. *That's her*. I watched in slack-jawed amazement as she approached the front door, tried the knob and found it locked, then simply *walked through*.

I blinked, thinking the camera must have glitched.

"What is she, a fucking ghost?"

Vinny didn't answer.

On the footage, Jessamine strolled through the house, apparently searching for something. She entered JD's office and looked through the drawers. She found nothing of significance. She swiped a finger along a dusty shelf and frowned.

Finally, she tore a piece of paper off a pad and sat at JD's desk. The same paper the note was on. From her slim purse, she withdrew a small inkwell and a quill.

Who the hell carried ink and a quill with them? An ancient vampire, that was who. My stomach turned at the thought of someone carrying a container of blood around to write notes with.

She scribbled the note, then returned her writing supplies to her purse.

She stood, searching the room until she stopped to regard a spot where I knew a painting hung. She was looking directly into a camera. Was it coincidence? I knew it wasn't when she held up the note as if allowing the person watching through the camera to read it. She then set it on the desk and left the room.

How had she known a camera was there?

I must have asked the question out loud, because Vinny replied, "Probably sensed it."

When the video feed stopped, he added, "No more footage. Cameras went blank and stayed that way for about five minutes. Enough time for her to root around a bit more, then get out."

Whatever Jessamine had used to break in and sense the camera, she must have also used it to temporarily disable the system. Why hadn't she disabled the cameras before? The answer was clear as I sank back onto the sofa. *She wanted JD to see her come in here.* Knowing he was not likely to return, she had held the note up for him to read.

"Well, was she this Jessamine you were talking about?" Vinny asked.

I nodded, then wondered if I had shared too much information. At least by coming here, I learned that Jessamine had already searched the place. It didn't look like she had come up with anything.

I twisted to face Vinny. "She came to my office. She told me what she was. What JD is."

Vinny paled.

"Are you one?"

"One what?"

"A…vampire?" I remembered what Jessamine mentioned about their kind not preferring the word, but I didn't know what other word to use.

At first, Vinny's face reflected shock and horror. Then he laughed nervously. "Fuck no, and I'm glad for it. Imagine having to live as one of them? A lot easier to blend in when you're…" He trailed off.

"When you're what, Vinny? You're enhanced, too, aren't you?"

He arched a brow. "Enhanced, eh? Is that what you're calling it?"

"Anomaly?"

Vinny frowned.

"Magical?"

"That's better."

"What are you?" I repeated.

"I'm a person, Miss Sterling."

I cringed. "Sorry, I only meant…"

He sat. "I know what you meant, and I'm a warlock. Usually vampires and witch-kind don't get along well, but I'm not exactly coven-bound, and JD isn't pals with his kind, either. So, we're sort of a likely pair when you think about it."

When *I* thought about it, the whole thing sounded ridiculous.

"Technically, I'm not even a full warlock. My powers don't go beyond basic spells and an elongated life span, but I still need to be careful. This lady who visited you, did she say anything other than her name and what she was?"

"She was looking for JD. Said she represented something called the Rose Conclave?"

Vinny's eyes widened. "Shit."

I waited.

"This is what JD was trying to avoid."

From the fear in Vinny's eyes, he seemed to think the Rose Conclave as dangerous to JD as the humans who wanted to experiment on enhanced individuals. "JD has always, at least as long as I've known him, wanted human connection. Who could blame him? He started acting so he could have that, if only for short periods of time. I'd seen him develop an attraction to some of his clients, but nothing like what he felt for you."

I bristled at the first part of his sentence, then my heart ached as he finished. I couldn't believe I'd fallen for an escort who was secretly a 1700s-born vampire.

"I told him he was getting too close, that the truth would

come out eventually. He wanted to tell you, I think. He was trying to come up with the best way to do it. Before, he kept the truth from you because he wanted to protect himself, but also you."

I was surprised when my eyes began to glaze. I blinked the emotion away.

"We magicals must protect one another. I didn't mean anything against you when I told him he shouldn't work for you anymore."

Suddenly, I was back in my apartment kitchen, and JD was telling me he wanted to leave my firm. It made sense that his friend and manager had recommended it. If JD had left sooner, maybe he wouldn't be hiding from human scientists and the Conclave.

"Some magicals protect their own kind better than others," Vinny explained. "Witches have covens, shifters have packs, and vampires have Conclaves. The strictest by far are the Conclaves. They're also the scariest and most ancient. Step out of line with them, and you'll be wishing you'd died decades ago."

The room suddenly felt chilled. I imagined Jessamine roaming this space and shook the image away.

I had a dozen questions about the world Vinny came from. For one, I wanted to know more about how a warlock had become a vampire actor's manager. But there were more important questions. "Is that all JD is doing? Hiding?"

Vinny paused. "I'm not sure."

"Do you know where he is?" When Vinny suddenly became very interested in a loose button on his shirt, I pushed him. "Tell me."

"At first, he went to his place in Switzerland. I know he isn't there anymore, but I don't know where he went. He did recently give me an address to send paperwork to."

"What kind of paperwork?"

"Legal documentation. Deeds, IDs, and so on. I doubt he would be staying in the same place, or at least not for long."

"Can I see it?"

Vinny's face hardened. "I don't think so. Look, JD sent me here to collect his things and send them as soon as I could. He ordered me not to show anything to anyone. I doubt he expected we would run into each other, but all the same."

Again, I wondered if JD was watching us on the cameras. "If you speak to him again, will you give him a message for me?"

Slowly, Vinny nodded.

I swallowed, trying not to sound too emotional. "Could you tell him that I hope he is okay? An-and that I miss him?"

Vinny's face softened. "I can do that."

"Thank you." I barely got the words out as I blinked away fresh tears.

Vinny stood as if ready to go. "It would be best if you didn't come back here. You should stay out of it from here on out. Go back to your life. Focus on your family and your work. For your own good and his, forget that you ever knew Jackson Dale Shade."

CHAPTER FIVE

TATIANA

Vinny didn't know me too well. I wasn't good at *staying out of it.*

I was determined to get to the bottom of this before Jessamine and whoever else was in her Conclave did. Vinny wasn't the only one of JD's friends I'd met. I had kept Beck's phone number after helping her with security last year.

Beck and JD had known each other for years, and now that I knew Jordan Davenport's true age, I wondered if Beck was like him. Maybe not a three-hundred-year-old vampire, but a friend for at least a few decades. They'd dated at one point, too. JD was the last man Beck had ever dated, as far as I knew. They had stayed in touch throughout the years, and I envied their mutual fondness.

I wasn't jealous of their former romantic connection, but of the fact that Beck knew things about JD he'd never shared with me. I didn't doubt that Beck knew his true nature.

I pushed away my envy and called her number, prepared to begin with something like, "This is Tatiana Sterling. I worked with JD. We met in November," certain she'd forgotten who I was.

It turned out I was mistaken.

"Tatiana Sterling. Isn't this a treat?" Beck greeted me when she answered the phone.

I was sitting in the Mercedes outside my apartment, not quite ready to go inside yet.

"Hi, Beck. I hope you're doing well. I know this will seem out of the blue, but—"

I didn't get to finish my sentence.

"If you're calling because you hope I can tell you something about JD's whereabouts, I'm going to disappoint you. I know he disappeared, and I don't know exactly why. I do know that he wouldn't vanish unless he thought he was in real danger." She paused before adding, "Or because he's trying to protect you."

"This isn't about me being overly curious or missing him," I hurried to explain. At least, not totally about that. "Someone else is looking for him, and I have a feeling it won't be pretty when they find him."

She paused, then asked, "Who?"

I hesitated. I had already told Vinny about Jessamine, but that hadn't been a big risk because he'd already seen camera footage of her. Telling Beck was riskier for both our safety.

Beck heard my hesitation and breathed, "Shit. It's that bitch Jessamine, isn't it?"

"You know her?"

"I met her once. Let's just say it wasn't pretty. And you're right. If she is looking for JD and finds him, he's going to be in thick mud. We can't talk about this further on the phone."

I expected her to hang up, but she stated, "You're welcome to come up for a visit. Miranda and I just got back from a trip out west and will be around all weekend. Unpacking, probably. I like to unpack right away, but Miranda needs to take a vacation from the vacation when she's home." Her soft laughter lightened my mood.

"That would be wonderful!"

"I'll send you the address."

I thanked Beck and prepared to end the call, but before I could, she added, "You're taking a big risk, Sterling. I hope it's worth it."

I exhaled. "Me, too."

After she said goodbye and hung up, I dug in my purse for a slip of paper. Vinny might have been a warlock with magical abilities, but he didn't have the training I had. We had left the house together after he returned to JD's office for the papers he'd come to collect. He hadn't noticed when I took the small note attached to the stack as I hugged him goodbye.

Hugging someone I barely knew wasn't characteristic of me, but he didn't know that.

I gave the paper a good look now. An address somewhere in Vermont was scrawled across it. Was JD staying there? Why send the paperwork to this place? I decided I would make a whole weekend trip of it. Beck might even be able to help. She sure as hell would be more useful than JD's manager. Vinny might have cared for JD like a brother, but he was playing this game too defensively.

I headed inside, planning to promptly remove my heels, then grab a hot shower and tumble into bed. However, when I entered my apartment and found the living room light on, I froze.

My mother sat on the sofa, legs folded under her and a glass of wine in one hand. The TV was on. She smiled. "There you are! I expected you home earlier. I'm not unhappy it's so late, though. You must have had a wonderful time. I was beginning to think you went home with him."

I was too surprised to see her to react properly to her insinuation. "Mom, what are you doing here?"

I slid off my heels and jacket, then set my purse on the kitchen island. I glanced at the stove clock. It was nearly 10:00 PM. Late for a Monday night, considering I was usually in bed half an hour before now.

An early bedtime meant early rising and getting a good

workout in before I headed to the office. I was a creature of habit, addicted to routine, and my mother knew it. It had not felt like I was at JD's for that long. The drive in and out of the city took a while, though.

"I wanted to hear how the date went! It's been too long since we had time together. I knew if I called or texted you about birthday plans, we wouldn't get anything figured out."

I grinned. "So you decided to confront me?"

She patted the spot beside her on the sofa. "Let's talk, dear."

I didn't want to talk about the date. Not because I had a bad time, but because I would need to explain where I'd been and what I'd been doing between seven and ten. I couldn't tell my mother I had gone to my ex-boyfriend's house—could he even be considered an ex?—to find out where he might have disappeared to, and ran into a warlock carrying off JD's personal information.

As I settled onto the sofa beside her, I came up with a good enough excuse. "Date went well, but there was no spark. I don't think there will be a second. I went for a drive afterward to clear my head." It wasn't a total lie. I had spent more time in the car than in JD's house.

"Poor dear," my mother murmured, patting my knee. "You've been so busy that you haven't given yourself time to sit and think about everything."

She was right. Any moment I wasn't filling with work or sleep, I was at the boxing club, the gym, or with my mom. On the rare nights I was alone, my new friend Valeria stopped in for a bottle of wine and reality TV. Despite all the distractions, I hadn't been able to get JD out of my head.

"You didn't have to come here, Mom."

"Let's talk about something more exciting. Your birthday!"

"I already told you what I wanted to do." I was considering fleeing the state. Now that Beck had invited me up north, I had an excuse to leave for the weekend. I could turn another year old in peace.

"How about a girl's weekend away? We could go to this lovely spa in Maryland that Linda recommended. A weekend with no interruptions. Just you and me."

The idea didn't sound all that bad, and I missed spending time with my mom.

"I wish I could, but work is taking me somewhere else."

She arched a brow. My mom didn't ask many questions about my job because she preferred not to be in a perpetual state of worry, so I was surprised when she questioned, "Where?"

No point in lying. "New York." I didn't mention the detour I planned on taking into Vermont.

She clapped. "Perfect! You tell me where exactly you're going, and I'll book us the closest spa! I don't imagine you'll be working the entire time, and we can enjoy some relaxation when you're off the clock."

"It's not an 'on the clock' sort of job, Mom…"

She was already opening a search engine on her phone. I didn't want to pull my mother into whatever web I was getting myself into, but she was too excited about the idea for me to tell her no. It would be good to spend time together, anyway.

"Okay, we'll do it, but you have to promise me you'll let me go and do my work. I expect you to be in full relax mode while I'm gone."

"It's a deal, darling." She squeezed my hand. "You won't regret it!"

I silently prayed she was right.

CHAPTER SIX

JORDAN

This wasn't a good idea.

The bar couldn't have held more than fifty people, and in this small town, everyone knew everyone. It was a Thursday night, so traffic in and out of the establishment wasn't high.

Despite this, I'd received a few wandering glances toward my end of the bar. Folks wondering who the handsome guy ordering Bloody Marys was. I either didn't return their looks or stared them down long enough that they looked away and chose spots across the room.

A jukebox in the corner pushed out the strained, static chords of a Johnny Cash song. One kick, and that thing would break for good. A few guys were gathered around a pool table. The clack of balls against one another would have been a lot more satisfying if I was in on the action, but drawing more attention to myself wasn't wise.

I should have stayed home and avoided all contact with humans. However, I couldn't stand being inside any longer, and I'd taken a walk to clear my mind. Before I knew it, I'd strolled into this bar on the fringes of the town.

Maybe it was the constant yearning for human connection,

something I'd had very little of over the last several months. Maybe it was innate stupidity, the ever-present inclination inside me to dance with danger. I'd left my burner phone at the house to prevent the temptation to call someone.

The bartender tonight was a young woman with red curls framing her face. She kept stepping outside, probably to smoke. She smelled like cigarettes and cheap vanilla perfume. The scent was almost overpowering.

Down the bar, two middle-aged men in ball caps leaned toward one another, muttering over bottles of Coors. One kept stealing glances in my direction. I'd opted for a simple T-shirt and jeans instead of my usual suit. This way, I blended in. I didn't feel like myself in such casual clothes, but that was exactly what I was trying to avoid. *Being myself.*

I had put on many names throughout the years to hide Jordan Davenport. Tonight, if I could manage it, I was Nobody.

"Aw, Charlene, don't be like that." The mocking voice of one of the men down the bar drew my attention away from my drink. The woman behind the bar scowled as she dried a glass she'd just cleaned.

"I told ya, Kevin. Once was enough for me." Her voice was low. Apart from Kevin and his buddy, only I could hear her, and that was because of my enhanced hearing. The others around the pool table and jukebox were oblivious to the interchange.

Kevin, the taller and thinner of the pair, braced his hands against the bar's surface and pushed himself up, nearly staggering. His glazed eyes announced he'd had too many beers. "Come on, Char. You know I showed ya a good time." He reached over and touched a curl.

She swatted him. "Hands on your side of the bar, Kev, or I'll have you thrown out."

Kevin's buddy snickered. "And who do ya think is gonna throw him out, sweetheart? Your daddy isn't around tonight, and you're..."

"Done serving you," Charlene cut in. "I'll close out your tab now." She turned to the register, and the men shared looks.

When she came back with their check, Kevin tried again. "Charlene, you know Kathy won't find out. And if she does, who cares? You and me are meant to be together, ever since school, ya know?" He snagged her hand, holding it tightly enough that she couldn't let go.

Her face scrunched. Blowing up at him now would cause a scene, and folks would wonder what part she'd had in the affair.

I wasn't interested in helping anyone hide their secrets, despite having plenty of my own, but I couldn't sit by while a grown man harassed a woman.

I sighed, slurped down the remainder of my drink, and stood. With an easy stride, I reached Kevin's side in an instant and placed a hand on his shoulder. "Is there a problem over here?"

Charlene blinked in surprise.

Kevin's nameless buddy swiveled toward me. "No problem. Not that it's any of your business."

Kevin turned and glowered. "Hey, I've seen you around. Always in here drinkin' yer sorrows, eh?" His words were slurred.

It was only my second time, actually. But the fact that he'd noticed wasn't good. Had I really looked sorrowful? "I recommend you call it a night and go home to the good wife," I told him, squeezing his shoulder like we were old school buddies.

Kevin shook me off. "Hey, leave me alone."

"Yeah, leave 'im alone!" The other guy got up.

I dropped my easy manner, becoming the cold predator that lurked beneath my skin. "You asked Charlene here who would see you out. I think that'll be me."

By now, everybody was looking in our direction.

Kevin laughed. "Yeah? I'd like to see you try."

I reached for his arm. He moved it, and his fist flew at me. The move was clumsy and predictable. I caught it in my larger hand.

The men were too drunk to realize I'd moved at an impossible speed for a human. However, Charlene gasped. I realized I'd be showing off too much if I didn't let the guy get a few punches in.

Kevin's other fist drove into my gut. I doubled over despite the negligible pain and couldn't help but grin as a thrill shot through me.

I let his buddy hit my jaw before I started hitting back. I punched the side of Kevin's face, sending him staggering against the barstool. He shouted a curse and clutched his bleeding nose. Before his buddy could respond, I grabbed the front of his shirt and slammed him onto the bar top. I could have easily broken a few ribs, but that seemed like taking it too far.

Charlene cried out. Several people across the room also let us know how they felt.

"Take it outside, boys!" a male voice boomed.

I was too focused on the second guy grabbing the glass that had shattered when I threw him onto the bar. It sailed toward me, and the jagged side struck my face. I hissed as my skin sliced, and a thin line of blood appeared. I swiped at it and flashed a fiendish grin.

However, before I could retaliate, we were surrounded. I considered taking on the whole lot of them, but most of the group only wanted us out of there.

I put my hands up. "All right, I'm done."

Kevin and his buddy were cursing when I walked out the door. No one followed me, and I sucked in the cool night air as I stood in the red light of the bar's neon OPEN sign.

"Stupid," I muttered. The last thing I should be doing was drawing attention.

The parking lot was full of pickup trucks. One guy had even driven his tractor here. I was wiping the last of the blood from my cheekbone when the figure stepped from behind a dumpster, wearing a frown that could have silenced a preacher behind the pulpit.

"Stupid is right," he snapped. "What the hell were you thinking, coming here? Let alone getting into *a fight*?"

The man—if he could be called that—was about four feet tall, but his crossed arms and heated glare *almost* scared me. "What are *you* doing here, Elias?" I demanded. "I told you not to leave the house."

"I'm not staying locked up while you get to come out here and make…unwise decisions."

So I wasn't leading by good example. "You're wise for a ten-year-old," I muttered.

"Seventy," the kid reminded me. "Now, let's get home before dawn."

"It's not even midnight."

He responded by walking away.

I huffed and went after him. I hadn't driven into town. I'd left the house wanting to clear my mind and breathe in the fresh air. I had ended up at the bar without meaning to and thought I would have one Bloody Mary before heading back.

"I hoped you would be too busy poring over your books to notice I was gone," I remarked.

He cast me a glare. "The house was too quiet without your lengthy philosophical tangents. I figured you were out here up to no good. I was right."

We turned from the parking lot down a desolate country road under moonlight. "Those men in the bar will remember you. Word will spread. We'll need to move on soon. Why do you have to be so flashy?"

"You sound like the fucking Conclave," I replied mildly. Elias was right, though.

"Good. Because it will be them who finds us. I hope you're working on a good explanation."

For why I was in hiding with a seventy-year-old vampire who looked no older than ten? Yeah, that wouldn't be easy to explain to the Conclave. Not after everything that had happened.

I recalled the footage of Jessamine Lane in my house. Vinny had texted me, saying I should have a look. He only messaged when it was necessary. I wouldn't admit it to Elias, but part of the reason I'd left the house tonight was because of the footage of Vinny and Tatiana in my house a few nights ago.

Seeing her again had done things to me I couldn't explain. I'd fought tears and pangs of guilt and regret. It had taken every ounce of my willpower not to call her. To tell her I was sorry and was coming back.

The need to protect her stopped me, as did knowing it would put Elias in danger. I wouldn't tell him this, but I'd gone into the bar trying to cope. Throwing my fists around made me feel better for a minute, but the thrill had worn off now.

I had been too flashy, though. We'd need to get on the move again.

I slid my hands into my pockets. "How's Montana sound? Imagine us riding stallions across the plains, those big blue skies going on forever."

"Dark skies," Elias reminded me.

"You can handle more sunlight than me."

He only shook his head, then murmured, "I've always wanted to see Yellowstone."

I slung an arm around his shoulders. "We can go to Yellowstone." Whatever Elias wanted, I would do my best to give him. He'd had a harder life in the last seventy years than I had.

While I had traveled from city to city, adopting different names and taking on different personas, he'd lived in hiding. He was a seventy-year-old vampire stuck in a child's body, aging at a much slower rate than any vampire I had met before. No one deserved to be turned against their will, but especially a child.

If I ever came across the bastard who'd done it, I'd rip him limb from limb. Elias' brain had never quite fully developed, much like his body. So, though he made much wiser decisions than me, he still had the mind of a child.

The Conclave had first summoned me in December, furious at my flashy heroics during my time working with Tatiana. While meeting with them, I'd discovered they were searching for a vampire called Elias.

A rogue named Callum was also hunting him. I'd heard of the guy before. A century ago, he'd exposed a group of vampires hunting for a meal in the Andes. Some vampires couldn't control their bloodthirst. The Conclave brought Callum in and punished him accordingly, and he was only released a few years ago. If they'd asked me, I didn't think he should have ever been released.

Callum believed that Elias' slow aging was the key to creating Day Walkers—vampires who could withstand sunlight, at least for much longer periods than we could now. Throughout the centuries, we had developed different ways of being in sunlight or working around it. However, Elias didn't have to worry about it much.

His greater worries were being hunted and exploited by people like Callum, or humans catching onto the fact that he didn't age. An adult male could get away with it for far longer than someone who looked like they were ten.

The Conclave would be no better for Elias than Callum was. So, when they let me off with a stern warning, I'd gone looking. It beat sitting around in my cabin, and I could still lie low while looking for Elias.

Images of the night I'd found him sliced through my mind. A burning house, and Callum lurking in the shadows. A bloody fight that I'd barely made it out of alive. Elias thrashing in my arms. Me telling him, "I'm here to help you. I don't want to hurt you."

Callum was still out there, but he was the least of our problems. No doubt the Conclave had heard about my stunt and would be hunting us both down. And Tatiana…

My heart ached. I tried not to think of her. I hoped she'd found a way to move on, that she would forget about me. That footage of her in my house said differently. Part of me loved seeing her there, knowing she still cared. The other part of me filled with dread. Tatiana was fierce and determined. If she wanted to find me, she would do anything in her power to accomplish it.

Vinny was like a brother to me, but under Tatiana's questioning, he was sure to break. Yes, Elias and I had to move on before anyone found us.

At last, we reached the end of the road and a narrow path leading up a hillside. Set against dense trees was an old stone house. It was nowhere near as grand as my home outside D.C., nor was it quaint, like my cabin in the Alps. It was old enough for the nearest town to consider haunted, and no one lived here. Elias and I had been here only two weeks.

I smiled as we started up the path. "Well, we made it back before dawn." It was barely past midnight.

Elias didn't respond. His gaze was fixed on the house, his expression full of longing, a haunted look in his eyes.

I regretted everything I'd done tonight, and I promised myself I wouldn't make that mistake again. I squeezed his shoulder. "Let's get some rest. We can start dreaming about Yellowstone."

CHAPTER SEVEN

TATIANA

"This place will be perfect, at least from everything I read online," my mom announced as I navigated the wide drive.

A Colonial-style mansion came into view, surrounded by rolling hills and forests. Idyllic was the perfect word to describe the grounds the hotel sat on. A sign leading onto the property read *The Silver Swan*. Behind the hotel was a large pond with several docks and a gazebo up one of the banks. A pair of swans glided across the water.

"We will have access to a full spa, walking trails, and an assortment of nighttime events. Our room even has a jacuzzi! I've heard they host weddings here throughout the year. Imagine getting married in such a beautiful place!"

I won't have much time to lounge in a jacuzzi, I thought, but I smiled at my mom. "It sounds perfect." Staying the weekend at a mountain hotel and spa was a tad too extravagant for my birthday, but at least it would only be Mom and me.

I stopped at the top of a U-shaped driveway, and a young valet approached. We took out our bags—a simple duffel for me, and my mom's two full suitcases. How she planned to use everything she had brought over one weekend was beyond me. One suitcase was probably solely for shoes. Ever the over-packer.

I handed the keys to the valet, and we headed inside. The lobby was all marble and crystal, the perfect blend of cozy and opulent. I didn't want to ask my mother how much money she'd dropped on our stay here. I promised that when it was her birthday, I would take us somewhere equally nice. Considering how well the firm was doing, I could afford to spoil her now.

"Sterling," my mother told the woman behind the desk when she asked for a reservation name.

The woman smiled and handed us each a key. "Your room on the top floor has the best view! You made a great selection."

My mother beamed and took my arm. "Nothing but the best for my daughter. It's her birthday this weekend!"

I tried not to groan. I wouldn't be surprised if the entire hotel knew it was my birthday by the end of the weekend.

The woman's brows furrowed, and her gaze flitted between us. Why did she look confused? She pressed a smile to her lips. "I hope you ladies enjoy your weekend. And happy birthday."

I thanked her, then steered my mom toward the elevator before she told the poor desk woman her entire labor and delivery story. In the elevator, I looked at our keys. "Mom, you reserved the honeymoon suite."

"Did I? I didn't mean to. I asked for their best room!"

I chuckled. "No wonder the lady was confused."

The room had not only a jacuzzi, but also a clawfoot tub and a stone-tiled shower with a waterfall head. The bathroom was double the size of mine at home. The room only had one bed, a California king with the most comfortable pillows and blanket I'd ever felt. And the view was magnificent. It overlooked the back portion of the property with the pond and floating swans.

I couldn't help but remember the last time I'd stayed in a hotel room with only one bed. I banished the image of JD from my mind. Until I visited Beck, I vowed not to think of him.

I turned from the window. "Mom, you really didn't have to do this."

She waved me off. "Nonsense. I wanted to. I'm going to change, then see if they accept walk-in massages downstairs. Are you coming with me?"

I shook my head. "I have work to do, remember?"

She looked ready to ask me where I was going, so I added, "I promise to be back before dinner." She seemed satisfied with this as she changed clothes and left the room.

I freshened myself up before leaving. The address Beck gave me was only ten miles away, and the drive was as scenic as the one to the hotel. The winding roads were more enjoyable in JD's Mercedes.

My GPS lost service halfway there, and I had to follow my memory of the directions up a winding, narrow road. A small cabin by a lake appeared through the trees. From what little I knew of Beck, this was very her.

As I parked, Beck appeared on the porch, waving. She wore a pair of dark-wash jeans and a flannel shirt, the sleeves rolled to her elbows.

"Welcome," she greeted when I mounted the porch steps.

"It's beautiful here," I told her, remembering the reason she and her partner had moved. During his series of art thefts and targeting people JD knew, Victor Hume had sent burglars to steal from Miranda's private collection. I suspected now that they might have been in danger for other reasons.

"Come inside," Beck invited.

The place was small but cozy. Art lined the walls, and ceramic vases and abstract shapes decorated various surfaces. "Sculpting and pottery are a few of Miranda's many interests," Beck murmured as she led the way into the kitchen.

There, a pretty woman with silvery-blonde hair braided down her back emerged from a sunroom. She wore an apron splotched with paint. In the room beyond, I spied a canvas and easel. The painting appeared to be half-finished and depicted Utah's grand arches.

"You must be Tatiana!" She hugged me like an old friend.

Beck drew her to her side. "Tatiana, Miranda. Miranda…"

"Oh, I know. You've told me all about her! I can't thank you enough for helping us last year." Miranda clasped my hands in hers.

"It was my pleasure. I'm glad you're both safe."

Beck tilted her head toward the adjoining living room. "Shall we?"

Miranda waved us away. "I'll whip up something to eat while you two talk."

The living room had a sofa positioned across from a large stone fireplace. Two armchairs were angled on either side. Beck plopped onto the sofa and motioned for me to take a seat. I perched on the other end of the couch. "So…you want to know more about Jessamine. I'd like to know why she paid you a visit," Beck began.

I leaned closer. "Are you like JD?"

Beck arched a brow.

"A vampire?"

Both brows rose this time. "Jessamine told you about JD."

"She *confirmed*." I decided I might as well tell Beck everything that happened leading up to Jessamine's visit. I explained the truth about Victor Hume and what he had done to JD. What he had been planning to do. Beck paled, and she cursed under her breath.

I told her about Lola, the shifter, and something in Beck's eyes flickered. Finally, I explained Jessamine's visit and running into Vinny at JD's home outside D.C. "Now I'm here, wondering where he is and if I can get to him before Jessamine does."

"You're wasting your time," Beck replied quietly. "JD probably already knows she's onto him. You going near him will only draw Jessamine and the Conclave closer."

My heart sank. Was I making matters worse by getting involved?

"But no, I'm not a vampire. Thank God." Beck chuckled roughly. "Don't get me wrong, I've had a hard time among my own kind, but I'm sure as fuck glad I've never been subjected to the Conclave."

I remembered Vinny's speech about covens and packs, and how he, too, was glad he wasn't a vampire.

"I'm a shifter. Something like your friend Lola, actually. I was born into a pack, but I didn't stay long."

I leaned forward with interest.

"When I was sixteen, I broke one of the pack's most sacred laws. I told someone what I was. Someone who wasn't a shifter. Non-magical. I ran away, yearning for freedom outside my people's strict laws, but they came after me. I'll spare you the details of how they punished, then excommunicated me. I was a loner for a long time after that." Light came into her eyes. "Until I met JD."

Her smile was sad. "He was a loner, too. Had no interest in hunting with other vampires. He hated the laws of the Conclave almost as much as I hated the laws of my old pack. We hooked up and got into some mischief together."

Dated, until Beck decided she didn't care for the pleasures of men.

"He was my best friend for a long time. He was family, the only person I had. I got the feeling I was the only one he had, too."

An ache formed in my chest.

"And that brings us to Jessamine." The fondness vanished from Beck's face, replaced by something hard and cold.

"What happened?" I asked.

"The Alpha, the leader of my old pack, died, and my older brother rose in his place. He decided he didn't like me wandering by myself and tried to bring me back in. I knew that would only result in more torture, so I refused. And I ran. Jordan came with me."

Beck swallowed. "He protected me as well as he could, but there was an…incident. My brother and his alphas tracked me down. When they tried to drag me back to the pack, Jordan intervened. It was bloody, to say the least, and the whole situation brought attention to vampires in general. So, the Conclave stepped in."

Beck crossed her arms. "Let's just say that Jessamine wasn't happy. She suggested JD not have friends outside 'his own kind.' Vampires and shifters have never gotten along, and don't get me started on witches."

I remembered Vinny saying something similar.

"Magicals can be territorial about their groups. Most packs, covens, whatever you want to call them, are led by greedy, power-hungry pricks. It would be better if we stuck together, but I don't think a world could exist where that is even possible."

"What happened to you and JD after Jessamine stepped in?" I asked.

"They kept him on a tight leash for a few years. We didn't see each other, but we've stayed in touch here and there. I felt like I'd lost a brother." Beck smiled slightly. "But we both moved on. JD to his…acting. I wandered for a while, eluded my pack time and time again. Then, I met Miranda."

"Is she…"

Beck shook her head. "Miranda is human. That's all. Well, that and the love of my life." Her eyes brightened.

"Is it common for magicals and humans to have relationships like yours?"

Beck's eyes shadowed. "No. It's risky, as you can imagine. For one, I couldn't be certain Miranda would accept me. I thought she might see me as a monster and never want to speak to me again. She did, though. She has never looked at me differently because of it."

"And do you ever feel like you're putting her in danger?"

Beck nodded. "Of course, but by the time we met, I hadn't heard from my pack in a decade. I was sure they would finally leave me alone. I also knew that if anyone came for us, I could defend her."

I sat back, admiring their bravery. Beck's for opening her heart to Miranda. Miranda for accepting Beck despite a story that had probably sounded impossible. Insane, even. I thought of JD and everything we had shared together. Was there a world where we could be together despite the truth coming out?

I pushed him from my mind. "What else can you tell me about the Conclave?"

"Not a lot. I am not a vampire, so there isn't much I'm allowed to know. Only what little JD once told me. Even vampires who aren't part of the Conclave don't know exactly how it's structured. I do know there are different seats. There's a North American Conclave, and a High Council that oversees all Conclaves around the world."

"And Jessamine? What sort of position does she hold?"

"Liaison. Fancy messenger, basically. I don't think she makes executive decisions. She's more their bounty hunter."

I recalled the predatory nature I had sensed in the female vampire. I certainly wouldn't want her hunting me down.

Beck snorted. "She's old as shit, too, though she doesn't look like it. Pretty bitch, isn't she?"

I nodded. Pretty and terrifying.

"What I know most about the Conclave is that they are not to be screwed with. They aren't as messy as packs, but they are clever. They have intricate law systems and extreme ways of enforcing them. If they're coming for JD..." Fear shone in her eyes.

I swallowed as dread curled in my stomach.

Beck's face softened. "You know, I think he really loves you. I saw it the first time I was in the same room as you both."

Tears pricked my eyes.

"If he's avoiding you, it's because he wants to protect you," Beck added.

I was sick of being protected. All I wanted was to find him, to help him get away from Jessamine and whatever the hell the Conclave had planned for him.

Beck must have seen these thoughts play across my face, because she stated, "I would advise against getting yourself involved. JD would want you to stay away."

"But I can't," I managed.

Beck looked like she wanted to object. Finally, she nodded. "I understand. You must be careful, Tatiana. I wish I knew where JD was, that I could help more."

"He hasn't reached out to you?"

Beck shook her head. I didn't tell her about the address Vinny was sending paperwork to or that I planned to go there.

Miranda bustled into the room, carrying a tray of sandwiches and drinks. "Anybody hungry?"

CHAPTER EIGHT

TATIANA

I arrived back at the hotel an hour before the agreed-upon time for dinner. A text from my mom flashed onto my screen as I stepped into the suite.

Went out shopping. See you at dinner!

We had agreed to eat in the hotel's dining room at 7:00, which meant I had an hour to myself. I stepped under the hot stream of the shower and processed everything Beck had told me, then took my time with hair, makeup, and getting dressed. I'd selected a simple, dark green dress with off-the-shoulder sleeves. I curled my hair before pulling it up into a ponytail.

My mother arrived shortly before our meeting time, her arms lined with shopping bags. "Looks like you've done some damage," I teased her.

Her eyes sparkled. "Just a few things here and there." How she planned to fit it all in my car, along with her two suitcases, on our trip back was beyond me.

While she freshened up for dinner, I wandered the hotel. The downstairs lobby was connected to a courtyard where a stone fountain dominated the center. Small firepits and comfortable outdoor sofas were arranged at the courtyard's four corners.

A lawn extended beyond, then the pond. The sun was close to setting as I stepped out under the awning. A few guests were enjoying glasses of wine or cigars in the outdoor area. Inside, I heard the low tune of stringed instruments. I closed my eyes, letting the warm, late spring air brush my skin.

I opened them when I heard a low, heated voice. "I'm telling you, I've found the right place."

A man paced at the far end of the courtyard with a phone pressed to his ear. His head was shaved and his clothes disheveled. He looked harried and kept rubbing his jaw. When he moved his hand, I glimpsed a row of thin scars. Letters were tattooed across his knuckles, but from this distance, I couldn't read them.

He must have sensed me looking, because he abruptly turned, his heated stare meeting my gaze. He lowered his voice, and I looked away.

I glanced at my phone and realized it was seven o'clock, so I headed inside for dinner. A hostess greeted me at the dining room entrance and led me to the table where my mother was already seated.

"Marvelous view, isn't it?" my mother remarked when I had taken my seat. Like our room upstairs, this spot overlooked the back portion of the grounds. I checked the courtyard, but the man with the tattooed knuckles was gone.

A waitress came with a bottle of white wine. "Your favorite," Mom remarked, smiling.

"You didn't have to."

"For your birthday, yes, I did." She raised a glass. "Happy early birthday, dear. And congratulations to me for pushing you out. I was in labor for nearly two days, you know. I'd never known longer hours in my life."

I braced myself to hear the same story she told me every year. Fifteen minutes and several sips of wine later, her eyes misted. "Every second of labor was worth it the first time I held you. I think that was the best moment of my life. Second to marrying your dad, of course. My third-best moment was when he held you for the first time. I don't think I'd ever seen him so charmed. He loved you with his entire heart, Tatiana."

I ached at the thought of my dad not being here. He would never see a birthday of mine again, nor I one of his. I raised my glass. "To you and to dad, for being the best parents a girl could ask for. Even if I was never the plan."

My mother laughed. They had never called me a mistake. Rather, a happy accident. "The best plan we never had," my dad had often told me.

Mom set her glass on the table. "Sometimes the best parts of life are the ones you never plan. I can't imagine my life without you, Tatiana."

She reached across the table to squeeze my hand. Once, neither my mom nor I could imagine a life without my dad. Yet here we were, sharing a bottle and remembering him with a fondness that ached.

The waitress came to take our order. The sun had nearly set by this point, and the dining room was filling up. Fires started in the pits outside, and I felt I could stay here a long time and be content. Part of me longed to curl up in bed tonight, comfortable and fulfilled, and pretend I had no troubles.

Vinny's last words to me at JD's house echoed between my ears. *It is better that you forget you ever knew Jackson Dale Shade.* What would my life look like if I did forget JD and move on? Maybe we'd both be safer. I could marry a nice man like Landon Greene, settle down, and have children before it was too late. I could still run the firm but take fewer jobs for myself. I had plenty of staff to delegate to.

The thought of my life becoming so simple made my heart ache with longing, but it also turned my stomach. I could attain that life, but JD would always linger at the back of my mind. If I was honest with myself, he'd be in my heart forever.

My mom's voice broke through my thoughts. "Everything okay, honey?"

I pasted on a smile. "Of course. This is lovely, Mom. Thank you for everything."

"I know how much you like Thai food on the couch, but this is so much more elevated. You should have a special time on your birthday."

"As long as you don't have a secret surprise party waiting for me upstairs."

Her eyes glimmered. "Only cake."

Cake, I could do.

She leaned her elbows on the table and examined me. "I wish Marcus could have joined us. He has a way of lighting up a whole room." She chuckled, and I managed a small smile. He sure did.

Then came the question I was dreading. "Did something happen between the two of you?"

My mom had taken on the greatest challenge of her life in recent months, second only to my dad's passing. She had not asked me about Marcus Smith. After he left, everyone could tell I wasn't happy about it. By some miracle, both my mom and Linda had given me space to process it.

"Marcus and I have different ideas about the future, that's all." It wasn't exactly a lie. Was a future possible between us now that I knew the truth? I couldn't quite wrap my head around the idea of him being practically immortal and me being…well, *human*. "It was never going to work out. We shouldn't have gotten involved romantically," I added, hating how dismal I sounded.

My mom gave me a look that said, *You're holding back*, but she didn't push. She squeezed my hand a second time. "Different ideas of the future can change. Maybe one day, you two will find a way back to one another."

A lump formed in my throat. I couldn't believe I was more upset about JD not being here than my father. It almost felt like

JD had died, too. Would I ever see him again? Was this trip going to pay off, or was I wasting my time?

I pushed a smile to my lips. "Maybe."

Our meal arrived, and mercifully, my mom moved on to other topics. She didn't press for details about work or Marcus. She talked about what her book club was reading and mentioned that she was starting tennis lessons next week. We wondered if Harry was finally the man for Linda and if we could expect to attend their wedding later this year.

Our conversation stalled when heated voices rose from across the dining room. "I'm going," a male voice growled.

I glanced over to see the same man from the courtyard earlier. He'd stood from his table, where he'd been sitting alone, and was shaking off a waiter. Whatever happened, the restaurant staff was trying to remove him. He huffed and stalked out of the room.

"Pleasant man," my mother remarked.

"I saw him earlier. I don't think he's having a good day."

"Even so, that's no way to act in public."

I agreed but said nothing more.

We finished our meals, and when the waitress came to clear our plates, my mom turned to me. "What cake shall we eat tonight?"

CHAPTER NINE

I woke and headed out early the next morning, before my mom was up. I left her a note, saying I would be back later in the afternoon and that I hoped she enjoyed the spa. I was a smidge jealous I wouldn't be with her for it, but duty called.

I snagged a quick breakfast in the hotel dining room before asking the valet to pull my Mercedes around.

"Right away, ma'am."

I settled into the driver's seat with a contented sigh, then typed the address I had swiped from Vinny into the GPS. I had a three-hour drive east ahead of me. At least it would be scenic. Fog draped the trees and the gently winding roads.

After the morning air had warmed, I turned on the radio and rolled the windows down. The drive gave me time to think about what I'd learned from Beck yesterday.

The world of magicals, from vampires to shifters and whatever lay between, was kept secret for many reasons. Mainly so greedy, hateful humans wouldn't hurt them for being different. It was easy to fear something you didn't understand. A Conclave whose function was mostly unknown made sense in light of this.

I considered everything I thought I knew about vampires.

Sunlight and silver hurt them, didn't they? They consumed blood and had supernatural abilities like heightened senses, speed, and dexterity. I'd seen evidence of JD's abilities and wondered about the other things.

It made sense that JD had been more prone to joining me on nighttime jobs than daytime ones. In the daytime, he preferred to be at the office. Several times, he had lowered the blinds and explained, "Sun was in my eyes," when he could have easily sat in a position to avoid that.

So many small things I had written off. JD had his quirks, regardless of vampirism. He had never lied to me, but he had allowed me to believe a truth I'd concluded myself. The reality was too absurd for me to reach the right conclusions. I still felt like an idiot for not seeing what he really was, but until six months ago, I hadn't known "enhanced" humans existed. I had to give myself some grace.

My thoughts roamed for hours. When I was thirty minutes out from the address, I pulled into a small town. The main street had nothing more than a tiny post office, a bar, a general store, a gas station, and one diner that looked like it served cheap but delicious food.

The streets were mostly empty when I pulled into the one-pump gas station. I had to wait behind a station wagon for several minutes. In the meantime, I checked my phone. My mom had texted me a photo of the spa with a message.

Wish you were here!

An hour later, she had added that she met a nice woman named Clarice over breakfast and the two had booked a couples' massage. I shook my head, chuckling. My mom made friends everywhere she went.

The station wagon finally pulled away from the pump, and I drove up for my turn. At the same time, two men strolled out of the station building. One of them, tall and lanky, whistled. "Sweet ride." His gaze slid over the Mercedes, then up to me. "And an even nicer-looking lady behind the wheel. What's your name, sweetheart?"

My dad had called me sweetheart nearly my entire life. Anyone else who said it made my skin crawl. I almost rolled my eyes. Unless the guy wanted to pay for my gas, he could get lost.

His companion thumped him on the back and snickered. "Careful, Kevin. Talk up another pretty lady, and you might get your ass kicked again."

Kevin glowered. "If I see that guy again, I'm running him over."

Mercifully, Kevin's friend led him away, and I was left in peace to pump my gas. When I finished, I decided to go inside for some snacks. I could function without a proper lunch, but I needed a little something before I reached my destination.

The interior was small, and an elderly man wearing a baseball cap sat behind the counter, flipping through a fishing magazine. I started down an aisle of snacks and halted, stunned at the sight of a man standing at the end of the row. His back was to me, but I knew instantly he was the same man who had been removed from the hotel dining room last night.

The odds of him being three hours away from the hotel in the same direction I'd gone were nothing short of incredible. Was he following me?

He turned, a different bag of chips in each hand, weighing his options. "Shit. Both of 'em," he muttered and shoved them back onto a shelf. I turned to walk away before he noticed me, but it was too late.

"Hey, you."

I cringed and turned. "Yes?"

He stepped toward me, eyes narrowing. "I saw you at the hotel last night. Are you following me?"

I shook my head. The coincidence was remarkable, no denying that. "We must be working in the same area."

He wagged a finger. "'Cuz if you're following me, you'll regret it!"

I put up my hands. "I swear I'm not."

He glanced around as if expecting someone might jump him at any moment. "You with the law or something?"

In a way, I was, but it had nothing to do with us running into each other in this small-town gas station.

I decided the conversation wasn't worth it. The guy was clearly paranoid. I went up to the counter to pay for the snacks I'd selected. Meanwhile, the man stomped from the building. Tires squealed as a car pulled out onto the road. He hadn't bothered buying anything.

"That all, miss?" the man behind the counter asked.

I nodded and handed him some cash. As he counted out the change, I leaned on the counter and asked, "I'm just passing through, and I wondered about the house up on a ridge outside of town here. Big old house. Do you know anything about it?"

I told him the road it was on, recalling details about the house I'd seen online. Not a lot of information had popped up. The county auditor's site had shown me the current owner, a Douglas Smith. Other online searches revealed that Douglas Smith had been dead for several years. Why didn't someone else own his house?

"Oh, yes. Big house. Haunted, folks say." The man behind the counter chuckled. "But they say that about all old houses. Place has been abandoned for years now. Nobody wants to clean up the dump."

"Good piece of property, though," I remarked.

"Buy it, then."

I smiled, thanked him, and wished him a good day. Outside, the Mercedes waited for me. I found a note attached to the windshield.

Call me – Kevin

A number was written beneath it.

This time, I did roll my eyes. I balled up the paper and tossed it into the nearest trash can. The guy was probably married.

The sun beamed fully overhead as I neared my destination. I turned down a narrow road with overgrown foliage on either side. I crested the ridge, and the house loomed into view.

The three-story Colonial mansion had long fallen into disarray. The yard was overgrown and full of weeds. A tree had fallen at the side of the house. Paint peeled along the exterior, and the porch looked about one more rainfall from completely rotting into the ground.

I parked in the only spot available before the tall grass sprang up and exited the car. A soft wind blew, scattering hair across my face. The place had to be abandoned. Who would want to stay in a shithole like this?

Despite my reservations, I stepped onto the porch and knocked. As I expected, no answer came. I picked my way through weeds, rocks, and the trash that had blown across the property until I reached the back of the house. Here, the land descended steeply into dense forest. The back door was locked, but I noticed a cracked-open window. I peered through it into what was once a kitchen. No appliances remained, but the counters, sinks, and cabinets were there. Everything was outdated and covered in dust and grime.

As I lifted the window, it emitted a horrendous creak. When it was up enough for me to climb in, I swung a leg over the side. It was only a two-foot drop into the room. I glanced around, then into the hallway. This place was a mess.

I brushed off the back of my pants. When I stepped forward, something crunched. I glanced down at the piece of loose, broken tile under my foot, then sniffed. The place smelled about as rotten as it looked. Why the hell did JD have Vinny send his mail here? Because few people would think to look?

I approached the hallway, passing an open doorway into what might have been a living room. I barely caught sight of a figure moving toward me before a wooden board studded with nails swung toward my head.

I yelped and dove out of the way. The plank swung again with a speed I could barely register. I sprang aside but landed against the counter and had to throw my hand out to catch myself. Something sharp sliced my palm. Broken glass.

The board smashed down and splintered against the sink beside me. On instinct, I drew the Ruger strapped to my side from beneath my jacket. "Stop!" I called. At the same instant, I got a good look at the weapon wielder and gasped.

He couldn't have been more than ten years old.

I lowered the gun and held up my hands. "Don't hit me, okay? I'm not here to hurt you."

The kid—a boy, by the looks of it—aimed for my head again.

His speed and strength impressed me. He was frail-looking and wore jeans and a faded gray T-shirt. The jeans were too small, and the shirt was too big. Grime and dirt streaked his face.

This time, I caught the end of the plank. Thankfully, the one without nails in it. He was surprised enough to lose his focus, and I took it from him and flung it aside.

"I'm not trying to hurt you," I repeated.

The boy stumbled back, chest heaving. His gaze swept me. "Wh-who are you?"

"My name is Tatiana, and I'm looking for a friend. Are you okay? Are you lost?"

His face hardened.

I relaxed my expression and voice now that I knew the threat was over. "What is your name?"

He didn't answer. His eyes were wide with fear.

"I'm sorry if I scared you," I told him, stepping back. I deposited my gun on the counter, hoping he would see I wasn't a threat.

"A-a friend?" he asked finally. "What friend?"

A friend who wouldn't be living here with a ten-year-old, I thought. Then again, many strange, inexplicable things were attached to Jordan Davenport.

Before I could answer, I noticed the kid's teeth. His incisors were elongated and pointed at the ends. *Fangs.* My heart skipped a beat or two.

He was a vampire.

CHAPTER TEN

TATIANA

"What is your name?" I asked again when the kid had settled down. I couldn't let him see my alarm at those fangs. I squashed the instinct to run. At least in this case, I had no urge to fight. Not when my would-be assailant was a full head-and-a-half shorter than me.

The kid balled the end of his dirty shirt in a fist and trained his eyes on the floor. Finally, instead of answering, he asked, "Are you with the Conclave?" His lower lip wobbled, and his shoulders slumped.

I knelt in front of him. "No, I'm not with the Conclave," I explained, then took a chance. "You're staying with JD. He's protecting you, isn't he?"

The boy's eyes misted as he met my gaze and nodded once.

I laid a hand on my chest and told him again, "My name is Tatiana. JD is the friend I'm looking for. I know the Conclave is after him, and I came to warn him. To find him before they did."

The boy's face hardened. Something flashed in his eyes. "Well, you might as well be leading them right to us. Did you think of that?"

Such a question coming from what appeared to be a ten-year-old startled me. As I considered it, though, I concluded he could be any age. He might have been made into a vampire as a child, however that worked. And now he was stuck in this body.

The thought chilled me. I didn't ask him how old he was. Somehow, that seemed rude to ask a vampire, though I knew little about the situation.

"What is your name?" I tried again.

He hesitated. "Elias."

"Elias. That's a nice name."

I didn't push for a last name. Maybe he didn't have one. Or if he did, maybe he didn't know it. JD seemed to be the one looking after him, not his parents. Unless…

JD doesn't have kids, does he? I'd learned crazier things about him, but somehow, I was convinced I'd have known if he was a father. I glanced into the hallway past the kitchen again. "Is there somewhere we can sit and talk?" I asked.

Elias nodded, then led me into a dusty living room. It seemed to be the only room on the main floor with furniture. A moth-eaten sofa was angled toward an empty fireplace. Dust and cobwebs covered the mantle. I lowered myself to the sofa, trying not to think of how much mold it might contain. Elias sat on the floor and crossed his legs.

"How do you know JD?" I asked, folding my hands.

Wariness still shone in the boy's eyes, so I added, "I'll tell you how I know him first. He came to work with me last year. I own a security firm, and I needed someone who could act as my partner to help me land more clients. JD was perfect for the job, but he also helped me solve a handful of cases." And made my job the most fun it had ever been.

I continued. "It is my job to track down the bad guys and protect innocent people. JD helped me in more ways than I could ever have imagined."

"As Marcus?" Elias asked.

I nodded. "How did you know?"

"He told me he used to act, that his last role was a security firm owner named Marcus Smith."

I wanted to ask Elias if JD had ever mentioned me, but that seemed desperate, even in front of a kid.

He went on anyway. "Jordan rescued me from a rogue vampire named Callum, who's been hunting me for years. We have been on the run and in hiding ever since."

My eyes widened. "Hunting you?"

"Yeah," Elias confirmed. "Real jerk."

"I'd imagine so." I had a dozen questions about how JD had heard of Elias' troubles, how he had rescued him, and why they were staying in this dilapidated mansion. Of course, I also wanted to know how the kid was a vampire and how long he'd been stuck in a child's body.

However, I could see my questions were making Elias feel like I was interrogating him. I needed to back off and make it clear he could trust me.

Elias eyed me. "I can see why you two liked working together. You're both stupid in the same way."

I was too taken aback by his statement to be offended. I laughed. "What makes you say that?"

Elias did not share my amusement. "You go where it's not safe. You shouldn't have come here. Now, they'll be hunting you, too."

Elias told me JD had gone out for supplies. The last run before they headed west. He didn't tell me where, but they had about the entire country in that direction. "He left about ten minutes before you arrived," Elias informed me.

Ships passing in the night. I decided I might as well stick around until JD came back, as long as Elias didn't come at me again with another nail-spiked board.

I returned to the kitchen and went through the cupboards and pantry, trying to scrounge up something for dinner. I found a few cans of soup that looked like they'd been sitting on a shelf since the Reagan administration. With a huff, I closed the pantry door.

Elias stood in the kitchen doorway. "Follow me."

He walked down a long hallway toward the front of the house. Rectangular outlines on the wallpaper revealed where frames had once hung. This house might have been quite nice years ago. I remembered the man in the gas station remarking that folks around here thought the place was haunted. I bet no one guessed a kid vampire lurked behind its walls.

Elias tugged open a hall closet and uncovered a box. Inside it were several cans, some dried meat, and a box of crackers. "We're running low. JD is coming back with more."

"Do vampires eat regular human food?" I asked.

Elias nodded. "I do, but I'm different. I don't think JD eats all that much."

Now that I thought about it, I'd rarely seen JD eat. The few times I had, he might have been doing it for show.

Elias selected a few cans and the box of crackers, then headed back for the kitchen with his arms full. I trailed after him, wondering how Elias was different and how much blood JD needed to consume to feel normal. As normal as a vampire could, anyway. I had questions about sunlight, too, but it seemed rude to ask someone I had just met.

"Soup?" Elias asked.

"Is there a pot?"

He nodded. The pot he produced from a shelf under the kitchen sink was surprisingly clean, and he showed me that both sink and stove worked. Someone was still paying bills out here.

I got to work dumping cans of vegetables into a pot and simmering them. It wouldn't be a great supper, but it was better than nothing. I took out my phone and texted my mom, letting her know I was caught up with work and wouldn't be back until later.

Have dinner without me.

My mouth watered, thinking of the food I could be having at the hotel, but I ignored it as I stirred the soup with a wooden spoon Elias found. How much of the stuff they'd brought versus found in this house I didn't know, and I didn't particularly want to ask.

Elias scooted onto the counter. "So, what are you? You're not a vampire."

I nodded. "I'm a regular old human. And a friend, if you'll have me."

He studied her. "Jordan says you're a friend."

It still felt odd to hear his first name. His *real* first name. I thought of several occasions when I could have considered JD much more than a friend. "Good friends. He saved my life a few times. I think you and I have that in common."

Elias didn't smile, but he relaxed a little. At least he no longer viewed me as a threat.

I stirred the soup more, then told Elias, "Food's almost ready." I wondered what was taking JD so long to get back and wished he was here baking pastries. They were much better than this hodgepodge dinner.

My thoughts shattered when a noise came from the front of the house. It sounded like a window breaking. Elias jumped, and I turned, startled.

Elias went white as a sheet. "It's him."

Not JD, but Callum. The rogue vampire hunting him.

Well, shit.

I moved silently to the other side of the kitchen where I'd laid my Ruger on the counter. I picked it up and crept into the hall. Outside, the sun had nearly set, and I could not see who was causing the commotion.

I signaled for Elias to stay where he was, then stole across the hall into the living room and crept along the wall. Here, I was closer to the front without being exposed. I peered into the hallway and found an arm reaching through the broken center of a window.

I nearly gasped at the sight of that hand. The knuckles were tattooed with letters. The hand moved too quickly for me to make the letters out, but I knew who that hand belonged to.

Shit.

The hand grappled with the lock, then the door swung open on creaking hinges. I pulled back into the room, weighing my options. Callum, if this was him, would not be a simple target. He was a vampire, which meant he had bloodthirst and the same supernatural abilities I'd seen JD display. *This might not end well,* I thought.

Part of me considered running. The front door was open. I could make it to my Mercedes before the vampire realized I'd been in the house. But that would mean leaving Elias vulnerable. He might have similar vampire abilities, but he was much smaller. No, I couldn't do that.

I raised my Ruger and went around to the other side of the living room. When I stepped into the hallway, Callum's back was to me. "Hands up," I stated evenly.

He turned, eyes flashing and nostrils flaring. "You. Bitch. You *are* following me."

I wouldn't bother explaining that he had it all wrong, and it was a coincidence that we were looking for the same guy. "You with the law?" he demanded, stalking toward me. He didn't give two shits about the gun I held to his face.

In a flash, his hand shot out. His fingers closed in an iron grip around my wrist and twisted. I cried out. My gun went off, and a bullet punched through the hallway's ceiling.

I kicked at him, and he doubled over and released me. He shouted a curse as I backed into the living room.

Whatever I had to do to keep him away from Elias. Maybe the kid could get away.

Callum lurched toward me, baring fangs that made my stomach turn. I didn't want to consider what he might do with them. I fired at him, and he hissed as the bullet grazed his shoulder. "You'll pay for that." His low, threatening voice sent ice through my bones.

"Not another step farther," I breathed.

"Or what? Bullets won't stop me."

I believed him.

He flew toward me. I barely evaded the first blow, but the second wasn't avoidable. His arm wrapped around my neck, and his chest pressed into my back. I cried out as hands—no, *claws* raked my side, tearing my shirt and flesh. The vampire's breath smelled metallic. He'd recently fed.

I tried shoving him off me, but he was too strong. I didn't have fangs, but that didn't mean I couldn't hurt him.

So, I sank my teeth into his arm.

He yelped, releasing me more out of surprise than pain. I rammed my elbow back into his chest, then up into his jugular. That gave me enough time to scramble for the hallway.

I reached a rickety set of stairs leading to the second floor. The instant my boot landed on the first step, I knew they were dangerous. Nevertheless, I climbed up. At least upstairs, I would be getting Callum farther from Elias.

The vampire pursued, but only as far as the bottom of the stairs. Had he not seen me go this way? It wasn't possible.

But Callum's attention was fixed toward the back of the house. He loosed a growl that made the fragile railing shudder, then lurched for the doorway and vanished into the darkness.

I started after him, my heart pounding. Perhaps Elias had run out that way, and Callum had sensed him and given pursuit.

A hand touched mine, drawing me back. "Don't."

I whirled. Elias had grabbed me.

"D-don't go after him," he stammered.

I looked through the open back door. Beyond lay darkness and dense trees. I didn't know how far the woods stretched. Why had Callum gone out there if Elias was in here?

Elias' gaze fixed on the rectangle of darkness, his breath catching. Something or *someone* was out there.

"Jordan," Elias whispered.

<u>Jordan</u>

I halted a few feet from the tree line and sniffed the air. Something wasn't right.

Slowly, I lowered the sack of goods I'd bought an hour ago from my shoulder, letting it fall to the ground with a soft thud. Beyond the trees, the blue hues of twilight washed over the property. Not long now before it would be fully dark. I followed my nose a few yards down the tree line, not yet emerging, and halted when I found the source of my disturbed senses.

Lying against the wide trunk of an ancient oak tree was a doe's carcass. She'd clearly died not from a shotgun wound or a natural occurrence, but at a predator's hands. A wide gash opened her side. *Claws.*

My heart skipped a beat. No wild animal had done this, unless the vampire who'd fed on her could be considered one.

I'd come up the back of the property. The road from the neighboring town where I'd bought supplies led through the woods, a shorter route than the main road. This way, I could also avoid being seen and perceived as a hitchhiker.

None of that mattered now.

I glanced toward the house. All seemed still, except that the kitchen light was on. Strange. Elias kept the lights off as much as possible.

Someone else is in the house.

The thought sent a chill down my spine. I trekked back to

where I had left my sack of goods. At the same time, a figure filled the back doorway. I could tell by his outline, those broad shoulders and fisted hands, who it was. I released a low snarl. "Callum."

I couldn't deny the fear sliding through me. Callum had gotten here before me. There was a good chance he had already done something to Elias. The thoughts racing through my head weren't helpful. Not in a moment where I need focus as clear as the night sky.

I shouldn't have left. I should have taken Elias with me. I thought it was safe here.

The wards only worked if I was here to hold them, and Elias wasn't trained well enough to throw his own out.

Yet Callum, the rogue bastard, had found us.

Callum sensed me, and his gaze cut toward me. A slow smile curled his lips, revealing bloodied fangs. I could only hope the blood was from the deer and not Elias. He stalked toward me, passing the tree line with the swagger of a centuries-old vampire who's known nothing but bloodthirst in his long, miserable life.

"This time, you're not getting away," he snapped when we were within feet of one another.

I rolled up my sleeves as casually as I could. This was not the time to demand what he'd done to Elias. Not the time to show my cards, or the truth—that I was *afraid*. Not of the rogue bastard standing in front of me, but of what I had failed to do. *Protect the kid.*

"You should really consider getting a hobby," I told him. "Once, I spent a year doing little other than reading Shakespeare. He really has a knack for articulating the human condition."

"Saw one of his plays once," Callum spat. "It was bullshit."

I shrugged. "Beats hunting kids for sport."

Either this pissed Callum off, or he was too impatient. Whatever the case, he flew at me. My back slammed against the trunk of a tree, and claws dug into my front.

The next several moments were mostly a blur. We traded blows—claws, teeth, fists, feet, anything we could use. My jaw ached, and I swore one of my teeth had been knocked out. Blood dribbled from my nose.

We threw each other against trees and the ground. I'd have more cuts and bruises than I could count when this was over. To make things worse, Callum had just fed. Deer blood was nothing compared to human, but it was worlds better than the synthetic shit I'd been relying on—and running low on—for weeks now. All that pent-up rage inside him helped his cause, too.

What kept me going was Elias. Beat Callum, get Elias. Get the hell out of here.

Finally, I pinned Callum to the ground and didn't hesitate to pound my fist into his face. Over and over again.

"Stop following us. Go back to whatever slimehole you crawled out of. Miserable bastard." I spat the words through clenched teeth with each strike. I was reminded of the days after I'd first been turned and couldn't control my bloodthirst.

I recalled the first time I'd encountered another vampire. How we'd fought over the body of a dead fox, of all things, and beaten each other to a bloody pulp. I remembered the thrill of that first fight, of feeding during those early days. Back when I did not know how to pace myself and control the hunger.

Callum's hands grappled with my shirt and threw me off him. I landed hard against another tree, giving him enough time to scramble to his feet. He hissed and spat blood. His gaze was so hateful, I thought if he didn't kill me soon, he'd explode with the need.

Instead of coming at me again, he took off through the trees, leaving a trail of blood behind. I'd injured him enough for now, but that didn't mean he would stay away for long. Elias and I should have left this shithole days ago.

My body would heal, but I felt like I'd been tossed around hell by the devil himself. I barely managed to peel myself off the ground. Then, I braced a hand against the tree, steadying myself. When I could walk without the whole forest swimming in front of my eyes, I hobbled toward the back door.

"Elias?" I called as I stumbled toward the living room, fearing the worst.

Callum wanted Elias so he could figure out how to become a Day Walker. He wouldn't have killed him. That didn't mean he wouldn't hurt him, though.

I froze when I entered the living room. Elias was fine, to my great surprise. The greater shock was that he wasn't alone.

Beside him on the sofa, bleeding but very much alive, was Tatiana.

CHAPTER ELEVEN

TATIANA

I wondered if I was dreaming.

JD stood before us, cut, bruised, and bloody. Like he'd been in a fight with another vampire. Callum hadn't returned, so JD must have gotten the upper hand.

"You look like shit," Elias remarked dully.

I pushed myself up, using the sofa for support. My other hand clutched my still-bleeding side. "JD…"

A dozen emotions played across his face. First was the relief at seeing Elias alive and unhurt, then recognizing me. Following this was concern over my wound as it dawned on him who'd caused it. Last, of course, were all the emotions at seeing a lover for the first time in months, after no contact.

The same emotions flooded me.

"JD," I started again, not sure if I should sit again and let him come to me or embrace him. God, I wanted to kiss him.

"You're hurt." His voice was low and gravely. His pupils were blown wide, chest heaving. The predator that had come out while fighting Callum lingered.

I huffed. "You should see the other guy."

JD's grim smile made my heart ache. I had missed that smile.

It faded, and the concern returned. "I don't think the bastard will be bothering us again anytime soon." He turned to Elias. "Will you go and get the first aid kit, please?"

Elias rose, but before he left the room, JD stopped him with a hand on his shoulder. "Are you okay?"

Elias simply nodded. My heart ached at witnessing JD's tenderness toward the kid.

Elias headed from the room, and JD sank onto the sofa beside me. "Here, let me see." His voice was soft, and his touch was cold but gentle. My eyes misted at his mere closeness. I'd imagined how seeing him again would go. In none of my imaginings had I pictured *this*.

Slowly, he peeled my shirt away from my side, revealing three long gashes oozing blood. I clenched my teeth against the pain as his fingers pressed along an unhurt rib, too close to the actual wounds.

"Did that hurt?" he asked.

"Your fingers are cold, but that's nothing new. All this time, I thought you had poor circulation." I pushed out a hard breath and tried a tone of amusement. "I can't believe I'm seeing *the* Jordan Davenport in a T-shirt and… Are those *jeans*?"

His half-smile didn't reach his eyes. "Tragic, I know. Alas, good fashion sense takes a back seat when you're on the run." His amusement died away as he added, "You shouldn't have come here, Tatiana. It's too dangerous."

"For me or for you?"

"Both of us. Elias, too."

For that, I felt a pang of regret. But if I had not been here to distract Callum, Elias would be in trouble. I wouldn't let my mind stray to what might have happened to me if Callum hadn't sensed JD outside.

I sighed. "Don't worry. Elias gave me a similar speech."

JD didn't lift his head, but he responded, "I've gotten a few lectures from him, too."

"For good reason," Elias stated as he walked back into the room, first aid kit in hand. He seemed prepared to lecture us again, but seeing as how we had both saved his life, he let it rest. "I'll go make some tea now."

He left again, and JD opened the first aid kit. He began to clean the wound, brows furrowed. "I've seen nastier, if that makes you feel better. Especially from vampires."

I winced as he cleaned and dabbed. "Me, too. In the military." I remembered plenty of times when I'd treated my own wounds or those of the soldiers fighting alongside me. I had never been attacked by a vampire before, though. At least, not that I knew of.

"Elias told me you're protecting him from Callum."

JD nodded. "Callum is a rogue vampire who wants to experiment on Elias. He thinks Elias is the key to creating Day Walkers."

I gave him a questioning look.

"Vampires who can resist sunlight. Perhaps not entirely, but much longer than usual. Elias can, and he ages much slower than others."

An anomaly, you could say. The joke felt too soon to crack. I knew what JD was now, but still, hearing the word "vampire" from his mouth after he'd spent months hiding it from me felt surreal. His mention of Day Walkers confirmed that the sunlight thing was legit.

"Shit," was all I could say.

"Yeah. Real stinking shit."

With the wounds cleaned, JD selected a salve. I clenched my teeth as he spread it across my side. I wasn't sure if the probing or his cold touch hurt more. As long as we kept talking, I could withstand the pain. "And the Rose Conclave? Do you think they will do something to Elias?"

Finally, JD's head snapped up, his blue eyes meeting mine. "How do you know about the Conclave? Did Elias tell you? You know, for all his lecturing about being careful, he sure talks a lot."

I shook my head. "Elias was quite wary of me. Actually, he tried to knock me out with a wooden board. He almost managed it, too." I paused and sighed. "Your old buddy Jessamine Lane paid me a visit. That's how I know." I reached into my back pocket and produced the card she'd given me.

JD stared at it like it was a bomb about to go off in my hand.

He cursed. "Jessamine is using you as bait. She knew that by going to you, you would get concerned about me and come looking. She's probably tracking your every move."

"I thought about that. You don't think I've been careful?"

JD's face softened. "Tell me everything that happened."

I started with how Jessamine had approached me after I'd finished a security job, then her visit to my office. I explained what I'd learned from Vinny, and finally, my visit to Beck's.

"You went to *Beck*? Tatiana, you shouldn't have gone to my house or to Beck's. It was safer when you were far away from me." His tone was both pained and earnest.

I couldn't help but feel hurt. "You disappeared, JD. For good reason, but I hadn't heard from you in so long. Then, some fancy vampire lady shows up and tells me you're in hot water, and she plans to bring you in. What was I supposed to do? Sit on my ass and let her do whatever the hell she wanted with you?"

"Yes," he answered simply, but I wasn't finished.

"And that was before I knew anything about Elias. Look, I'm sorry if I've complicated everything, but I won't apologize for putting myself in danger. I'll always do that for the people I..."

I trailed off. The big word lay between us, creating thick tension in the air.

JD's hand slid from my side to rest on my thigh, and he hung his head. "I know. I would have done the same."

I swallowed the emotion that formed a lump in my throat. "I-I hadn't heard from you. I wanted to know that you were okay."

His hand tightened on my thigh, and I slid my hand over his. "JD, I missed you."

I hadn't let myself admit how much until that moment. I'd missed him like crazy. I could barely remember how my life was before he came into it. After he'd gone, I'd felt I was missing a limb. Now, he was here, smelling like blood and looking wrecked. Far from the professional actor in expensive suits driving sports cars. But he was so *him*, and I had missed him more than I could express.

I cupped his cheek with my other hand. "JD, I know what you are now, and I'm not afraid."

The words seemed to break something in him. His face shifted through several emotions before he reached back into the first aid kit for bandages. "We have a lot to talk about. You know enough of the truth now. I want to tell you the full story."

As he had promised in the note he'd left before disappearing.

"I would like that very much."

JD swallowed. "But first, I must say I'm sorry. I'm sorry for letting you believe lies about me, for pretending to be someone I wasn't, and in the end, for leaving. For not reaching out."

"You did what you thought was best." I blinked so tears wouldn't form. "JD…was it real? How you felt about me?"

"Fuck, of course it was real, Tatiana. Do you know how hard I tried to make it *not* real?" He laughed roughly, then slid a palm against my cheek, down the side of my neck. Goosebumps erupted across my skin. "You are the hardest thing I have ever had to resist."

I offered a tired smile. "I'm going to take that as a compliment."

"I should begin by explaining recent events." As he bandaged me, he told me how he'd answered a Conclave summons in December and was charged a steep penalty for his "flashy heroics." At the same time, he'd heard of a rogue vampire named Callum going after a very slowly aging vampire boy named Elias.

"How old is he really?" I asked.

"Seventy."

"And is a vampire like Elias common?"

JD shook his head. "No one like him has existed as long as I have been alive. Sure, there are kids who get turned, and they age slowly, but not like Elias. If he were a normal vampire, he would look twenty by now."

The words "normal vampire" weren't computing.

JD told me the Rose Conclave was tracking both Callum and Elias. "They said that if I helped them find the pair, they would waive my penalty. I agreed, mostly because I think Callum is a bastard. I knew what the Conclave wanted to do to Elias would be no better than what Callum would do. Maybe more humane, but still the same end goal."

Dread curled in my stomach. "Experiment on him?"

JD nodded. "Get to him before he learns how powerful he could become. I found Elias and had to fight Callum off. When that was over and I thought Callum was gone, the Conclave told me to hand Elias over. Instead, I ran. We've been running ever since."

"And both Callum and the Conclave haven't stopped looking for you." I cursed under my breath. "If Callum was able to track you down…"

JD finished my thought. "Then Jessamine and the Conclave won't be far behind." He lowered my shirt over my bandaged side, adding, "I can get you something cleaner to wear."

I looked him up and down. "Maybe you should do that for yourself first. I don't imagine you brought all your suits here."

JD seemed to have forgotten all about his blood-soaked clothes or the fact that he smelled far from good. Already, the bruises and cuts I'd noticed on his face, arms, and hands were fading. Vampire healing abilities, probably.

He barely smiled. "No suits. I haven't felt like myself in months." He stood, and I felt suddenly empty without him so close. "I'll shower and change. But first, let's find Elias and make plans to leave."

My heart lifted at the thought of going with them, but JD quickly dashed my hopes. "You must return to D.C. as soon as possible, before Jessamine catches wind of you here. If she hasn't already."

"I can handle Jessa—"

JD stopped me with his hands on my shoulders. "You're the bravest woman I've ever met, Tatiana, and you've dealt with some real hard-asses, but Jessamine is not to be underestimated." Real fear filled his eyes. "You will go back to D.C., and I will take Elias far away from here."

"Tell me where you're going, JD." *Far away* wasn't good enough.

His hands slid away. "It's not safe, Tatiana." He paused, then added before I could protest, "I'll send word after we've settled somewhere. I promise."

It was the best I'd get, so I nodded. "Okay."

We headed for the kitchen, but before we were down the hallway, headlights beamed across the front of the property. "Shit." I hurried to the front windows. A black SUV with heavily tinted windows rolled up the driveway and halted behind my parked Mercedes.

JD came to my side, his mouth set in a thin line. I noted the license plate out of second nature, then crossed my arms. "Looks like one of us was followed here."

CHAPTER TWELVE

TATIANA

I'd seen JD scout a perimeter more times than I could count. I'd seen him creep around corners, scale walls, and hide in places he shouldn't have been able to hide in. Seeing him glide to the window and scan the property for danger felt different now.

Before, I hadn't been fully aware of his preternatural abilities. In the deep twilight, he could see much farther than I could. He could hear and smell things I couldn't.

His spine grew rigid, and his jaw tightened. For him, it wasn't merely training but a predator's instinct. A combination of thrill and fear shot through me as he slunk back into the shadows after watching the property for a minute.

"Three vehicles. One..." He pointed at the SUV parked behind my Mercedes, then turned slightly to the left. "Two." Slightly to the right. "Three." Two and Three were hidden among the dense trees surrounding the property. "All three with at least two operatives," he added.

He turned and walked toward the kitchen, his steps hurried yet purposeful.

"Vampires?" I asked, trailing after him.

He shook his head. "Humans. Well-trained, with military gear. Their equipment is government-issued."

"Do you have X-ray vision, too?" I demanded. I had no idea how he could tell all this.

He eyed me. "Of course not."

I opened my mouth to demand an explanation, but as we reached the kitchen, I realized now wasn't the time for questions. We had to get out of here.

"We've got company," JD told Elias. "We should have moved last night."

The thought of arriving at this house and finding it empty a mere day after JD had been here made my heart sink. At least that wasn't the reality. Instead, we had company we weren't expecting.

"How do you think human authorities got involved?" I asked as JD and Elias hurried to gather what few possessions they had in the house. Among them were the first aid kit JD had used to patch me up and the remaining pantry items. The soup sat on the stove, untouched. I wasn't too mad about it. I never expected it to turn out very good.

"Do you think someone from the Conclave tipped them off? Or Callum?" I asked.

JD peeled off his bloodied shirt, and it took all my willpower not to gawk. All that time in hiding hadn't prevented him from working out. "No. Callum is brash and idiotic, but he knows better than to let that sort of thing slip to the public, especially law enforcement. The last thing Jessamine or anyone else in the Conclave wants is risking exposure. That's why they were after me in the first place, and now Callum."

Then who? JD didn't seem to know and wasn't interested in finding out when these guys came knocking. He pulled on a fresh shirt and glanced at me. "No time for a shower." He reached into a large backpack, pulled out another shirt, and tossed it to me.

Light beamed through the front window into the hallway, and

footsteps sounded on gravel. Time was running out. "How do you plan to get out of here?" I asked JD.

He glanced toward the back door leading into the forest, but decided against it.

Some of these guys would come around back before long. With my Mercedes parked out front, the operatives already knew someone was here.

"This way." He shouldered his backpack. Elias also wore one. I shrugged my jacket on and grabbed my Ruger, keys, phone, and wallet. I shoved the smaller items into pockets and holstered the Ruger.

JD opened a door leading down a narrow staircase. We descended into a cold, dank cellar, where he approached a wood-paneled wall and pried one of the panels back. "This will lead us out."

I had a dozen questions about this place. How he'd found it, why he knew where the secret tunnel was, and why he had come here. But I kept my mouth shut as he ushered Elias inside, then me. JD stepped through last and replaced the panel.

A flashlight ahead of me turned on. Elias waved it across the tunnel ahead of us and commented, "Good thing I'm not claustrophobic."

I felt JD's hand on my shoulder. He squeezed lightly, a small comfort in this otherwise less-than-ideal situation. It was all the communication I needed to follow Elias.

We walked for what felt like an eternity, but according to JD, we'd only gone a mile and a half before we started ascending. Elias halted at the end of the tunnel, where a ladder led to a square of wood above.

JD moved in front of us, climbed the ladder, and removed the panel, then hoisted himself up. He reached down to pull Elias through, then me.

I emerged in the midst of dense trees, dark all around me. In the distance, I caught flashing lights. We were too far for me to hear voices, but JD and Elias seemed to. They shared a look as if to say, *Let's keep moving.*

When Elias switched off his flashlight, I realized he'd only used it before for my sake. They were both vampires and could see in the dark. It wasn't so dark that I couldn't follow them, though.

We started through the trees, skirting fallen logs and broken trunks, boulders, and even a creek. The night air was cool enough to be pleasant with my jacket on. I burned with curiosity about where we were going, but I didn't ask. I would know soon enough.

Finally, JD halted ahead of us, and I glimpsed the tree line. Beyond was a ramshackle-looking house. A fishing shack, I realized, along the banks of a river that gleamed in the moonlight.

We weren't here for the shack, but for an old pickup truck that looked one bad pothole away from falling apart.

Elias dug around in his backpack and tossed JD a set of keys. "Don't drive so fast you nearly throw us off the side of a mountain, okay?"

JD flashed me a smile, the first real smile that night, that said, *You aren't the only one who has a problem with my driving.*

The truck was hardly a replacement for my Mercedes, but getting that back right now wasn't an option. Was it even mine now that I'd found JD again?

JD opened the driver's side door. It emitted a low creak. Elias climbed in first and settled in the middle. I stepped into the passenger side. Seconds later, JD perched in the driver's seat, and the beater rumbled to life.

"Where are we going?" I finally asked.

JD put the truck in reverse and backed down the driveway leading to the shed. "An old contact of mine owns a cabin in a remote area. We can crash there for a day or two, but it will take several hours to get there. We'll figure out how to get you back to

D.C. when the coast is clear." Which would be as soon as possible, if he had his way.

It occurred to me as we drove along winding backroads that the human authorities might have been looking for me as well as JD and his sidekick. If so, they might have also contacted Beck or my mom.

JD glanced at the dashboard and grumbled, "We'll need gas."

Fifteen minutes later, he pulled into a gas station. In this remote area after dark, the lot was empty of customers. "I'm going to make a few calls," I told him as I climbed out of the truck. JD filled up while Elias rifled through the glovebox, presumably for anything interesting.

I walked a few yards away, dialing Beck's number.

She didn't answer, so I left a voicemail informing her to be careful, because human authorities might be watching her.

Next, I called my mother.

"Honey, I was beginning to worry. I've just had dinner in the hotel. The oysters were *delicious*. Are you on your way back? We can order dessert and a bottle of wine, and sit out by one of the firepits."

"Mom, I'm not going to be able to make it back tonight."

"Oh, honey, is anything wrong?" The worry in her voice was unmistakable.

"Just caught up in my work. Look, it's a sensitive case, and I can't come back to the hotel for a few days. You should head back to D.C. in the morning. You won't have my Mercedes, so you'll have to rent a car. I'll cover the cost and arrange it for you."

"Go home without you?" My mom sounded offended.

"I'm really sorry. You should, for your safety."

"But what about your safety?"

"I'll be fine."

After a pause, my mother lowered her voice and asked, "Does this have to do with Marcus? Are you with him?"

I glanced at the gas pump and the truck parked beside it. JD looked so ordinary in his jeans and T-shirt, waiting for the tank to fill up. This was not the Marcus Smith I had worked with for months.

"It does," I admitted, hoping that my being with JD would give my mom some semblance of comfort.

"Okay, good. I'll go back tomorrow, then. Call me when you can, dear. Please."

I promised to do that and said goodnight. Before returning to the truck, I texted Jake and asked him to run the plates from the SUV we'd spotted at the house.

I'd pocketed my phone and was returning to the truck when JD asked, "Everything okay?"

"As okay as it can be. That was my mom. I was letting her know that she should head back to D.C. as soon as she can. I think I forgot to tell you we were in upstate New York together."

"Mother-daughter trip?"

"She wanted to go to a nice hotel and spa. We compromised on the location because of my work."

"To find me." His gaze was trained on me.

I nodded.

"Special occasion?" he asked.

I paused, then admitted, "My birthday."

Something in JD's eyes deflated. "Your birthday." He repeated it almost mournfully. "I'm sorry I couldn't be around for it. Was it yesterday?"

I nodded again. "Don't worry about it."

"Well, happy birthday." He leaned forward and kissed my cheek.

I smiled. "Thank you."

We climbed back into the truck and set out. Urgency laced the air. The operatives would find the house empty, but they'd know at least one person was there. Though they shouldn't be able to track us to the next location, at least not anytime soon, human authorities being involved was clearly a problem.

Callum was injured, according to JD, but far from dead. How did one kill a vampire, anyway? I didn't want to start thinking again about Jessamine and the Conclave.

"Here, some snacks. I got them from the gas station while you were on the phone." JD handed me a package of beef jerky and some cheese crackers.

"Thank you," I murmured as I accepted them. I hadn't realized until then how empty my stomach felt. As I ate, we basked in the quiet of the truck rumbling along the country roads. Elias remained silent between us, staring through the windshield.

When I finished eating, and exhaustion trickled in, JD suggested, "Sleep, if you can. I'll try not to hit too many potholes."

CHAPTER THIRTEEN

TATIANA

I jostled awake when JD stopped the truck.

"We made it," he stated softly.

I raised my head from where I'd been resting it against the window, shivering. The heat in the truck didn't work, which came as no surprise to anyone. I peered through the windshield at a small log cabin situated against a thick forest. Then, I glanced at the clock. It was nearly midnight.

Silently, we filed out of the truck and approached the cabin. JD fished in his pocket for a key.

The front room had a tiny kitchen, table, sofa, and a hunky, box-shaped TV covered in dust. Taxidermied animals and oil paintings of mountain landscapes decorated the walls. The place looked like it hadn't been used in months, maybe years.

"Cozy," I muttered.

"We won't have to stay long," JD assured us.

Elias wandered toward the back of the house, which had a small bedroom with an attached bath. The only other door led out the back to a stoop and a small circle of stones that served as a fire pit. The place had no heating or cooling functions other than a wood stove.

I took out my phone and found a message from Jake Molina.

Call me.

I turned to JD. "I'm going to call Molina, ask what he found out about the SUV we saw." JD only nodded, and I stepped back outside.

The sky was clear, the moon emitting silvery light. I felt far removed from civilization, the quiet night dancing between serene and eerie.

"Sorry I'm having you do all this so late, Jake," I greeted when he picked up the phone.

"You know I keep late hours, Sterling." The man was practically nocturnal.

"What do you have for me?"

"Plates are registered to a Patrick Goth, a private security operative. I traced him to his boss, a Malcolm Ellwood."

"The Ellwood running for senator in Virginia?" I asked.

"Same guy," Jake confirmed.

Ellwood had already served a term as senator before bowing out of the political spotlight for years. I'd worked a function for him when my firm was just getting started. My rival, Dan, hadn't been able to cover the event and begrudgingly recommended me to Ellwood's wife.

I remembered being in their opulent Virginia home for the simple security event. I'd had little interaction with the Ellwoods and was certain I'd faded into obscurity with them.

Why the hell was a previous senator running for another term sending security up to Vermont? Was he after me or JD? I had been very careful about not being followed and hadn't noticed anything unusual.

"If I learn anything more, I'll be in touch," Jake promised.

We told each other goodnight and hung up. I paced across the porch and thought everything over.

"Everything okay?" JD stood in the doorway, arms crossed. He still wore his bloodied jeans, though his shirt was clean.

I told him what Jake had reported.

JD's face tightened. "I spoke with Vinny. We don't call often, mostly so I can keep him safe. The fewer people I get wrapped up in this, the better. He sent me an urgent message, though, saying we needed to talk."

"And?"

"He says someone has been leaking information about magicals to human authorities. Some agent lady came knocking at his door, wanting to ask him a few questions. He's heard from others in our community about similar situations."

My blood ran cold. "What kind of questions?"

"How long he had lived there, what he did for a living, if he was connected with any 'unsanctioned' groups."

I lifted a brow.

JD ran a hand through his hair. "It wouldn't surprise me if human authorities start catching onto us, and what they'll categorize us as. Domestic terrorists, threats to national security. You name it."

"Did Vinny give her anything?"

He shook his head. "He didn't have to answer any questions, so he didn't. I wonder if these 'human authorities' include this senator Molina has told you about."

In that case, the guys following us couldn't be working with the Conclave or Callum. They were a shared enemy. What were the chances? Could Ellwood be connected to the work Victor Hume had been doing?

JD leaned against the door frame. "There is a lot more going on than meets the eye, but I can't be too concerned with that right now. I have to focus on getting Elias somewhere safe."

That, we could agree on.

JD's gaze lingered on me. Gone was the grim focus of our escape and drive, replaced by unnamed emotions. Whatever he was feeling, he didn't share. All he said was, "I'm going to shower."

I decided to check on Elias. He was perched on the edge of a twin-sized bed pushed up against the wall. The bedroom wasn't much bigger than my closet at home. The floorboards creaked as I approached the doorway, but Elias didn't need the sound to know I was there.

"Everything okay?" I asked, noting his downcast expression.

When Elias didn't answer, I sat beside him. My instinct was to treat him like a child in need of comfort, but did he feel like a child after being alive for so long?

"I'm afraid," he admitted when I'd settled onto the worn, quilt-covered mattress.

"Of Callum and the Conclave?"

"Of Jordan and I being separated."

The words cleaved through me. *Me too, buddy.*

"I've spent my whole life feeling alone," Elias murmured. "Ever since I was turned..." He trailed off, his gaze fixed on a distant point.

I didn't know what "turning" entailed, but it didn't sound good, especially for a kid.

Elias stared into his lap and picked at a loose thread on his shirt. "Jordan was the first vampire to treat me like a person instead of a curiosity or resource."

I'd had experiences with non-vampires who acted the same way. "I'm sorry for what has happened to you. We're both lucky to have met JD." I couldn't quite get "Jordan" to roll off my tongue yet. It made me feel like I was talking about a distant stranger.

Elias' gaze met mine. "And we would be unlucky to lose him."

My heart ached, but I smiled and bumped my shoulder against his. "JD would be unlucky to lose you, too."

Elias swallowed. "He didn't have to come and find me. He doesn't have to keep running with me, but he does. I don't understand it."

"He cares about you," I told him.

Elias nodded, his eyes misting. "But why? He only learned I existed six months ago."

"Maybe he sees some of his old self in you. But even if he doesn't, what reason does he need to care? Having a heart and a brain should be enough."

Elias managed a smile. "I'm going to bed now," he stated after a beat.

I stood to give him room on the bed, with the fleeting thought that it was the only one in the cabin. Where I would sleep was such a small problem compared to what we'd already dealt with tonight. "Do vampires sleep as much as non-vampires?"

"We either sleep very little or enter a meditative state, usually during the day. Tonight has been particularly…taxing."

I nodded. "Get some rest, then."

I left, closing the door behind me, then glanced at the stove clock. It was almost one in the morning, but the night felt far longer. I noticed the shower was no longer on, and the bathroom door was open. So was the front door.

JD stood on the porch, his back to me. I was caught between leaving him alone to process and finally having a conversation that Elias didn't need to be present for.

I drifted toward the doorway. "JD?"

He didn't answer, so I stepped closer and brushed the back of his arm. When my hand made contact, he jerked away, then turned quickly. His pupils were so wide that his irises were nearly invisible. His gaze was pure hunger, and not the kind he had shown before. This was the hunger of a predator.

I stepped back. "JD…"

He didn't seem to recognize me as he growled softly. His lips parted, revealing the points of his fangs. He stalked toward me, bracing his hands on the door frame.

"JD, what's wrong?" I asked.

He leaned toward me, his fangs going for my neck.

I moved out of the way, but his fingers caught my wrist. "I can hear your heart," he murmured.

My heart was beating faster, but not in the exciting way I'd come to expect around him.

"JD, let go." My voice was firmer.

His grip only tightened. He wasn't himself. He stared me down for a solid heartbeat or two, then suddenly released me. He stepped back out onto the porch, and I noticed his fingernails had extended. *Claws.*

My side throbbed where Callum had wounded me.

Shit.

JD threw his head back, arching his spine, and released a sound halfway between a whimper and a snarl. Something was happening to him, and it wasn't good.

"JD," I tried again.

He came toward me, and I moved out of the way before he could snatch me. He barreled past me into the cabin's main room.

I watched, stunned, as he tore into the sofa, wrenching those claws through the upholstery. He dragged them down the wall and shredded the wallpaper. The sounds he made were guttural. Animalistic.

He whirled on me again, his eyes wild and darting all over the room.

"JD, come back to yourself," I pleaded. I reached for him, commanding myself not to be afraid. I took his hand and gripped hard, then slid my other hand to his jaw.

He grew very still, his gaze fixed on me.

"It's me," I murmured. "You're safe. Come back to yourself."

The change happened in an instant, like a switch was flipped.

JD's pupils returned to normal size. He blinked, then in a normal voice murmured, "Tatiana?"

I smiled grimly. "It's me. What happened?"

He stepped back, chest heaving, and moved to drop onto the

sofa. Then, he backed away when he saw the damage. "Wh-what did I do?"

"You're looking at it."

His gaze returned to me, full of fear. "Did I hurt you?"

I shook my head but didn't tell him, *I thought you might try to.* "Does that happen…often?" Was this not being himself normal for a vampire?

JD sank to the sofa and ran his fingers through his hair. "It isn't normal. It only started after Victor."

My heart sank. I lowered onto the sofa beside him and kept my voice low to avoid disturbing Elias. "The drug he gave you?"

"Whatever was in it made me have these…blood rages. That's what Elias calls them, anyway. This is the third I've had since I met him."

"And before that?"

"Once. I was alone."

"Blood rage?"

"A thirst I feel I cannot control. I feel the same as I did when I was first turned. Like I'm going to die if I don't drink."

My stomach coiled.

"It's slowly leaving my system, the drug. The rages are fewer and farther between, but…"

But it had been *months* since Victor abducted and drugged JD, and we knew little about what was in the substance. "I'm sorry," JD stated huskily. "I wasn't aware of myself. I think the stress of the night triggered it, and—"

"Hey." I put a hand on his shoulder. "I'm not afraid of you. I hope you know that."

His eyes were hungry, but not for blood. They were filled with longing. "Tatiana…" My name on his lips was soft, the yearning unmistakable.

"JD."

His lips crashed into mine. One hand slid up my jaw, into my hair. I reached for him, hauling him closer. He tasted exactly as I remembered, and I couldn't get enough of him.

His other arm snaked around my waist, and our bodies were flush together. He smelled much better now that he'd showered. After a moment of bliss, he tore his mouth away. "Tatiana," he repeated like it was the most beautiful word he could speak.

I smiled. "This is hardly the place for a proper reunion." The sofa was too small for us to sleep on, and Elias was on the other side of the wall.

JD stroked my side, the one that wasn't wounded. "And you're still hurt. No, hardly the time." But promise filled his voice.

I cupped his face. "Another time."

He kissed my cheek, then my forehead, before planting a softer kiss on my lips. "You should get some rest."

"What will you do?" I asked.

A far-off look entered his eyes. "Plan what's next."

I could see that he didn't want to be pushed. I squeezed his hand. "We still have a lot to talk about."

JD nodded. "I know. Later, I promise. For now, you sleep."

CHAPTER FOURTEEN

TATIANA

I awoke the following morning on the sofa. My limbs were stiff, and the blanket JD had covered me with was itchy. I sat up, groggy, and peered through the window. The sky was beginning to turn gray. The place was quiet, with no sign of JD.

"He went for a run," a voice stated. Elias appeared in the bedroom doorway, looking refreshed.

I understood. Anytime I had a lot to think about, a run or a boxing session usually helped.

I checked my phone and found a message from Jake.

Call me when you're up.

I stepped outside so as not to bother Elias. The early dawn air was cool against my skin. "Molina," I greeted when Jake answered the phone.

"Good and bad news. The good news is that I found out more about what Ellwood is up to. Bad news is…well, what he's up to."

My anticipation built.

"It appears he's assembled a task force that focuses on tracking activity among, as Victor Hume called them, 'enhanced individuals.' This task force has been going directly to individuals they suspect are either enhanced or in close proximity to enhanced individuals."

I thought of what Vinny had told JD last night.

"No evidence points to them having worked together, but it's quite possible through mutual connections that Ellwood learned about Hume's research and experimentation and has taken an interest of his own." Jake paused, then added, "It gets worse."

Of course it did.

"They seem to believe you're involved. I found a file in their system labeled 'Sterling and Smith, Person of Interest – Proximity to Anomalies.'"

My heart thudded. How long had they been watching me? The men who followed us last night, had they come after me or JD? Were they aware of Elias? If they were, did they know as much as Callum and the Conclave? We were swimming in shark-infested waters.

I had not mentioned the slowly aging vampire to Jake or even that I was with JD again. It was better to keep us all safe, so I gave as little information as possible.

"I'll keep looking. I wanted you to know that, so you can be careful," Jake told me.

"Thank you. We can talk about this more when I'm back in town."

"Watch yourself out there, Sterling."

As I hung up, JD came jogging up the path toward the cabin. A mist rose behind him. He didn't look like he'd been running. Not breaking a sweat must be one of the benefits of having an enhanced body.

He spotted me and smiled, though weariness lurked in his eyes. It was not the fatigue of a sleep-deprived body. He tilted his head toward the porch. I joined him there, and we sat on a bench pushed against the exterior wall while Elias puttered around inside.

"Sleep okay?" JD asked.

I nodded. "I haven't slept that hard in…" I had to search my memory, then flushed as I realized it was the last time JD and I had spent the night together. We'd awoken mid-morning in my apartment and spent a good hour in bed before getting up and making brunch.

That was when I'd noted it was strange JD didn't want to eat. "I only have an appetite for one thing," had been his excuse then. He'd kissed my neck in such a way that I'd nearly forgotten about my growling stomach.

JD appeared to access the same memory, but his eyes glimmered. "That's good," he murmured.

"Molina called." I shared the new information.

JD's expression darkened. "This isn't good."

Understatement of the week.

I reached for his hand. "We can discuss what to do about Ellwood later. Right now, I want you to tell me more about you." It was the conversation I'd been dying to have since my first taste of the truth six months ago.

JD sighed. "It's a long story. Are you sure you want to hear it?"

"Every detail."

He smirked. "I've been alive for a little over three centuries. We don't have time for every detail, but we can start. First, I want you to know that everything I've ever told you was true."

He'd told me that he was orphaned at a young age and took care of his siblings. That he had traveled far and wide. I recalled the fragments he'd given me, and the picture came into fuller focus. I remembered his insistence that I stop digging for the truth, that I would find something I wouldn't like.

"Tell me about getting turned. How does that work?"

JD's face hardened. "It can happen in many ways. Some of us are turned with full consent. Some are at the brink of death, and are brought back by a vampire who desires to expand their family. However, many are turned without even knowing what's happening to them."

"That was what happened to you," I guessed.

A grim nod. "A bloodthirsty vampire with no control sank his fangs into me."

It was as easy as that?

"It's…complicated. A vampire in control of himself can feed without turning the person, but it can go too far," JD elaborated.

I tried not to shudder at the word "feed."

JD noticed. "It has been decades since I last fed in the way you may be imagining," he told me. "Most of us now drink a synthetic blend, supplied by… Well, it doesn't matter."

"That flask you always carry around?"

He almost smiled. "I'm not an alcoholic, I promise. At first, I had no idea what had happened to me. Sunlight was painful. I had a thirst I could barely quench. My body began to change in ways I didn't understand. Something lurked under my skin."

A predator. I'd seen it in him a handful of times. I'd glimpsed it in Jessamine, and Callum's had been more obvious.

"I didn't understand what I had become until I met another like me." His gaze grew distant. "Her name was Isabella. I met her a year after I was turned. By that point, I was a hopeless, wandering beast. I knew the instant I saw her that she was like me. The look in her eyes said she knew what I was. She took me into her home, taught me what to do."

His expression suggested something tragic had happened to her. "She's gone, isn't she?"

A curt nod. "They stabbed her through the heart with a silver dagger, then burned her body."

He didn't need to tell me who. I knew. Humans hunting vampires. I knew there was far more to the story, and he would tell me in time, but I asked, "What about Callum? Did you know him before learning about Elias?"

A cold glimmer entered JD's eyes. "You could say that. We met shortly after Isabella… After she was gone. Callum was always hotheaded, but so was I, back in the day. He was well integrated into a community like ours, and he brought me in.

"That was when I learned about the Conclave, an institution of ancient, powerful vampires who oversaw our affairs. The rumor is that it was established during the Black Plague, but I've never learned if this is true.

"Callum and his clan were hunters. They would enter villages and prey on the weak and starving. Back then, I had tendencies that leaned more toward beast than man, but I always felt what they were doing wasn't right. I never felt I belonged among them."

JD paused as if weighing his words before continuing. "Callum gradually became more obsessed with our evolution and the power it could afford us. He believed, and no doubt still does, that vampires should rule over humans instead of hiding from them. I cut ties with him and went off on my own again."

I couldn't imagine the difficulties JD faced in being alone for so long.

He straightened. "I don't trust the Rose Conclave to protect Elias. They are more concerned with protecting their power. It doesn't surprise me that they see Callum as an issue. Once, I might have trusted them. Lucien Castain, Isabella's father, used to be an elder."

No more? I wondered.

The hollow look in JD's eyes said he didn't want to speak of it further.

"So what do we do now?" I asked.

Part of me wanted to hide away in this cabin and pretend the outside world didn't exist. I wanted to hear all of JD's story and make up for the time we had lost together. He wanted that, too. It was clear in the way he looked at me.

But there was Elias, and I had a life back home. People I needed to protect. I answered my own question. "I'll go back to

D.C. and see what I can do about Ellwood. You and Elias stay hidden until we know more."

As for Jessamine and Callum, I wasn't sure. *One step at a time,* I told myself.

The last thing I wanted to do was leave them, but I could be more help to JD back home.

JD slid a hand around my neck and rested his forehead against mine. His voice was a husky whisper. "You don't need to help me, Tatiana. You would have a better, less complicated life without me in it."

He didn't realize that so much of my life now had come about because of him. My firm was bigger, and I could lead the lifestyle I enjoyed. Yet none of those things mattered as much as what I felt for him.

I smiled grimly. "You're right, but I don't want that life. I want a life with *you* in it."

His smile was sad, but he didn't say anything. JD's lips pressed against my forehead, and I closed my eyes, holding onto the moment for as long as I could.

CHAPTER FIFTEEN

TATIANA

I headed to work Monday morning after getting little sleep the night before. JD and Elias had taken me back to the abandoned mansion so I could get the Mercedes. The coast was clear, and I'd left from there.

The whole drive back to D.C., I couldn't stop thinking about JD's kiss goodbye. How he had whispered against my forehead, "I'll see you soon."

I returned to my apartment wanting to text him and tell him I made it. Instead, I had called my mom to let her know I was home, safe and sound. I rolled into bed late and spent most of the night tossing and turning.

I'd awoken early, unable to fall back to sleep, and decided to go to the apartment building's gym to blow off steam. I'd gone easy on myself since the wound in my side would not heal for a while.

I walked into the office, still wearing my leggings, sports bra, and cropped workout jacket. Linda was already there, clacking away at her keyboard, with Whiskers in her lap.

"Good morning," she greeted with her usual cheer. "How was your weekend?"

I had to pretend I didn't have the most interesting weekend of my life. "It was nice. Good for me and my mom to have some time together. How was yours?"

Linda told me about a new Hawaiian restaurant Harry had taken her to. According to her, it was "divine" and "you must try it as soon as you can."

"But enough about my weekend. Your mother told me…" Linda's eyes glimmered.

I nearly groaned.

Linda clasped her hands. "Is he back? Marcus?"

I wasn't surprised my mom had passed word along to Linda, and I had to be careful how to play this. I took my sweet time setting down my gym bag. Whiskers hopped down from Linda's lap for a scratch behind the ears. "He is, but he's working on a case out of state. I don't know when we will see him again." It was true enough.

Linda's brows furrowed. "But I haven't logged anything about an out-of-state job."

I straightened, and Whiskers rubbed against my legs. "It's a sensitive case. I took it directly from the client." Elias flashed through my mind. Hardly the typical client, and I wasn't technically working for him, since he wasn't paying me. I pulled off my jacket and added, "Don't tell any of the other staff, okay? The fewer who know what Marcus is up to, the better."

Linda gave a solemn nod, then jumped from her seat. "Oh, I have something for you!" She opened a desk drawer and took out an envelope. "Something small."

I opened it to find a birthday card. Inside, I spotted a gift card with a familiar logo and gasped. "Linda, what is this?"

"A year's pass to the boxing club you and Margo go to. I know how much it helps you to go. Everybody pitched in. See? The card is signed, too."

Linda's signature was big and curly. Margo's was simple. Brando and Marco had added their names along the bottom.

I hugged Linda. "This is too kind."

She smiled as we drew apart. "You deserve it. I wish we could do more, but you're so difficult to buy for. You're also the best boss."

Maybe it was the lack of sleep or coffee, or all the emotions I'd felt over the weekend, but the gesture almost made me cry.

"Oh, honey. You're a sweetheart," Linda cried when my eyes misted. "Oh, there is something I need to tell you! I came in on Saturday morning because I'd left something Whiskers needed, and someone stopped by. An odd man. He asked strange questions."

I stilled. "What are you talking about, Linda?"

"He didn't give a name, but he seemed very FBI."

"Did he show you a badge?"

Linda shook her head. "He asked me who I was and who I worked for. He was very interested in hearing about our staff. He wanted names, to know how long everyone had worked here. He was especially interested in Marcus."

"Did you give him any information?"

Linda glowered. "Really, Tatiana, I thought you would know I'm smarter than that. Of course I didn't. I told him if he wanted answers, he could come back on Monday and talk to you."

"You didn't tell him Marcus' name, right? He already knew it?"

A nod. "He seemed to know a lot about Marcus. I wondered if they knew each other. The whole thing seemed strange."

Indeed. "Did he mention who he worked for?"

Linda said no, but I had a feeling the guy had come from Ellwood's camp. "Well, I suppose we'll see if he shows up today to talk to me," I finally remarked.

I told Linda I needed to change and went into the office bathroom. There, I replaced my workout clothes with a simple pair of charcoal slacks and a matching blazer. I dabbed on a bit of makeup and brushed my hair into a ponytail.

Linda got the coffee machine going and brought me a cup, along with muffins she had picked up before coming in. I didn't know where I would be without her.

I opened my email to find an influx of new security requests that had come in over the weekend, which Linda had forwarded to me. I assigned two of the small but more urgent jobs to Margo, Brandon, and Duncan, then asked Linda to send replies to other clients that we would provide service as soon as possible.

Jake called at the perfect time, just as I completed this. Over the last twenty-four hours, he'd been focused on getting into Ellwood's office network. At this point, I should have hired him as a part-time employee. I could only ask for so many favors, even if he was willing to help me out every time.

"It's been an interesting morning," he stated when I answered the phone. "I've found at least a dozen files on 'enhanced individuals.' I think you'll find one particularly interesting. Check your email."

Anticipation building, I opened my inbox and clicked the top email from Jake. Attached was a video, and I quickly realized it was surveillance footage Ellwood's office had obtained from...

"The Baltimore Art Museum." Where JD and I had stopped a theft Victor Hume had organized to distract law enforcement from what he was really doing, while luring JD and me into a trap.

The footage was damning. It showed JD sprinting after a moving van at a speed no human was capable of. Him wrenching open the driver's side door and forcing the driver out with remarkable strength didn't help matters. Worse, the camera caught me coming out of the building behind him.

This was probably why my company was listed in their system as "close proximity to anomaly."

"Shit," I muttered.

"At least you have solid proof of Ellwood's interests."

It wasn't a stretch to believe Ellwood was trying to get back into office so he would have the resources necessary to track someone like JD down.

"I have a list of Ellwood's staff members, if you would like to look into them," Jake offered.

"Yes, please."

A minute later, a new email appeared. I scanned the list, my gaze snagging on a name I recognized. "I don't believe it."

There it was. Adeline Pike, Chief of Staff

"Know someone there?" Jake asked.

I told him about a security job I'd done over a week ago for a woman named Adeline Pike. "I thought she ran a fashion magazine. That was all I found when I looked into her."

"She may have been hired recently, but still."

I blinked, dumbfounded. What if Pike had hired me so she could assess whether they could recruit me to Ellwood's cause? *Or eliminate me. I could visit her under the guise of her payment not going through and see what's going on.*

"If you can find that out, that would be great. Thanks for everything, Jake."

"Anytime." He hung up, and I sat back, processing. It would be better if I simply showed up at Pike's office instead of calling ahead for a meeting. I didn't want her preparing for it.

First, I called Marc to ask if he could watch my mother's house for the next week. Only at night, and he didn't need to follow her when she wasn't at home. Since I had been followed into Vermont, I needed to ensure she was safe. Marc was by far the most discreet of my staff. He wouldn't tell anyone else he was on this job.

"Don't let my mom find out, either," I instructed. "I don't want to worry her."

Marc accepted the job without question. "Your mom is a sweet woman. I wouldn't want anything happening to her."

When I got off the phone, a text from my friend Val waited for me.

Drinks this evening?

I weighed my options. I had a lot going on with everything involving JD, Elias, and the Conclave, but not much I could do after I visited Adeline Pike. Seeing a friend would be better than pacing my apartment like a penned animal.

Sounds great. Send me a time and place.

I gathered my things. I had the whole afternoon ahead of me and hoped I would find Adeline at her office.

It was noon when I reached Adeline Pike's downtown office. The whole building was for her company, *The Silk Society*.

I stepped off the elevator onto the floor where Adeline's office was supposed to be located and entered a bustling hive of reporters—mostly young women hunched over desks and either clacking away at keyboards or sifting through printouts for upcoming issues. The place was so busy that it took a moment for anyone to notice me.

I approached a front desk behind which a flustered woman sat. She pressed a phone to her ear and switched between a keyboard and a notepad, pen in hand. "We will have that shipment out by tomorrow," she stated into the phone. "Good day, thank you."

She gave me a crisp smile that said, *This had better be good.*

I tried to appear as friendly as possible. I wished JD was beside me, playing his ever-charismatic Marcus Smith. He'd have this whole floor charmed in seconds, whereas I had to come up with a good excuse.

"Hello, I'm here to see Ms. Pike. Is she in?"

The woman blinked. Her cheeks flushed as she searched her notepad. "I'm sorry, you are…"

"Tatiana Sterling. I worked security for Ms. Pike last week. There was a problem with—"

The secretary interrupted, "Ms. Pike doesn't have any appointments scheduled for today. You will have to call ahead to make one, and come back another time."

I pretended not to have heard her and breezed past the desk, having already noticed a door at the end of the hall with Adeline's name engraved into a plaque. "This way? Thanks!"

The secretary tried to call after me, but she was too flustered. Within seconds, I reached the end of the hallway, well aware of the many pairs of eyes turning in my direction. The door was open a crack, so I pushed it inward and stepped into the office.

Adeline had her back to me, facing a window with the blinds closed. At this time of day, it wouldn't have been possible to sit at the desk without squinting. Framed issues of past magazines lined the walls. Two comfortable chairs were angled on the side of the desk nearest me. Adeline stood on the opposite side.

When she heard me enter, she started, "Not right now, Leslie. I—" She turned, halting as she realized it was not her secretary who'd come in.

She recovered quickly and smiled. "Ms. Sterling, what a surprise! My apologies. My secretary didn't tell me you were coming today."

"She didn't know until about thirty seconds ago," I replied, smiling back. "There was a problem with the payment. I'm afraid it didn't go through. I called ahead, but no answer. I thought it would be easier if I swung by while I was in the neighborhood."

The lies slid off my tongue. I'd practiced them all the way here and hoped Ms. Pike wouldn't feel the script. I wasn't here to confront the woman, merely feel her out.

Adeline set a stack of papers on her desk. "I'm terribly sorry. I was certain it went through, but I'll talk to Leslie and see that it does."

Her cheer sounded forced, as if she wished I'd sent this in an email. I glanced around her space. "Your office is lovely. I was looking at the most recent issue of your magazine this morning, too. I admire you, Ms. Pike. We women in business have to stick together."

She gave a knowing smile as she sat behind the desk and folded her hands. "You're right, Ms. Sterling. One of the reasons I was keen to hire you last week was because I know how difficult it can be for us, especially in male-dominated industries. I have no doubt you've experienced it."

I nodded. "More than you know. I hope your old business partner hasn't made any trouble for you since the dinner."

Ms. Pike took a moment to register what I was saying, then laughed. "Oh, him! No, he hasn't been a bother. I think you scared him off."

I stepped closer to the desk and pointed at the stack of papers. "Is this the upcoming issue?"

Adeline beamed and turned the stack around so I could read the top page. "It is. This is the sample print. I've been noting a few adjustments that need to be made."

The front page featured a woman in an elegant dress, her dark hair styled in soft waves below her chin. Where had I seen her before? I read the script along the side.

Emily Ellwood makes her comeback to D.C., elegant as ever!

I picked up the stack, disguising my surprise with admiration. "The finest-dressed members in D.C.," I read. "Are you featuring politicians?"

Adeline nodded. "It's an exciting issue!"

I tapped the page. "And this is Senator Ellwood's wife?"

"Good friends of mine."

Of course.

She made no mention of working for Senator Ellwood.

I smiled. "I hope for the sake of your business that he wins the election." I set the stack back on her desk. "Thank you for looking into the payment. I'll leave you be now. I'm sure you're very busy."

I noticed a hint of annoyance in Adeline's eyes, but her smile did not falter. "Thank you for coming in, Ms. Sterling. Rest assured that I will be contacting you again the next time I need security help."

I offered a pleasant goodbye and saw myself out of the office. My phone buzzed in my back pocket as I stepped onto the street. I thought it might be my mom, or Val sending me details for drinks later, but the number wasn't one I had saved.

The message was brief.

Meet me at Meridian Hill Park. 8:00 PM.

The sender had not left their name, but I had a good guess.

Jessamine Lane was ready to confront me.

CHAPTER SIXTEEN

TATIANA

Jessamine stood by the reflecting pool below the thirteen-basin cascading fountain. Twilight cast the area in shades of blue, and many of the park's visitors had already left.

"I was wondering if you would heed my message," she greeted as if I were some servant of hers to be summoned. She spoke without looking at me. Instead, her gaze was trained on the ripples in the reflecting pool.

"I imagine this has something to do with JD," I commented as I halted a few feet in front of her.

Jessamine wore a dark teal blazer and black slacks. Her hair was pulled back into a braid. She was beautiful in an other-worldly way. Others would think she had fantastic genes or a good plastic surgeon.

I wondered how old she was, how long she had worked for the Conclave, and what was at stake for her if she never found JD and Elias. Was the vampire world harsh on its women the same way the human world was? Had Jessamine clawed her way into the Conclave, or had it been granted to her?

I didn't ask her these questions, despite my vast curiosity. I wasn't thrilled with the idea of being alone with a vampire in the dark, especially after my run-in with Callum. I imagined Jessamine was far more capable of fucking me up.

My military training would give her a run for her money, but I doubted I could outlast her. That was a skill I had learned to use well—understanding what I was up against and backing down when necessary. I would not be able to work with Jessamine by exerting brute force.

So, I slid into diplomat mode as she stated, "I know you have seen him, and the boy. Where are they?"

"I don't know," I answered truthfully. "And JD isn't who you need to be worried about right now. Callum is one of your issues, but so is the person leaking information about you and your people to human authorities."

Jessamine's eyes glimmered. "What are you talking about?"

"Senator Malcolm Ellwood and his chief of staff, Adeline Pike. Considering how concerned you are about your safety, I'd think you have already heard of them." I explained what I'd learned but left out Jake Molina's involvement. Jessamine didn't need to know how I came by my intel.

"You know how dangerous Victor Hume was. You called JD in for being too flashy because of it. I promise you, Ellwood will be worse for everyone involved. You and the Conclave are better off focusing on them. JD could help, you know. I could too." I hoped I sounded as sincere as I felt. Neither JD nor I wanted to be on Jessamine's bad side.

"We need to work together, unless we want Ellwood to become a much bigger problem. The whole goal of the Conclave is to keep you a secret, right?"

Jessamine was silent for a long moment. Eventually, she remarked, "If Mr. Davenport wanted to help us, he would have already done so. Instead, he has actively gone against us at every opportunity. You are proving to be much the same by working with him."

Her eyes met mine before she went on. "As for the other

matter, the Conclave has known about Ms. Pike's betrayal for weeks. We have not yet acted because we are divided. Some wish to eliminate Pike quietly. Others want to negotiate directly with Ellwood. We could offer our cooperation in exchange for legal protection."

"Hold on," I cut in. "*Betrayal?*"

"Yes." Jessamine seemed to take satisfaction as reality dawned on me. I remembered the closed blinds in Adeline's office. *She is a vampire, and she betrayed her kind to Ellwood.* "Ms. Pike has been working for Ellwood for far longer than her chief of staff position indicates," Jessamine continued, as if this were obvious.

"Why?"

"She wants his resources and protection, I assume."

We needed to backtrack, because she was starting to lose me. "What do you mean, *negotiate* with Ellwood? He probably wants to wipe you all out!"

"You don't know that," Jessamine retorted crisply. "Ellwood wants *information*. He may plan to get back into office and use that information against us, yes, but what if we made him a sweeter deal? We give him information, and he uses his sources and government protection to help us improve our standing in human society.

"Think about it, Sterling. One day, we will be exposed. There have been too many close calls. It is better if we have the power to protect ourselves when that day comes. Ellwood may be one way to do that."

"And what if he doesn't? What if you're actively making an enemy for yourself?"

"The Conclave will take care of him," she responded.

I imagined a well-timed car accident and a smooth cover-up. I stammered, wanting to ask more questions but also to protest this plan. What would JD think of it all? *That it's ridiculous,* I thought. Jessamine and her colleagues were playing with fire.

"This matter is far too complicated for a security guard with mere military training to handle."

I bristled.

"We will handle Ellwood and Callum. Though I can respect your effort to try to work together, I have already proposed all that we are willing to do. Bring us Jordan Davenport and the boy, and we will leave you and your family alone."

The implied threat was unmistakable. I thought of my mom, with Marc watching her home. Despite his training and skills, Marc would not be enough to take on anyone Jessamine might send.

Jessamine smiled. "Do it our way, and everyone wins."

Bullshit.

"You will use Elias, like Callum wants to, and you'll punish JD for helping him."

Jessamine considered this before saying, "I'll make it easier for you. How about this? We will let Jordan go without punishment if he brings the boy to us. This is his last chance. He has seven days."

She turned as if to go, but I stopped her. "And what about Elias? What will you do to him? Turn him into a fucking experiment?"

Jessamine's eyes were cold and predatory. I half expected to see fangs when she spoke again. "Our interests lie in protecting all our kind, including the boy. He is dangerous to himself more than anyone, and Jordan Davenport doesn't know what he's doing.

"He thinks he is protecting the boy because he sees a younger, vulnerable part of himself in him. In the end, Jordan will only be hurting himself, the boy, and everyone else involved. He is allowing himself to be blinded by emotion."

Her gaze trailed over me. "It seems this isn't the first time he's done that."

I was tempted to push her into the fountain, but I balled my hands into fists at my sides.

"If you do not cooperate with us, you will be complicit in Mr. Davenport's crimes. Do you understand?" Jessamine turned and walked away, but before she reached the path out of the park, she added, "Your choice, Ms. Sterling, but I recommend you don't cross us."

I drove to, parked, and entered my favorite restaurant—a Brazilian place with sliders that had dropped from heaven itself —in a daze. Val had already claimed a table. She threw up a hand to signal me, and I managed a smile as I approached. She stood and hugged me. "Hey, darling. How ya doin'?'"

Val wore leggings, a crop top, and sneakers. Her days as a professional trainer meant she was always dressed in synthetic fibers. She smelled like vanilla perfume and an obscene amount of hairspray. She looked good, with her toned, tan body, hair that never seemed to be affected by sweat or the weather, and a smile that could charm a whole room.

She had already ordered us drinks. "White wine, right?" she asked as I scooted into the booth.

"You're the best," I told her. I tried to shake all thoughts of Jessamine's threats and wished more than anything I could reach out to JD and tell him about our meeting. I was still in shock over Adeline Pike being a vampire, and a traitorous one at that.

Deep down, I also admired Pike for operating so well in human society as one. Knowing the lengths JD had gone to himself, it was nothing short of impressive.

"Anything the matter, honey?" Val asked.

I liked having a new friend. I had missed having women my age around. Making new friends in your late twenties and thir- ties was harder than it seemed. Val was my only friend who didn't work for or with me. For that reason, I wasn't interested in putting her in danger by telling her the truth, so I settled for, "Just had a long day of work."

Val smiled. "Then order those sliders you love. On me tonight!"

"You don't have to do that," I told her.

She waved me off. "I want to."

A manager sauntered over, grinning from ear to ear. "Tatiana, why didn't you come in on Saturday for the birthday special?" He glanced at Val. "Any drink and app you want, on the house. But only for our most special customers." He winked at me.

"Your birthday?" Val asked. "Why didn't you tell me?"

Freddy leaned closer and lowered his voice. "Tatiana is quite the private woman, but she got drunk one night as I was explaining the new birthday special, and she let it slip."

I was embarrassed that the manager knew me so well. Even knew my birthday, when people like Val and some of my other friends didn't.

"Well, any chance she can get that free drink and appetizer a few days late?" Val asked.

I laughed. "That isn't necessary."

"This one time," Freddy agreed, winking again before striding off. "Sliders coming right up!"

"So what did you do for your birthday?" Val asked.

I told her about my trip with my mom to upstate New York, but left out anything pertaining to work. Val stirred her straw in her frozen margarita. "You're lucky. My mom and I can't be in the same room for more than twenty minutes before we want to kill each other."

The appetizers arrived, and we enjoyed them with our drinks. The more we talked, the less I thought about Jessamine, JD, and Ellwood. However, by the time we walked out, the spell was breaking. Our cars were parked next to each other in the now nearly empty lot. As we approached them, I sensed we were not alone.

I turned, but didn't see anyone lurking in the shadows of the building.

"What is it?" Val asked.

I stared into the darkness. "I don't know. I guess I thought we were being followed."

Val laughed. "I'm impressed with your spy skills, but maybe you think so much about it that you think things are happening when they aren't."

"I'm not a spy, Val."

"Spy sounds cooler than security guard."

"I'm not exactly that either, but I get your—"

I didn't have time to register the figure materializing from behind a dumpster before he grabbed the back of Val's head and pressed her against him, a pistol aimed below her jaw.

His gloved hand slapped over her mouth as she tried to cry out. He wore a dark hood, so the only feature I could make out was the hard set of his bristled jaw. "Keep quiet, ladies, and we won't have any problems."

"Let her go. You're here for me," I commanded.

A smile spread across his lips. "But this one is so pretty."

"Who are you?" I demanded. "Are you working for Ellwood?"

Val's eyes widened, and the thug's expression faltered. Bullseye. "Tell your boss that if he has a problem with me or my friends, he can come and tell me directly."

The thug studied me, then growled and shoved Val toward me. She stumbled, crying out, and I caught her. She clutched my arm as the armed man darted off into the dark. "Wh-what was that?"

"Someone trying to scare me," I replied grimly. I didn't think he planned on harming either of us. As far as I could tell, the thug had not been a vampire, so I was certain Ellwood sent him. Why? I had done nothing to him.

"Val, you should go home."

She nodded, her lower lip wobbling.

"I'll follow you there to make sure no one else does, then I'll have one of my security people stay outside your apartment tonight." It was the least I could offer. I blamed myself for her being in danger.

"B-but what about you? Will you be safe?"

I nodded curtly. "Don't worry about me."

After Val stopped shaking and felt good enough to drive, we left. No one else had been in the parking lot to witness the altercation. I saw Val home safely, then called Duncan to see if he could take the night shift and stake out the place. He agreed and said he would be there as soon as possible.

On my drive home, I called Marc to ensure my mom was safe.

"She is. Nothing suspicious going on over here."

I felt relieved and wished him a good night.

At home, I let myself feel the weight of all that had happened. Only a few hours ago, Jessamine had threatened to punish JD and me for protecting Elias. Ellwood was on my ass, too. Shark-infested waters, indeed. I dropped my keys on the entry table in the hallway, then took off my shoes. I yearned for a shower and bed, but my mind was still racing.

It was time I did something about Ellwood.

Jessamine had told me she would handle it. *But Jessamine's friend isn't being held at gunpoint in a parking lot,* I thought as I began to undress. I wanted more than anything to call JD, but I resisted. I stepped into the shower and vowed not to reach out until I'd done my job here.

CHAPTER SEVENTEEN

TATIANA

I dumped protein powder into the blender and turned it on. I didn't have much of an appetite, but I needed to eat something. As I waited for the powder and fruits to become a blended mush, I weighed my options.

I could do as Jessamine had commanded. Reach out to JD and tell him he had seven days to turn himself and Elias in. Even if I pleaded on my knees, I didn't think he would. And I didn't want him to.

I believed Jessamine when she said they would let JD walk free without punishment, but they would keep a close eye on him. The next time he did something "too flashy," they would either drag him in or he would be on the run again. He might as well stay on the run now, if that also meant protecting Elias.

I wondered where they were and if they were safe. What rundown place were they hiding in now? I thought of JD's comfortable home outside the city and how he must miss sleeping in a real bed, wearing his favorite suits, and driving his cars. The image of JD in jeans and a T-shirt behind the wheel of a beater truck was somehow more unbelievable than him having fangs and blood thirst.

I considered his blood rage, as he called it. Had it happened again since I left? It had only been two days since I last saw him, but it already felt like years. I wanted nothing more than to call him, but that wouldn't work. The only number I had for JD had been disconnected. I'd found that out about four months ago, in a moment of great weakness when I had tried calling.

I'd gotten lost in thought and forgotten about my smoothie. I turned off the blender and removed the lid. The contents were runnier than I liked, but at least it would go down fast.

I poured the sickly-looking brown-green liquid into a cup. It tasted much better than it looked. As I finished the smoothie and gathered my things, I decided what I would do.

I needed to confront Malcolm Ellwood, but it wasn't wise to march into his office and pray for a miracle. I needed to be more covert. I would look into Ms. Pike's previous business partner first, see what dirt I could dig up on her. As Ellwood's chief of staff, eliminating Ms. Pike would weaken him.

Her former business partner had made strong claims about her the last time I encountered him. Now that I knew she was a traitor to her fellow vampires and had a sleeve full of secrets, his claims might ring truer than I'd previously thought.

I slipped into a pair of loafers and pulled on my favorite dark blue blazer. As I headed to my car, I got online to find contact information for him. When I'd last worked for Ms. Pike, I had looked into Mr. Andrew Spencer. I hadn't found much online, and considering the job's last-minute nature, I couldn't dig further. A small job like that didn't require much research, anyway.

By the time I reached my car, I had located Mr. Spencer's downtown office. It was still early, but I decided to call anyway.

A female voice answered. "Andrew Spencer's office, how can I help you?"

I introduced myself as Tatiana Sterling and asked if Mr. Spencer was in.

"He just arrived. One moment."

This secretary was much easier to work with than Adeline's had been.

"Good morning, how can I help you?" a male voice asked a moment later.

"Hi, Mr. Spencer? This is Tatiana Sterling, with Sterling and Smith Security Solutions. I was wondering if we could meet for a talk. I have questions about your previous business partner, Ms. Adeline Pike?"

He paused. "Are you investigating her?"

"You could say that."

I expected he would hang up or say he wanted nothing to do with this. His response surprised me. "I can meet you for lunch. How's Jovi's Diner downtown work?"

I scribbled the restaurant name onto a napkin I found in my console. "Noon?"

"Noon works. See you then, Ms. Sterling."

He hung up. I had the weird feeling that his voice had sounded different, but then, he hadn't been angry and throwing a tantrum today. I was surprised he'd agreed to meet me, since the last time I saw him, I'd thrown him out of a hotel. He had asked so few questions, too.

I thought over the matter as I drove to the office. I decided I would spend the morning on admin tasks and checking in with Marco to ensure all had gone well the night before at my mother's house. The sun had risen by the time I arrived, casting splendid rays across a pale sky.

Inside, I checked my phone and found a text from Linda.

Taking Whiskers to the groomer! I'll be in after.

I didn't mind. It meant an hour or so of peace and quiet in the office. I settled in at my desk and got to work, counting down the hours until I met with Mr. Spencer.

I arrived ten minutes before noon. Jovi's was a '50s-style diner I had been to before. Because it was a Tuesday, most of the diner's patrons were getting carryout for lunch. Plenty of seating options were available when I walked in. I chose a corner booth and sat on the side with a good view of the door, as well as the windows and the street beyond.

I scanned the menu, unsure what to get. The smoothie had carried me through the morning, and I was vaguely hungry but still didn't have much appetite.

Someone cleared their throat, interrupting my menu scrutiny. "Ms. Sterling?"

I looked up to see a man wearing a simple button-down shirt under a leather jacket. He was tall, with a neatly trimmed beard complementing his combed-back brown hair.

I didn't recognize him.

"Yes?"

He stuck out a hand, and I noticed a wedding band on his left ring finger. "Andrew Spencer. Good to meet you."

I shook his hand, bewildered. "*You* are Andrew Spencer?"

He chuckled as he released my hand, then slid into the other side of the booth. "Last time I checked. I'm sorry, have we met before?"

I set down the menu and was about to answer when a waitress bustled over and took our drink orders. Andrew asked for a coffee, two creams. I told her water was fine.

When the waitress left, I stated, "I thought we'd met before, but now I think there's been a horrible mix-up. You are not the same man I thought I was meeting. You *did* used to work with Adeline Pike, right?"

He nodded. "Emphasis on 'used to.' We were business partners until she screwed me over." He clearly wasn't happy about the situation, but he was far from the blustering fool I'd met at Adeline's business dinner.

After our drinks arrived and we ordered food, I explained the situation. I told him Ms. Pike had hired me to work a business dinner in case her old business partner, Andrew Spencer, showed up and caused issues. I explained that a man had arrived, claimed she was a back-stabbing bitch, and I'd had him removed from the premises. "But that man wasn't you."

"No, it wasn't. I would have remembered you if you'd thrown me out of a hotel." Mr. Spencer's expression was grim. "Though I wouldn't be surprised to hear she'd hired someone to pretend to be me."

I leaned forward. "Has she done something like that before?"

"Not that I know of, but she's gone to drastic measures to convince people she's someone she isn't."

No shit. Any vampire had to. Maybe Ms. Pike had gone the extra, unnecessary mile. I doubted Mr. Spencer knew that aspect of her nature, though. "Mind telling me what happened between you two?" I asked.

"We were friends for a long time, started in college together. She always had an interest in fashion, and I thought she had great ideas. I agreed to help fund her startup as long as I was made a partner. I had the connections, you see, as well as the money.

"We got up and running, and the magazine was successful for years. I won't go into details, but she had me removed from the company. She owes me a lot of money, even now."

"Have you pursued legal action?"

He nodded. "Her lawyers are sharks. Same guys who work for…" His mouth tightened. "Perhaps I am saying too much. I still don't know why you wanted to meet."

Mr. Spencer clearly wondered if I'd been sent here on Ms. Pike's behalf. Quickly, I assured him this was not the case.

"As I told you, Ms. Pike hired my company to work this event. I have recently come to learn she may have hired me as a test. I have it on good authority that her boss, Senator Ellwood, has it out for me." I wasn't about to tell this man why.

Andrew blinked and echoed, "Senator Ellwood?"

"Yes."

He blew out a hard breath. "I'm not surprised to hear that, either. You know, she only met Ellwood because of me? The senator's father is an old business buddy of my dad's.

"I don't know Malcolm too well myself, but we were invited to an event of his years ago. I took Adeline along as my business partner. I thought she'd like to meet the people I was already connected with. Look, I said I wouldn't get into details because I wasn't keen on bringing Ellwood up, but now you have. It was Ellwood who helped her turn me out, and his shark lawyers who have kept me there."

"But why? It can't all be about money, can it?"

"Why not? These people are shrewd. I'm more interested in knowing why they have it out for you."

"I'm investigating," I replied simply. "Maybe they don't like how close I'm getting to uncovering something." It was true. Still, it didn't answer why Adeline had hired me to begin with.

Mr. Spencer finished his soup, then remarked, "You need to be careful with Adeline. She has no trouble stabbing a partner in the back."

"Can I ask you how long she has been Ellwood's chief of staff?"

"Must be a new position. This is the first I'm hearing of it."

Jessamine seemed to think the position was new as well, though Adeline had been working with Ellwood for far longer. "One more question. Do you know anything about a Patrick Goth?"

Andrew shook his head. "Haven't heard the name before."

I thanked him for his help and paid for his lunch. He didn't have to tell me anything, and I was grateful for his candor. With some people I interviewed, it felt like throwing my questions against a wall.

"Whatever this investigation of yours is, I hope it goes well and that you don't encounter too much trouble," Andrew told me as he rose from the table.

I watched him leave as I left a tip. When I stepped outside the diner, my phone rang. "Hey, Linda. I'm heading back now."

"Good!" she chirped. "I was calling to tell you there is someone important at the office to see you. I would have told him to come back or make an appointment, but he said it was urgent, and when he said what he was—"

"Who is it, Linda?"

She lowered her voice. "Must be a big job, Tati. He says he's a senator!"

I was glad I'd kept my lunch light as I entered the office. Linda wasn't at her desk, though Whiskers was curled up in her seat. I heard her voice in the adjoining room.

I entered the meeting space to find Linda chatting up a tall, handsome man wearing a suit. "You know, I grew up in Stafford County. My whole family is still there! Virginia natives and all. Isn't it—" She halted when Senator Ellwood's gaze slid to me. "Tatiana, there you are! I've been keeping Mr. Ellwood company."

I pressed on a smile. "Thank you, Linda. I can take it from here."

Linda smiled at the senator as if she were the one running for office, then scampered out of the room.

I closed the door behind me, examining would-be Senator Ellwood. His dark hair was combed back, and he was clean-shaven. He wore a wedding band on his left hand and a smaller ring on his left pinky. He held a politician's smile, revealing a row of perfect white teeth. He appeared in his mid- to late-forties and looked exactly as he did online and in papers.

"Good afternoon, Senator. I hope you haven't been waiting

long," I greeted as I removed my blazer and draped it over the back of a chair.

"Good afternoon, Ms. Sterling. I haven't been waiting long, and as your secretary stated, she has been keeping me company." He examined me with shrewd, dark eyes. "I'll cut to the chase. No doubt you have already concluded I am not here seeking your services."

I tried not to bristle.

Senator Ellwood slid his hands into his pockets. We both remained standing. "I have taken a great interest in you lately. Quite an impressive operation you have set up here."

I wasn't surprised he'd heard of me. He might have even if JD had no part in the picture. I'd led successful operations over the last several months and worked with a good number of high-profile clientele. Ellwood wasn't the first senator I had crossed paths with, either. In this case, he wasn't even back in office yet.

He stepped toward me, tilting his head. "I'm curious, though. The firm is called Sterling and Smith, yet there only appears to be a Sterling. Tell me, where has your business partner gone off to?"

He was not messing around. Ellwood slid on a smile that made my skin crawl. He might have been dressed nicer than the dickheads I dealt with before, but he was still a dickhead.

"I am quite aware of Marcus Smith's unusual...abilities," he continued. "An actor with no military or special ops training happens to partner with a security firm on the rise and accomplish great feats in the process. Marcus Smith isn't his real name, I have no doubt."

But he didn't know JD's real name, I realized. I still had an edge here.

"Are you connected with Victor Hume?" I demanded.

Malcolm Ellwood's eyes narrowed. "Hardly. Hume's methods are inhumane."

On that, we could agree.

Ellwood began pacing. "I am merely interested in learning

more, especially after getting to know Adeline Pike, a dear friend of mine. I believe the two of you have become acquainted."

Was he hinting at her abilities, too?

I crossed my arms, finding my in. "I doubt the remainder of your staff is aware of Adeline Pike's special abilities, as you call them. Would they like it if they found out what their boss was?"

People were afraid of and sometimes hated the things they did not understand.

Ellwood halted and turned to me. "You should be careful, Ms. Sterling. I came to say it is better for you to stay out of this matter altogether."

"You had me followed. Why?"

Ellwood took his sweet time answering. "We knew you could either be an asset or an obstacle to us, Ms. Sterling. We were simply watching. Recent circumstances suggest you could still be either. I want to make it clear where I stand, and where you *could* stand."

"You're going to have to elaborate," I replied dully.

Ellwood had sent his security thug after me and JD, and probably after Val and me last night. Goth, or someone like him, had also come to the office on Saturday when Linda happened to be in. When he realized his intimidation tactics weren't going to work that way, Ellwood decided to come and confront me himself.

"I am concerned chiefly about public safety. The existence of undocumented…enhanced individuals poses a problem there," Ellwood professed. "I know you share these concerns, considering your history and current occupation." He waved around the office. "I also know you have had close proximity to such an individual. I am not saying Marcus Smith poses a threat."

"Then what are you saying?"

"That I want to know more."

"So you can keep people safe?"

Ellwood nodded.

"Then why have me followed? Why have my friend and I attacked while we're out to dinner?"

Ellwood blinked. "Attacked? I did no such thing?"

"Last night, outside the restaurant. You sent one of your thugs to intimidate me."

Ellwood shook his head. "I did no such thing," he repeated. "How would you even know?"

Did I have this all wrong? Ellwood seemed to be telling the truth.

"What about my business partner? He's left you alone. Why can't you do the same?"

Ellwood recovered himself. "Marcus Smith is a special individual, and I hear he is harboring someone even more special."

He must have heard this from Adeline, but the timeline wasn't quite adding up. Adeline betrayed her own kind years ago, according to Jessamine. How could she know about Elias?

Ellwood headed for the door. "When I am elected again, I hope you will prove cooperative. I might think of giving you a good position working for me."

His audacity made me want to chuck the cup of coffee he'd left on the table at his head.

He winked. "In this dangerous world, I could use your protection."

He left, and I stood at the table, baffled. If Ellwood hadn't sent the thug after me, who had? Why did the attacker's face change when I mentioned Ellwood?

What if the senator didn't send him, but someone under him did? What if Pike was behind the attack and Ellwood didn't know?

I considered pursuing the would-be senator and demanding to know if this could be true. However, I stayed put. Further interaction would only hinder the plan I was forming. I needed a way to take Ellwood and Pike down, then deal with Jessamine and the Conclave.

It all felt too big to accomplish without JD at my side.

Maybe I didn't have to do it alone, though. Maybe I could get both birds by exposing Pike for what she really was. It would damage public trust, and Jessamine wouldn't want to align herself with Ellwood anymore.

The plan took better shape. I only had one problem.

For this to work, I'll need a good actor.

CHAPTER EIGHTEEN

JORDAN

<u>**France, 1736**</u>

A fist collided with my face, and I smiled. It was a feral smile that could make the strongest men piss their trousers, but these men were too drunk for fear. That was why they'd come after me, jeering and hissing.

I'd prevented them from taking the barmaid out back and doing with her as they had pleased, so when I left the establishment, they'd trailed me like a pack of skinny dogs looking for scraps.

I would be lying if I said I hadn't purposely slowed my walk so they could catch up. It was nearly dawn. I didn't have much time to loiter outside. But I couldn't help the thrill at the thought of a fight.

So when one of them knocked me from behind, and another pounded his fist into my face, I grinned like a feral beast.

"Tu aimes, ça fils de pute?"

My French wasn't very good yet, but I knew he'd said something along the lines of, "You like that?" I was fairly certain he'd added something about me being a whore's son, too.

"Oui," I answered, then delivered my fist to his nose.

The satisfying crunch of bone breaking was almost enough to make my gums sing. The fresh spurt of red blood made my mouth water.

The other three closed in, and a blurred fury of kicking, punching, and swearing passed, mostly in French. What these men did not understand was that not only was I quicker and stronger, but I could outlast them. By the time they were slumped on the ground in a heap of bloodied faces, my clothes were rumpled, torn, and dirtied.

"This shirt was new," I mumbled. "You're lucky I don't make you pay for it."

I walked off, wiping my own blood from my mouth with the back of my hand. The men were lucky I hadn't gone further. Merely cracking my knuckles did nothing to stave off the hunger inside me. I could have fed on all three, left them for dead instead of unconscious.

Still, I knew three bodies lying dead on the street would lead to questions, and I had drawn enough attention. It was nearly time I found a new city, but the dear woman I was going home to loved Paris so much.

The sky was beginning to gray when I entered through a narrow door and climbed an even narrower staircase. The second level of the ramshackle building was creaky. The floors and walls and doors, all of it creaked like an old man rising from a rocking chair. It might have once been a brothel or a warehouse. Now, it was a tenement building, and its occupants were poor. Or, like me, thieves.

Though the building seemed it might collapse with one good gust of wind, our space was decorated comfortably. I stumbled through the door, and the woman sitting at a dressing table before an open window raised an eyebrow. She eyed me through the mirror, not bothering to turn.

Her lacy nightgown exposed one shoulder and her slim collarbones, as well as the beautiful white pillar of her neck.

Masses of auburn curls fell to her waist, and those silvery-gray eyes were as captivating as the full moon. Or so I murmured against her skin time and time again.

"You're late."

"You still have the window open. Sun will be up soon," I replied, grinning despite my split lip.

Finally, she turned, curling her fingers around the back of her chair. Her skin was already ivory, but she clutched the chair hard enough to turn her knuckles even whiter. "You got into another brawl. You're a fool, Jordan."

I sauntered over, stripping off my torn and stained shirt. Then I leaned over her, tracing my lips along her jaw and up to her ear. "A mad fool, desperately in love. Do not be cross with me, Isabella."

She turned away from me, focusing on a pair of earrings she'd just taken off. "You draw too much attention to us. We will have to leave again soon, and my father won't be happy. You know how much I hate leaving Paris."

I circled her, placing my chin in the soft spot between her shoulder and her neck. "We will have to go anyway. Lucien said as much. We have stalked these streets long enough." I pressed my lips to her neck. When she arched, whimpering, I saw my invitation. I sank my teeth in, as easily as piercing ripe fruit, and drank until she pushed me away.

"You go too far," she whispered. "You need to learn to curb your hunger." Even as she said this, her pupils dilated. She wanted to return the gesture. "There is a difference between the beasts who drink human blood and those of us who can live forever."

Night Walker. Blood Stalker. Many names were given to them.

Isabella peered into my eyes. "Vampires who lose their humanity with all this killing and hunting and fighting stand no chance of sustaining themselves."

She looked for fresh kills before the blood was cold in the body. She was more vulture than predator and had taught me to be the same. She'd shown me how to go days, sometimes weeks, without feeding. And if I was becoming dangerous, she offered herself.

I drew her close, inviting her into our bed. She had adorned the place with all manner of beauty. A bed laden with sheepskin blankets and silk pillows. A canopy of fabrics woven above us. She'd collected paintings and jewelry and clothes. Her perfume made the room smell like a garden.

I tucked a curl behind her ear and whispered against her neck, "As William in *The Tempest* said, 'Of the very instant that I saw you, did my heart fly at your service.' We shall go soon. Tomorrow, if you please."

Slowly, she smiled and spoke Miranda's line back to me. *"Je souhaiterais avoir n'importe quel compagnon au monde, sauf toi."*

I would not wish any companion in the world but you.

———

The bed was empty when I awoke. My sleep had been brief, more meditative than actual slumber. Still, Isabella had crept from the room without me noticing.

I rose and pulled aside the curtain to find night had fallen once more. I washed my face in a basin of water, then dried it with a towel. Next, I dressed in a tunic and trousers that did not reveal the brawl I'd been in a mere twelve hours ago.

I thought little of Isabella being gone. She often went out at night, vulture that she was. I knew where I might find her. This would be her last night in Paris for some time, and she would want to see the moonlight along the Seine. I had only to walk its curve until I caught her scent and found her.

The night was cool and calm when I stepped outside. The streets were empty. It was quite late.

I reached the river and strolled along it with my hands resting idly in my pockets. My easy gait belied the close attention I paid to every corner and shadow. Ahead, two men stood outside a tavern. They hardly paid me any attention as I passed. I saw no one else for quite some time. I'd been walking for what felt like an eternity and not yet come across my darling Isabella.

I toyed with the small metal cross on a chain around my neck, a gift from her. "Where are you, *mon amour*?" I whispered into the night. The moon was suspended in her full glory above the Seine, but Isabella was nowhere nearby to watch it.

I halted at a bridge. Ah, there it was. Her scent. It led away from the river, so I followed. Before long, I encountered a stone church, much older than I. It was dark and at first seemed empty. As I neared its entrance, her scent grew stronger, but something was wrong with it.

Terribly wrong.

My heart thudded. The church doors were locked, but I wrenched one open and slipped inside.

I was not prepared for the horror I faced beyond those doors.

I hardly remember what happened, except that I fell to my knees and gathered her body to me. A silver dagger was embedded in her chest, and her eyes were glassy. Already gone. I screamed and clutched as agony tore through me. This wasn't real. It was only an awful dream. Isabella would shake me, pull me from this stupor, tell me all was well and she was alive.

The spell of sleep never broke, and I remained there until I was surrounded. They materialized in their dark robes, faces concealed. I might have been able to fight them off if I could have pried myself away from Isabella's body.

A hand closed over my mouth, and pressure built behind my eyes. I thrashed as more hands gripped my arms. They dragged me across stone, into the biting cold outside. A door thudded shut behind me, and I glimpsed beyond the hands over my face to the clear sky and the outlines of barren trees.

They had dragged me into a courtyard. Isabella, too. They'd torn off her coat, leaving her in only her boots and nightdress. The dagger remained in her chest, the blood pooling down her front the darkest red.

The gloved hand on my mouth muffled my scream. One man held me while another bound me with rope. I could not fight them off, try as I might. Whatever had been in the first man's hand drugged me enough to keep me docile. I was only strong enough to stay conscious.

Horror sluiced through me as I realized what they were doing with Isabella's body. They had killed a vampire in one of only two ways they could—silver through her heart. At least they had not separated her head from her shoulders.

She would not be able to rise from death, but they took every precaution. They placed her on a pile of wood, and one of the men wandered over, carrying a lantern. He broke it, and the flames leaped onto the wood.

I thrashed against the binding rope, loosing guttural sounds full of agony. I did not care who heard.

A heavy hand pressed on my neck, cold as ice, and a voice filled my ear. "You should have stayed inside, blood-thirster. Should have kept your little lady in the dark."

They would do this to me next, I knew. They only wanted me to watch her body turn to ash, so I would feel as much misery as possible before they sank a silver dagger into my heart.

Rage and sorrow welled within me, a cresting wave that gave me the strength to tear the ropes from my body. The man tried to grab me, but I was quicker. I wanted to rip him limb from limb and bathe the courtyard in their blood. But I knew better than to stay and fight.

My only choice was to run.

<u>Three hundred years later</u>

The memory was as clear three centuries afterward as it had been the night it happened. I woke from a rest that was more meditation than slumber, the images staining my mind. This time, it was not Isabella's lifeless eyes staring into the starry heavens, but Tatiana's.

I have been a great fool, I kept thinking. I had made myself wait centuries before falling in love again, and I feared it had been a mistake.

I needed air. I emerged from the ramshackle, abandoned farmhouse Elias and I had stopped at for the day. The sky was overcast, but I still stayed under the porch's awning to protect myself.

It had been only two days since I last saw Tatiana, and Elias and I hadn't yet made it out of the state. The beater truck was still chugging along, but we would need a more reliable vehicle soon.

Elias' small form appeared in the doorway. "Are you having one of your episodes again?"

I glowered. He called my blood rages "episodes," as if I were a mental patient. Sometimes, I felt like one.

Something rectangular and black flew at me. I caught it easily. "Message for you," Elias reported.

It was my burner phone, and only Vinny had this number. I checked the new text.

Beck is in trouble.

My bones turned to ice.

"Do we know Beck?" Elias asked.

Slowly, I lowered myself to the porch step. Elias and I had traded many stories of our lives, but I had yet to tell him of my old friend Beck. If she was in trouble, why was Vinny telling me about it? Why couldn't he go and help her?

This could be a trap, I thought. To Elias, I clarified, "Shifter."

"She needs our help."

"She needs *my* help."

I dreaded the worst-case scenario. Vinny had been questioned about being a magical. It was quite possible Beck had been, too. I stood. "If she's where I think she is, or was last I knew, I won't be gone long."

"I'm going with you," Elias insisted.

I shook my head. "It's too dangerous."

"It's just as dangerous for me to stay here."

He was right, but I had to at least consider what I was doing. "Fine. Come with me, but you do exactly as I tell you. We may be walking into a trap."

Still, I had to go. I wouldn't forgive myself if something happened to Beck and I wasn't there to stop it. I was convinced Vinny had been targeted because of me. The same would be true of Beck. I considered calling Vinny, but that could be dangerous for him. No, I would stay quiet, leave the message unanswered.

Elias disappeared inside and returned a short while later, hauling our meager supplies. "Let's hope the truck makes it."

CHAPTER NINETEEN

TATIANA

I stayed in the office long after Linda had gone home with Whiskers and treated myself to Thai takeout. Around eight o'clock, as I was chucking the empty containers into the garbage, someone knocked at the door. I opened it to find Jake standing in the hallway, bearing coffee. "I take it this will be a late night of planning?"

Earlier, I had asked if he could stop by the office tonight. He agreed without needing an explanation. I smiled as I accepted the coffee. "You know me well."

He grinned back. "It will feel like old times." He closed the door behind him and locked it. I started to tell him about Senator Ellwood's visit earlier in the day, but I'd barely gotten past the point of us meeting before he held up a hand, silencing me. He held a finger to his lips, then glanced around the office.

I frowned, mouthing, "What?"

Jake opened drawers in Linda's desk and emptied its contents. Not roughly, and he placed everything back, but with an urgency that told me exactly what he was thinking. I started looking as well, moving furniture, opening drawers, and checking among the snack baskets.

Jake balanced on Linda's chair and removed a light fixture. Nothing was in it. Next, he went into the conference room. It did not take him long to find the bug under the table, taped to the center of the side opposite the door. He did not remove it. He only showed it to me, then motioned for me to follow him into the hallway, where he asked, "Would there be any others?"

I shook my head. "I keep my office locked when I'm not here." We had already checked the front room and the bathroom.

I called Linda, and she picked up on the third ring.

"Odd question, but was Ellwood alone in the meeting room today?" I asked her.

"Why, yes. I went to use the restroom shortly after he arrived, then returned to my desk. That was when I called you. After I realized it would be a while before you were back, I went to keep him company. Whiskers wouldn't go near him, and he kept saying he didn't like cats. Who in their right mind doesn't like cats? Maybe he's allergic or something."

"Thank you, Linda. I'll see you tomorrow." I hung up before she could ask why I was concerned, then addressed Jake. "He was in there long enough to plant the bug, and no one has checked the cameras." I gestured at the camera in the corner of the room.

"Check it now, but let's have a casual conversation while you do that," he suggested.

We went into my office. The footage showed Senator Ellwood dropping a pen, seemingly by accident, then crawling under the table to fetch it. He emerged a minute later, still without the pen.

We returned to the hallway. "Now we can talk," Jake stated.

I told Jake about my entire interaction with Ellwood. "You were right about JD," I finished. I shared what happened within the last week, from meeting Jessamine to the truth I had learned from Mr. Spencer today. I only left out the reasons for the Conclave wanting Elias and what JD had told me about his past. I didn't mention the Conclave by name, but referred to them as a group who oversaw vampire affairs.

Jake listened with rapt interest. When I finished, he whistled. "You've had quite the week, Sterling. I knew you were on a hot case, but I didn't imagine there would be this much involved."

"As you can see, I'm in a bit over my head. I can't contact JD, and no one else knows about enhanced individuals. I need your help."

"I'm guessing you already have a plan."

"Half-baked, but yes. I need to draw out Ellwood's operatives by exposing Pike as one of the enhanced people he is tracking. I doubt his task force will be happy to learn one of the people they're supposed to go after is their supervisor."

"Turn his own people against him?"

"Right," I confirmed. "The sudden break between Ellwood and his chief of staff will raise eyebrows. The plan comes with great risks, though. Who's to say that after I expose her, one of those operatives won't go public and suddenly we have a much bigger problem on our hands? It could put JD at further risk."

The public was already learning more about what Victor Hume called "anomalies." Some, he even referred to as aliens, as though they had no humanity. He had displayed Lola Park, a wolf shifter, before a crowd of bio-tech investors who held no prior connections to the magical world. Exposing Pike could bring the veil down further, and I had to weigh the risks.

If I didn't do something about Pike and Ellwood, it would only be a matter of time before they made the information public themselves. I couldn't prevent damage, but maybe I could control it.

Jake was on the same wavelength. "You want me to help because I'm already aware of these people. What's your idea?"

I'd spent the afternoon after Ellwood's departure thinking over the details. "I want a ruse where we pretend Marcus Smith has returned to work. We'll need to leak the information somehow and get Ms. Pike here. We can keep the office bugged and do it that way. After we have her, I want you to pose as

Marcus. Only we'll make sure Pike learns you aren't the real Marcus and get her to reveal her true nature."

"We need to give her team a good enough reason to raid the office," Jake mused. "Make it seem like there will be anomalies here she can capture."

I nodded. "Exactly. We'll have cameras rolling, and when Pike shows who she really is, we'll leak the footage, exposing her to Ellwood's task force." It was the only idea I had to get them off my back.

Jake considered the plan. "Only problem is, I'm no actor. I don't think Pike or her people will believe for one second that I'm Marcus Smith. You can't bring JD in for this?"

"Not while the Conclave is breathing down my neck. I can't have them and Ellwood's task force on me at the same time."

"Do you have someone else? Someone who already works for you?"

I considered my options. Only three men worked for me. Duncan, who was too old, Marco, who was loyal and skilled but lacked JD's flair, and finally, Brandon. I groaned. "There is someone. One of my recently hired part-time guys has the same charisma and bravado as Marcus Smith. The problem is getting him to act the part of a vampire without telling him Marcus Smith *is* a vampire."

"Do you trust that he would keep the secret if you told him? Or that he would do the job anyway, without asking questions?"

I chewed my lower lip, considering. "It's worth trying. Seeing if he'll do it without asking questions, anyway. It won't hurt to ask."

"I can be here, running surveillance," Jake offered. "You and Brandon do your acting. It's almost a bulletproof plan. All you have to do now is leak the information."

And hope that Pike showed up at my office, not Ellwood or one of his cronies. Without her, the plan would fall apart. I needed a way to involve her personally.

More ideas came to me, but I decided to keep them under my hat. That part wouldn't involve Jake.

Jake raised his coffee cup. "Feels like old days."

My military training had prepared me in a lot of ways, but this was a whole new arena. "I feel like I've been swimming with the sharks since the first night Jessamine came to me," I admitted.

Jake's eyes glimmered. "Then maybe it's time you became a shark, too."

CHAPTER TWENTY

JORDAN

It was well after dark when I pulled the beater to the side of the road and killed the engine. We were about a quarter of a mile from Beck's lake house, and I wanted to be careful on approach. The rattling truck would signal our arrival before we reached the driveway.

I considered telling Elias to stay put, but he quickly jumped out of the truck. I pressed my lips into a thin line. "Be careful," I muttered to him as we kept to the side of the road. Up here, the countryside roads were vacant, especially at this time of night. If luck was on my side, we would have no trouble.

Before long, the lake and Beck's cabin came into view. One window was lit, the warm glow within inviting. Part of me wished I could live out here as Beck did, quietly away from danger with her partner.

"If these are your friends, why haven't we been staying here? This place looks much nicer than the dumps we've been using," Elias murmured.

"Our options are limited, and I have had no interest in placing my friends in danger," I replied.

Elias fell silent and kept his footsteps up the gravel drive quiet. When we were within yards of the porch, I signaled for Elias to stay behind a large oak. He frowned but did not protest. I slunk forward, keeping low and to the shadows. If Beck and Miranda were already in danger, I needed to know it before adversaries sensed me lurking.

I'd hardly stepped onto the porch before I sensed something coming at me. I whirled, but not fast enough. A growl sounded, and the next thing I knew, I was on my back, and the creature had collided with my chest. Hot breath, dripping saliva. Teeth closed around my upper arm.

I snarled in alarm, and my instincts kicked in. I shoved the animal off me with more force than I intended, but not without claws slicing through my shirt and chest. A red line appeared, dribbling blood. I surged toward the animal, and the coyote bared its teeth, eyes blazing.

I put my hands up. "It's *me*."

The coyote stilled, as if studying me, then backed up until it was nearly concealed in the dark. I only saw the outline of the creature's form as it turned from coyote to human. Slowly, she rose from all fours, then stepped into the dim light coming through the window. "Jordan, what the hell are you doing here?" Beck demanded.

I gave my shirt a rueful look. "You ruined one of my last remaining shirts. I don't have many clothes right now, you know."

Beck's gaze slid to Elias, who had appeared from behind the tree the moment he saw a coyote leap onto me. "Why do you have a kid with you?"

"I'm not a kid," Elias replied mildly, but his eyes reflected displeasure.

"He's very touchy about that," I whispered. "Why the hell did you attack me?"

"I didn't know who you were. I was coming back from a run when I saw a strange man on my porch. I didn't think my old friend Jordan Davenport had big enough balls to come here. Not after…"

"Tatiana came to see you?"

"She found you," Beck realized.

I nodded. "She's gone back to D.C. now. We have a lot to catch up on."

Beck glanced again at Elias. "Yeah, we sure do."

I stepped toward her, examining her face. "Are you okay?"

"Why wouldn't I be? Other than these strange arrivals, I've been… JD, what's wrong?"

My face must have revealed exactly what I was thinking. *This is a trap.* "I got a message from Vinny. He said you were in danger."

Beck glowered. "Well, I'm not, as far as I know, and I haven't spoken to Vinny in…well, forever. Why would I contact him? Does he want me to act for him, too? Not my thing. I've seen how much trouble acting has gotten you into."

The acting wasn't the problem. It was that I'd fallen in love with one of my clients and stayed in one place too long. I'd been Marcus Smith and Jackson Dale Shade long enough to attract the wrong sort of attention. At the moment, that was *any* attention.

"We should talk inside," I suggested, leading the way.

Beck trailed after me. "Jordan, what the hell is going on? You need to tell me now! Does this have to do with the Conclave? Tatiana told me that bitch Jessamine came to see her. If this involves her, count me out."

Elias was the last to enter. I quickly closed the door and locked it. "Look, I think someone captured Vinny and used his phone to send me a message about you."

Beck's eyes widened. "Which means you've just walked into a trap, and I'm bait. Terrific."

I told her what had happened over the last several days, from encountering Tatiana at the Vermont house to our escape when unknown operatives showed up to scout out the place. Beck's face grew grimmer the longer I spoke.

She cursed. "JD, you always get yourself into such deep shit. And what about this one? What's the kid got to do with anything?" She gestured toward Elias, who repeated, "I'm not a kid," this time with more bite.

"Sorry. Not a kid. Pre-teen?"

"He's seventy," I told her.

Beck's eyes nearly bulged out of her head.

"I'm a vampire, aging very slowly. The Conclave wants to experiment on me," Elias explained with the casual air of someone discussing the weather.

"That part is a longer story I can tell you at a later time. Right now, we need to leave. Where is Miranda?"

As if I'd rubbed a genie's lamp, she appeared in the doorway of what appeared to be a sunroom beyond. Such a useless room, I thought. She wore a paint-splattered apron and held a palette in one hand, a brush in the other.

"Beck, what's going on?" Miranda slowed her words at the sight of my torn shirt and the slowly healing cut. Her gaze slid to Elias, who announced, "I'm not a kid," before she could comment.

Miranda looked at Beck. "What is wrong?"

"We're leaving," Beck replied. "I'll explain on the way. Actually, JD will explain. Thoroughly. Without leaving anything out," she directed at me, clearly unhappy with this turn of events.

"If they came for Vinny, they're bound to come for you," I told her. "Let's hope we can get out of here before it's too late."

Bewildered, Miranda set her supplies aside and untied her apron. "Who came for Vinny? What the hell is going on?"

"Get the essentials," Beck responded. "Like we've drilled."

Miranda wasn't happy, but she turned and went upstairs without objecting.

Beck whirled on me. "Where are you going to take us?"

I opened my mouth, then shut it. I hadn't thought that far.

Beck blew out a hard breath and threw up her hands. "You show up at my house and tell me I'm in danger, but you have no idea what we're going to do? Fine. I have a friend up past the border we can stay with."

"My truck won't take us there. We'll need your car," I explained. "After I know you and Miranda are safe, Elias and I will be on our way. It's not safe for all four of us to be together."

Beck processed this information. "Tatiana was right. The Conclave is really after you. And your sidekick." She nodded at Elias. He frowned but didn't say anything. Maybe "sidekick" was better than being mis-aged.

Miranda returned with two duffel bags stuffed to the brim and grimaced at Beck. "I wasn't sure what to pack." At least they had far more possessions than the meager load Elias and I had been carrying around.

Beck slung one of the bags over her shoulder. "I'm sure you did perfectly." She led the way out of the house, locking up after everyone was out, then headed toward a detached garage. Inside was her SUV. She tossed the duffels into the trunk as I slid into the driver's seat.

"No way," she barked. "I'm driving."

"I'm faster," I insisted.

"You're *reckless*."

"I know I just met the coyote, but I vote that she drives," Elias piped up.

I shot him a glare.

"Beck is a good driver," Miranda added.

I sighed and tossed her the keys I'd snatched off the entrance table inside. Beck caught them with ease and addressed Elias. "I prefer the term 'shifter.'"

He saluted. "As long as you don't refer to me as a child."

She smiled. "Deal."

Miranda and Elias slid into the back seat, and I took the

passenger side. Beck started the SUV, muttering, "I've never started a road trip in the middle of the night."

She pulled out of the garage, hitting a button to close it after we were out, then drove down the gravel path toward the main road. The sky was overcast tonight, and the only light came from the car's headlights. Dense woods bordered either side of the curving road.

I twisted in my seat to regard Miranda. "Are both of you nocturnal? I haven't met someone who stays up so late to paint."

Miranda smiled. "Beck takes her runs late at night, and we like to go to bed together. I paint until she's back."

My expression softened. "I'm sorry to ruin an otherwise pleasant night."

"Uh-oh," Elias remarked, interrupting our conversation.

Beck's hands tightened around the wheel as the three of us came to the same conclusion, but Elias spoke the words. "We've got company."

Headlights appeared behind us.

"Might be a late-night trucker," Miranda suggested.

The rest of us were assuming the worst.

"He's picking up speed, whoever he is," Miranda observed.

Beck took a right turn without signaling, heading down a road away from the interstate. She huffed when he turned down the same road.

"Might be better to head for the interstate," Miranda proposed.

"And risk highway patrol pulling us over? No, thanks." Beck increased her speed, but so did the truck behind us. She reached a three-way stop and pivoted left without halting. I glanced in the rearview mirror and noticed another vehicle pulling from a nearby driveway. It fell in line behind the truck already pursuing us.

"Shit," Beck breathed.

Up ahead, a third pair of headlights appeared, and Beck grimaced. "You think…"

"Turn right here," I urged.

Beck took the turn, again without signaling. The two cars already following us did the same, and the third turned in the road to head back the way they'd come. "Third car is going around, probably to cut us off. Now might be the time to slam, Beck," I told her.

"Slam?" Miranda echoed.

Elias was already gripping the oh-shit handle, his jaw clenched.

Beck slammed her foot onto the gas and shot down the road. The car rattled over a pothole, then through likely the only stoplight in this nearly deserted area. We sped past farms with white houses and decrepit barns. Beck saw the third car coming toward us before I did and made a last-second decision to veer left into someone's field.

Miranda cried out, but Elias stayed silent. I wished more than anything that I was behind the wheel, though Beck was doing everything I would have done. She barreled the car through a fence, sending wooden boards flying.

The vehicles behind us didn't stop.

"Shit, Jordan! What am I supposed to do?" Beck nearly howled.

I racked my brain, trying to figure a way out of this. Who was following us? The senator's goons or the Conclave? Either way, not good.

Beck continued racing across the field, the uneven ground giving us all sore asses. Behind us, the three vehicles fanned out, trying to surround us. She wrenched the wheel hard to the left, then the right, but there was nowhere to go. We were in the middle of open farmland, with woods too far in the distance to reach.

"Beck, stop the car."

She didn't look away from the path she was forging in front of her. "Are you insane?"

"They're going to box us in anyway. Better we face them on our terms."

Beck's jaw clenched, but she knew I was right.

She brought the SUV to a skidding halt in the middle of the field, sending dirt and grass flying. The three vehicles formed a loose triangle around us, their headlights creating a harsh spotlight. Doors opened, and three figures emerged, one from each car, with a fluid grace I knew all too well. Vampires.

"Stay in the car," Beck murmured to Miranda and Elias.

"What are you doing?" Miranda's voice was pitched high with fear.

Beck was already opening her door. She didn't answer.

I stepped out into the cool night air, moving so I stood beside Beck in front of the car. Its headlights beamed behind us. The three vampires sauntered toward us, two men flanking one woman. I didn't recognize them. *The Conclave hired some muscle,* I concluded inwardly.

The woman spoke first, her voice carrying easily across the distance. "Jordan Davenport. We've been looking for you."

"Congratulations on finding me," I replied. "Though I have to say, your approach lacks subtlety."

One of the men laughed coldly. "We were told you had a mouth on you." His gaze slid to Beck. "And what's this? A fox caught in the trap, too?"

Beck tensed beside me. I could feel the heat rolling off her as her shifter nature rose to the surface.

"She has nothing to do with this. Let them go. It's me you want."

The woman tilted her head and flashed a predatory smile. "Oh, we'll take you. But we can't exactly leave witnesses, can we? The Conclave was very clear about keeping this clean."

"So Jessamine sent you?" I spat.

"You forget that Jessamine is merely a messenger," the second man stated. He was broader than his companion, built like a linebacker. "You've caused them a lot of trouble, Davenport. Time to answer for it."

Beck's breathing changed, becoming shorter, more rapid.

I gripped her arm. "Beck, get back in the car and go. Take them somewhere safe. This is my fight."

"Jordan—"

"I said *go*."

It was too late. The three vampires moved as one, closing the distance with inhuman speed. I shoved Beck aside and met the woman head-on, catching her arm as she swung at me. We grappled, vampire strength against vampire strength, neither giving ground.

Behind me, I heard the distinctive sound of bone cracking and reforming. Beck's shift was fast, thanks to years of practice. One moment, she stood on two legs. The next, a coyote launched at the broader vampire, its teeth finding his shoulder. He screamed with more rage than pain and tried to throw her off, but Beck held on.

The third vampire—the one who'd laughed—went for the SUV.

"No!" I roared, breaking free from the woman and intercepting him. We collided hard enough that I heard ribs crack. His or mine, I wasn't sure. We went down in a tangle of limbs, rolling across tire-torn earth.

He was fast, but not as fast as me.

I wrapped my hands around his throat and squeezed, cutting off his air. He didn't need to breathe, but the pressure on his windpipe would hurt enough to slow him down.

The female vampire was still a problem, though. She hit me from behind with something hard, driving me off her companion. Her claws raked my back, shredding my already ruined shirt and the skin beneath. The pain was bright and immediate, but I'd felt worse.

I spun, catching her wrist and twisting. She hissed and kicked out, her boot connecting with my stomach.

I stumbled back, and she pressed her advantage, moving in fast. I was ready for her. I ducked under her next strike and came up inside her guard. My fist connected with her jaw hard enough to snap her head back. She staggered, and I followed with a knee to her midsection that drove the air from her lungs.

Across the field, Beck was a blur of tawny fur and teeth, using her smaller size and speed to her advantage. The broad-shouldered vampire was bleeding from a dozen wounds. He swung wildly, trying to catch her, but she was too quick.

He grabbed a fencepost that had torn loose when Beck crashed through and swung it like a club. It caught Beck on her flank with a sickening crack. She yelped and went down.

"Beck!" I started toward her, but the laughing vampire tackled me from the side. We slammed down hard, and he got his hands around my throat, returning the favor. His face twisted with rage, eyes black with bloodlust.

I brought my knee up between us and rolled to my feet. He came at me again, but this time I sidestepped, grabbed his arm, and used his momentum to smash into one of their vehicles. The metal crumpled beneath the impact.

Beck had shifted fully back to human, one hand clutching her side where the splintered end of the post had penetrated her. She was breathing hard, but her eyes were fierce.

The broad vampire advanced on her, and I saw red.

I pushed every ounce of speed into my run and hit him like a freight train. We sprawled on the ground, and I didn't give him time to recover. His face became a bloody ruin. His struggles weakened until he stopped moving.

I stood, chest heaving, and turned to assess the situation. The woman was back on her feet, but she looked uncertain now. The laughing vampire pulled himself from the wreckage of the car, moving slowly, favoring his left side.

Beck had shifted again, back to her coyote form despite her injury. She loosed a savage snarl as if to say, *Come near me, and I'll rip out your fucking throat.*

"Leave," I commanded. "Tell the Conclave that if they want me, they can send someone worth my time. Not expendable grunts."

The woman and the laughing vampire exchanged glances. The broad one on the ground groaned but didn't move. They could take him or leave him. Their choice.

"This isn't over." The woman's voice dripped with contempt.

I didn't reply.

They moved to their fallen companion, hauling him up between them. They dragged him to one of the vehicles, loaded him in, and drove off separately, their headlights disappearing into the night. The third vehicle sat empty and abandoned.

I turned to where Beck was shifting back to human form. Her body trembled with the effort. Miranda had gotten out of the SUV and was running toward her, tears streaming down her face.

"Beck, oh my God…"

"I'm okay," Beck gasped, though she clearly wasn't. "Just bruised. I'll heal."

I approached slowly, giving Miranda space to check her partner. Elias climbed from the SUV, his face pale.

Beck leaned against Miranda, letting her partner support her weight. She leveled a grim expression at me. "Jordan, you can't keep doing this. Running, fighting…"

Putting everyone in danger. She didn't say it, but she might as well have.

"I know."

"What are you going to do about it?"

"If they came for you and Vinny, they're coming for Tatiana, too. They might already have her. I need to go to D.C."

Beck nodded slowly. "Elias can come with us."

I shook my head. "He's my responsibility."

"I can protect him." Beck's voice held bite despite her pain. "The worst thing you can do right now is drag him into the very place the Conclave is waiting for you."

She had a good point. My heart twisted as I looked at Elias. I had sworn to protect him, but now I was leaving him.

He spoke before I could. "You have to go. I understand."

I walked over and placed my hands on his shoulders. "I promise to come for you as soon as I can. Beck is my good friend. I trust her with my life."

He nodded, trying to be brave, but I could see the fear in his eyes. The fear of being left alone again, even for a little while.

"Hey," I murmured. "I don't break my promises. You know that, right?"

"Right," he whispered.

I pulled him into a brief hug, then drew back. Beck watched me, her expression softer.

"Go," she insisted. "We'll be fine. I'm harder to kill than I look."

I managed a small smile. "You've always been a good friend, Beck. Even if you were a lousy lover."

She barked out a laugh that turned into a wince. "And you've always been impossible. Nothing's changed there."

Miranda helped Beck back to the SUV, then got into the driver's side. I walked to the abandoned vehicle, a dark sedan with tinted windows. The keys were still in the ignition. I climbed into the driver's side and started the engine.

Beck's SUV made a careful turn before heading back toward the road. I watched until the taillights disappeared into the darkness.

The eastern horizon was beginning to lighten, the first gray fingers of dawn reaching across the sky. I would have to drive fast, find shelter before the sun rose fully. I put the sedan in gear and headed south, whispering, "I'm coming, Tatiana."

CHAPTER TWENTY-ONE

TATIANA

I felt bad about lying to Linda.

"Is he really? Finally!" Linda clapped. "He left for too long, but I knew he wouldn't be gone forever. How could he stay away from you?"

I managed to keep smiling despite my sinking heart. "Would you go and pick up some things he might like? Marcus will appreciate it."

"Of course. Anything he wants. When did you say he's coming back?"

We stood in the meeting room where the planted bug would pick up our conversation. "This afternoon."

Linda settled a palm on her cheek. "Oh, dear, I'm going to miss him! I have my doctor's appointment today."

I feigned disappointment. Of course I knew her appointment was today. I'd selected today for this ruse because I knew Linda would be out of the office. I didn't want her wrapped up in this mess.

I placed a hand on her shoulder. "You can see Marcus another day. Take the rest of the day off after your appointment."

"Are you sure?"

"It's on the other side of town, and you would only be coming back for another hour anyway. I'll see you next week."

Linda huffed. "All right, but you'd better tell Marcus not to disappear again. Not until I've had a chance to see him."

I sent Linda off with a list that would keep her out of the office for the next half an hour. After she was gone, I texted Jake.

Coast is clear.

A moment later, Jake's boots shuffled up the stairs outside the office. He entered in full tactical gear and armed to the teeth. "I'll need to keep you out of sight, or you'll scare Linda."

From his cat tower in the corner of the room, Whiskers stood and arched his back into a stretch. He settled again, not giving a care in the world for what was about to happen.

"This way," I told Jake, leading him into my office. The bug wouldn't pick up on much in here, but we kept our voices low. Jake began setting up his surveillance system. He would be watching and ensuring the footage was recorded as the scene unfolded.

He gave me a comm, and I shut the door and left him to it. It was perfect timing, because as I exited my office, Brando filled the doorway. "Well, what do you think?" He gestured at his navy blue suit and winked. "I bought it just for this."

I couldn't deny that, without seeing his face, Brando could convincingly pass as JD. He was no Jordan Davenport, but he was the best I had. "Thank you for doing this," I whispered, remembering our conversation from yesterday.

All I'd told Brandon was that some powerful people were after Marcus, and I had to expose their illegal activity. I needed him to pose as Marcus to pull it off. We had no photos of Marcus on our website, and I was certain all Adeline Pike had seen of him was the fuzzy camera footage from Ellwood.

I'd given Brandon a script to go by and crossed my fingers.

"I'll take any excuse to flirt with my boss," Brandon teased.

"That isn't part of the job."

"Everybody says you and Marcus had the hots for each other."

I glared, more at his volume than what he'd said.

He realized his hiccup and winced, mouthing, "Sorry."

We weren't in the meeting room, but I didn't want whoever had planted the bug to hear our plan.

Linda bustled in behind Brandon, her face lighting up. "Oh, Brando, I didn't know you were coming in today. What's the suit for?"

Brandon turned so Linda couldn't walk into the room, keeping her far enough away from the listening device. "Linda! Are those for me? Hmm, blueberry scones are my favorite."

"They're for Marcus, not for you. You know, when I saw you as I was coming up the stairs, I thought you might be him. He always wore navy suits, and with your dark hair... Though you are a tad shorter than Marcus."

"Thank you for bringing these, Linda," I called over Brandon's shoulder. I took the paper bag full of scones and the tray of coffees, knowing she would need to be on her way or she'd be late for her appointment.

"I'm going on a very important job," Brandon told Linda. "Needed a suit."

Linda only laughed. "Well, you clean up well. I'll see you all later!" She coaxed Whiskers to her and headed out.

I closed the office door and exhaled a deep breath, then turned to Brandon and whispered, "Show time."

We walked into the meeting room together, and I gestured for Brandon to take a seat at the conference table. I paced on the other side, exuding nervous energy that wouldn't be out of place for someone reuniting with a partner who'd vanished for months.

Brandon settled into the chair, crossing one leg over the other in a way that was almost like JD. *Almost.*

I started speaking loudly enough for the bug to pick up. "I can't believe you're actually here. After all this time."

Brandon looked up at me, his expression serious. "I had to come back, Tatiana. I couldn't stay away any longer." He reached into a bag he'd brought in with him and produced a box of chocolates. I glanced at it, then at Brandon, trying to transmit, *This wasn't necessary. The people listening can't see the chocolate!*

His eyes shone as if to say, *Have it your way. More for me.*

"Where have you been?" Genuine frustration crept into my voice. I wasn't sure if it was toward Brandon for the extra flair or because I was imagining it was really JD sitting across from me. "Do you have any *idea* what the last few months have been like? The staff wondering where you are, me having to cover for you?"

"I know," Brandon replied with actual regret. He was a better actor than I'd expected. "I know I left you in an impossible position, but I didn't have a choice. You know this."

"There is always a choice." I crossed my arms. "You could have trusted me. You could have let me help."

"It was too dangerous." Brandon stood, moving toward me with measured steps. "The people looking for me wouldn't have stopped at me. Anyone close is a target. I couldn't risk that. I couldn't risk *you*."

"Then why are you here now?"

His jaw tightened. Brandon had never met JD, which made his performance even more impressive. "Because I heard you might be in danger. I had to come and see for myself."

I turned away, letting silence briefly hang. "You should have let me make the decision about risking me."

"Would you have let me go if I had?"

I didn't answer immediately. Let whoever was listening think this was real. Finally, I responded, "No, probably not." It didn't require any acting to sound earnest.

Brandon took another step closer. He was really committing to this, playing it with more drama than I'd anticipated. If he tried to plant one on me, he'd find my knee between his legs. "Tatiana…"

I cut him off. "If you say you're in danger, and I am, too, we shouldn't be here. What if you were followed?"

"I wasn't. I was careful."

My hand moved unconsciously toward my hip, where my weapon was holstered beneath my blazer. "It isn't only the Conclave looking for you now. There's a senator with a full staff of operatives. If they find you here…"

Brief confusion flashed through Brandon's eyes at the word *Conclave.* He recovered quickly, though. "Then we deal with it. Together, like we always have."

The emotion in his voice nearly made me roll my eyes, but it was working. It felt real enough that I almost believed it myself.

"I've missed you," I stated quietly. That part, at least, wasn't a lie.

Brandon's expression softened. "I've missed you, too. More than you know."

Jake's voice crackled over the comm. "Four guys coming up the stairs. Tactical gear. Armed."

My pulse quickened, but I remained composed, only letting the barest smile touch my lips as I looked at Brandon. "Ready for a fight?"

His teeth flashed in an award-winning smile. "Woke up ready."

The office door slammed open with enough force to rattle the frame. Four men in tactical gear poured through, weapons raised. They spread out quickly, with one remaining to block the exit.

"Hands where we can see them!" the lead operative barked.

I raised my hands slowly, deliberately. Beside me, Brandon did the same, his expression shifting to confusion that looked entirely genuine.

"What is this?" I demanded. "Who are you?"

"Homeland Security," the lead operative barked, though I knew it was a lie. These weren't federal agents. They were

Ellwood's private muscle. "We have reason to believe you're harboring a fugitive."

"A fugitive? This is a *private security firm*. We don't harbor anyone."

One of the operatives moved closer to Brandon, studying his face. "That's him. That's the target."

"Target?" Brandon sputtered. "I don't know what you're talking about. My name is Marcus Smith. I *work* here."

"Save it." Another operative moved to flank us. "We know who you are."

I spoke up. "You have no authority to be here. This is private property, and unless you have a warrant—"

"We have all the authority we need," a new voice called from the doorway.

Exactly as I had hoped, Adeline Pike stepped into the office, her heels clicking against the hardwood floor. She looked every inch the professional in her tailored cream-colored suit, her hair pulled back in a severe bun. A predatory gleam that made my skin crawl sparked in her eyes.

"Ms. Pike." I injected surprise into my voice. By the time this was over, both Brandon and I would deserve an Oscar. "What are you doing here?"

"Securing a dangerous individual," she returned smoothly, as if this was an everyday task. She moved past the operatives with fluid grace, her attention fixed on Brandon, whose stony expression was convincing. "Mr. Davenport at last. I've been wanting to meet you." Her voice was low, almost sultry.

Genuine confusion flashed in Brandon's eyes. "I'm Marcus Smith. I don't know who this Davenport person is."

Adeline's smile held no warmth. "Is that so?" She circled him, and I saw the moment she realized something was wrong. Her nostrils flared, her eyes narrowing. She stepped back, her face twisting. "You *aren't* him."

"Like I said, I don't know who this Davenport is." Real frustration edged Brandon's voice. He glanced at me as if to ask, *What the hell is she talking about?*

Adeline moved faster than any human should be able to. One moment, she was standing five or six feet away. Then, in a blink, her hand was wrapped around Brandon's throat as she lifted him off his feet. His hands grappled with her wrist, his face reddening.

"Where is he?" she hissed, fangs extending. "Where is Jordan Davenport?"

The operatives stilled and lowered their weapons slightly. They looked uncertain. This wasn't part of their briefing.

"I don't…" Brandon gasped. "I don't know who that is. I'm Marcus Smith!"

Adeline slammed him against the wall hard enough to crack the drywall, and I winced. Brandon hadn't signed up to get his skull rattled. "Don't lie to me!"

I finally moved, drawing my weapon and aiming it at her. "Let him go. Now."

Adeline turned her head. Her eyes had gone completely black. "Or what? You'll shoot me? That won't do much good, Ms. Sterling, but I think you've already figured that out."

"Try me."

Full realization dawned on Adeline. She let Brandon go and stalked toward me with the grace and precision of a predator. "You did this. You had this man pose as Jordan to lure me in." Her laugh was raw and husky. "Perhaps I underestimated you, but you are still a fool, girl. You are one woman against four operatives and me."

A vampire. That was the part she didn't say.

One of the operatives stepped forward. "Ma'am, what…what is going on?"

Adeline ignored him, her attention still on me. "You set this up. This whole thing was a trap."

"I have no idea what you're talking about," I returned, but my voice was more mocking than innocent confusion. "If you and your men do not leave my private property now, I will put you down."

Adeline's laugh was sharp enough to break glass. "You *can't* stop me. None of you can! Tell me where Jordan is, or I'll kill you. Trust me, darling, it won't be a quick death."

One of the operatives behind her blinked. They'd been ordered to retrieve Marcus Smith, not hand out slow and torturous deaths. I felt a spark of victory. No doubt Jake had gotten all of this. The operatives weren't likely to follow Pike's orders now. If Brandon, Jake, and I could take her down, the show would be over.

It was too good to be true, as I quickly found out. Jake's voice came over the comm again. "Sterling, more company."

My stomach dropped. More of Ellwood's men? Had Pike somehow signaled for backup? We could handle four, maybe six, but if he'd sent a whole team…

Three figures stepped into the office. A female first, then two men slinking in behind her.

My heart sank. *Shit.*

Jessamine Lane wore black from head to toe, her hair pulled back into a sleek ponytail. Her expression was both cold and beautiful. The two flanking her were unmistakably vampires. Adeline's reaction—first shock, then open horror—confirmed my suspicions. I didn't recognize either of the vampires behind Jessamine, but they looked dangerous.

Jessamine didn't even look at me. "Adeline Pike." Her voice carried an authority that made Adeline's eyes glint with fear. "You have violated Conclave law. Step away from the humans. I suggest you cooperate with us, or face more severe consequences."

The operatives had no idea what to do. They kept their weapons raised, but confusion rippled across their features.

Adeline stepped away from Brandon and recovered herself. "Jessamine. I should have known you would show up."

"You've been trafficking information to humans," Jessamine continued, approaching with measured steps. "You have exposed our existence for personal gain. The Conclave has issued a retrieval order."

"For me?" Adeline laughed. "*I* am not the one you should be worried about. Jordan Davenport is the one who has been exposing us. Acting like a superhero, drawing attention—"

"Davenport's crimes are his to answer for. As are yours." Jessamine spoke with the frustration of a parent whose child was throwing a tantrum. Her gaze swept the room, from me to Brandon, then the four operatives who appeared to be seriously reconsidering their career choices. "And anyone who has aided him," she added.

My blood ran cold. "We haven't done anything wrong."

"You have been harboring a fugitive from Conclave justice," Jessamine countered. "You have helped him evade capture more than once. I warned you, Ms. Sterling. That makes you complicit."

"The seven days aren't up," I cut in.

Jessamine sighed as if I was another tantrum-throwing toddler. "Yet you have failed to contact Mr. Davenport and lay out the terms."

"That isn't Jordan Davenport," Adeline interjected, gesturing to Brandon. "You can see for yourself."

"Like I said, I'm Marcus Smith!" Brandon cried. He clutched the side of his head, where a trickle of blood ran from above his ear to his jaw.

I shot Brandon a look that said, *Shut up. Act's over.*

"I know this man is not Jordan," Jessamine snapped, then turned her gaze back to me. "You tried to deceive us, which means you know where he is."

I shook my head. My Ruger was still aimed at Pike, not that it would do much now. "I set this up to catch *her*. Actually, I was doing you a favor."

Jessamine laughed, deep and husky. "Your act is over, Ms. Sterling. Let us not waste time with lies. Now, either all of you can comply, and things can go smoothly, or we can do this the hard way."

I was still considering my options when Jake's voice spoke in my ear. "Shit. Our new friend disabled the cameras."

I didn't have time to process what that meant before the room exploded into chaos.

CHAPTER TWENTY-TWO

TATIANA

Pike and Jessamine collided in the center of the meeting room. Pike hit Jessamine with enough force to overturn the table behind her. The two vampires with Jessamine moved to flank Pike, but the four operatives finally recovered from their shock and opened fire.

Bullets tore through the air. I grabbed Brandon and threw us both behind the overturned table as rounds punched through drywall and shattered windows.

"What the hell is happening?" Brandon shouted over the gunfire.

"Welcome to my life!" I hollered back.

One of the male vampires, tall and dark-haired with features that seemed carved from stone, took three bullets to the chest and barely flinched. His expression was more mild annoyance than pain. He closed the distance between himself and the human who'd shot him in a blur of motion. The operative's scream cut off abruptly as the vampire's hand closed around his throat.

"Matthias, we need them alive!" Jessamine snapped, dodging a vicious swipe from Pike's clawed hand.

Matthias dropped the operative, who crumpled to the floor, gasping.

The other male vampire, shorter, red-haired, and wearing a smile that promised violence, was already disarming two of the other operatives with surgical precision. He moved like water, flowing around their attacks, his hands blurring as he stripped weapons, broke fingers, and left grown men whimpering on the floor.

The fourth operative realized he stood no chance and high-tailed it for the exit. The red-haired vampire moved to pursue, but Matthias called, "Let him go!"

"Sterling!" Jake's voice crackled over the comm. Whatever he said next, I didn't hear over Pike's scream. Jessamine must have gotten in a good strike.

I risked a glance over the table. Pike and Jessamine were locked in combat that was barely comprehensible to my human eyes. I saw a hurricane of fists and claws crash through my office door, taking half the wall with them.

"Now, Jake!" I shouted without using the comm.

A canister rolled out from my office doorway—a smoke bomb Jake had rigged earlier. It detonated with a sharp hiss, and thick gray smoke filled the room at an alarming rate.

The two operatives the red-haired vampire had disabled scrambled to their feet, not needing further encouragement to flee. They scrambled for the exit, half-crawling, half-running, desperate to get away from the monsters they'd found themselves fighting.

"Cowards!" Pike's high-pitched voice rang out from somewhere in the smoke, followed by the sound of something heavy hitting a wall.

I pulled Brandon to his feet. "We need to move."

Matthias was already there, materializing from the smoke like something out of a nightmare. His smile told us he'd been looking forward to a fight. "You're not going anywhere."

I didn't think. I grabbed the desk chair beside me and swung it with everything I had. It shattered against his chest, and wooden pieces flew. Matthias looked down at the broken chair, then back at me, one eyebrow raised.

Brandon grabbed a stapler from the floor and threw it at Matthias' head. It bounced off harmlessly. "Sorry?" Brandon croaked, unsure if he was apologizing to the vampire or me. "I-I panicked."

The red-haired vampire appeared behind us, cutting off our escape route to the main door. "Going somewhere? We were just beginning to get acquainted."

"Tatiana!" Jake burst out of my office, a laptop bag slung over his shoulder and what looked like a modified flare gun in his hand. He aimed it at the red-haired vampire and fired.

A burst of brilliant UV light exploded in the vampire's face. He shrieked, throwing his hands up to shield his eyes as he stumbled backward. His skin smoked where the light touched it.

"Move!" Jake shouted.

He didn't have to tell me twice.

We bolted to the door. Behind us, Matthias was already recovering from the surprise, and the red-haired vampire snarled in rage.

In my office, the sounds of Pike's and Jessamine's battle echoed. I was glad Harry's other tenants were no longer in the building thanks to his outrageous rent prices. Only a mover's company downstairs remained, and no one was in today. No one else to see this shit show play out to completion.

I led the way to the bottom floor, then into a tiny back office. Harry's. Jake slammed the door shut behind us and immediately shoved a filing cabinet in front of it.

"I don't know if you noticed, but bullets didn't stop those guys. I don't think a fucking filing cabinet will do anything," Brandon burst out.

"Maybe you should have thrown the stapler harder," I muttered back.

Brandon blanched, and I nodded toward the cabinet. "It doesn't need to hold long." Behind where the cabinet had been was a door. I opened it and revealed steel stairs leading down.

Brandon stared. "You have a secret passage in your office?"

"Not secret, exactly, and this isn't my office." I had no time to explain further.

As we filed onto the stairs, something hit the office door with enough force to crack it. The filing cabinet screeched as the blow shoved it aside. I pulled the door shut and locked it, knowing it wouldn't buy us much time.

We dashed down the stairs, then turned into a narrow maintenance corridor. Jake and I jogged side by side with Brandon bringing up the rear. "Where does this go?" Brandon panted.

"Basement, then the service tunnels," I replied. Our way out.

"You planned for those...things to attack us?" Brandon demanded.

"I didn't plan for the last trio to show up." And I was paying for it now.

A door shattered somewhere behind us. We emerged into a concrete corridor illuminated by flickering fluorescent lights. Old pipes ran along the ceiling, dripping condensation. The air smelled like mold and rust.

Jake was already ahead, his longer legs gaining more distance. We followed him through a maze of corridors, past old storage rooms and forgotten equipment. I heard the vampires behind us, pursuing with inhuman speed, their footsteps barely audible but growing closer. Our head start was quickly dwindling.

"Sterling, please tell me you have a plan," Jake tossed out.

"Working on it," I responded, pushing ahead of him.

I skidded to a halt at an intersection, almost slamming into a wall. I yanked open a panel and typed on the keypad behind it.

"Hurry!" Brandon urged frantically.

Matthias rounded the corner behind us, his expression pure, predatory focus. The red-haired vampire appeared from a side corridor, cutting off what might have been our retreat. His face was blistered and angry where Jake's UV light had burned him, but he was already healing.

"End of the line," he growled.

I stepped in front of Brandon and Jake, my hand moving my backup weapon, a knife strapped to my thigh.

The red-haired vampire smiled. "I'm going to enjoy this." He lunged.

Jake slammed his hand on the keypad.

The ensuing explosion was deafening in the confined space. Pre-planted C-4 charges I'd carefully positioned last night as part of our contingency plan detonated in sequence. The ceiling collapsed between us and the vampires in a cascade of concrete and rebar. Dust billowed through the corridor, choking and blinding.

I grabbed Brandon with one hand, Jake with the other, and we ran through the chaos. Behind us, the vampires screamed in rage as they dug through the rubble.

Jake coughed. "That won't stop them for long!"

"It doesn't need to!" I returned.

We burst out of the access tunnel into the alley behind the building. Blessed, beautiful daylight poured down from above. We came out fast enough that I slammed into the side of a fire escape. I hissed and staggered away. Jake caught me with a steadying hand.

The vampires wouldn't follow us out here, but we couldn't linger for long. They might have withstood the sun if we hadn't buried them under rubble after engaging them in the fight, then the chase. No doubt Jessamine and Pike were still going at it upstairs.

I bent over, hands on my knees, and gulped air. My shoulder

throbbed where I'd hit the fire escape, my ribs ached, and I was pretty sure I'd pulled something in my leg.

Brandon collapsed against the wall. "That was insane."

"Welcome to Sterling and Smith," I managed between breaths.

A vehicle screeched to a halt at the mouth of the alley, a black SUV that made my hand instinctively go for my weapon. Was it possible the vampires had gotten out and were cutting us off here?

The doors opened, and relief flooded through me when Margo jumped out, followed by Duncan.

"Boss!" Margo ran toward us. "We got alerts that the building alarms were going off." She scanned us. We were covered in plaster and dust. The side of Brandon's head was bleeding. It wasn't bad enough to need stitches, but he'd clearly been through an ordeal. "What the hell happened?"

Duncan was right behind her, scanning the alley for threats. "We saw armed men leaving in a hurry. Was that an explosion?"

I looked at the building. Smoke drifted from broken windows. The fire alarms wailed, and emergency vehicles were probably on their way. My office, my business, the place I'd built from nothing, was a war zone.

Jessamine, Pike, and the other two vampires would be smart enough to leave the area before first responders arrived. I considered staying, but the whole thing required too much explanation.

I straightened, tightening my jaw against the pain in my shoulder. "We need to head somewhere we won't be found. Ellwood is going to come after us with everything he's got. And the Conclave..."

"The what?" Margo asked.

"That's what I want to know!" Brandon declared.

Duncan fixed me with a steady but questioning look.

"You two need to decide right now if you're in or out. After this, there's no going back," I told them.

Margo and Duncan shared a look.

"There's a lot to explain, but not here," I added.

Margo grinned. "I didn't sign up for a boring desk job."

Duncan nodded in agreement. "We're in."

"Good. Get in the car."

Duncan jumped into the driver's seat, and Margo took the front passenger side. Jake, Brandon, and I piled into the back. Margo and Duncan knew Ellwood's men would be after us, but they didn't know about Jessamine and her brutish vampires. "Where are we going, boss?" Duncan asked, tires screeching as he pulled away from the curb.

I gave him an address, and Jake shot me a confused look. "Are you sure?"

I nodded. "It's secure and big enough for all of us. We won't need to stay long, but we can't go to my place."

I took out my phone to call Marc, ensure that my mom was safe, and ask him to extend his watch without letting her know. When I hung up, Duncan announced, "It will take a while to get there. We should take a route that isn't the main one."

I agreed and prepared myself for questions. There would be a lot of them when my crew realized we were going to a house that belonged to a man they once knew as Marcus Smith.

CHAPTER TWENTY-THREE

JORDAN

The sedan's engine ticked as it cooled, the sound loud in the pre-dawn silence. I sat behind the wheel and stared up at the crumbling manor. Gothic spires reached toward the lightening sky like skeletal fingers, and ivy claimed most of the exterior walls, creeping across crumbling stone.

The windows were dark, but I hoped the place was not abandoned. It would be just my luck if the man I hoped to find beyond those walls had gone for good.

Would serve me right for not reaching out all this time, I thought as I stepped out into the cold Virginia pre-dawn and sucked down a breath of air, bracing myself. Perhaps coming here had been a mistake. Already, the old wounds were opening. A lump grew in my throat, but I swallowed it. *You don't have to stay long,* I told myself.

I approached the massive front door silently, as if nearing a caged animal that might growl the moment it sensed me. The carved oak door, reinforced with iron bands that had rusted over the decades, loomed over me. I raised my fist and knocked, three sharp raps that echoed like distant gunshots.

I waited, hearing nothing, and began to think the place might be empty after all. "Waste of time," I hissed. I could have been in D.C. by now, at Tatiana's office or her apartment, wherever she was.

The moment I muttered these words, I heard the light shuffle of footsteps. The door swung inward, hinges groaning.

The butler who stood in the dim hallway looked more skeleton than person. His skin was papery and thin, stretched tight over his bones. His hair was wispy and white, and his eyes had the rheumy quality of advanced age. Human, decidedly so.

His posture was perfect, despite his age, and his livery immaculate. When he looked at me, the sharpness in his eyes attested to his state of mind.

"Good morning," I greeted with cheer that belied everything that had brought me here.

The butler scanned my torn, bloodstained clothes and frowned.

"Jordan Davenport. Mr. Castain will know who I am," I added.

"*Lord* Castain," the butler corrected, his voice like dry leaves. "One moment."

He shuffled away down a dim, grand hallway, leaving me to admire the portrait gallery filling one wall against faded, dark red wallpaper. The oil paintings depicted various landscapes, and men and women I did not know. The ceiling of the cavernous hall soared thirty feet overhead. A chandelier hung in the center, wrought iron and crystal, though half the crystals were missing and the iron had blackened with age.

"This way, sir." The butler had silently returned. He motioned toward an adjoining room with a glimpse of firelight beyond a heavy wooden door standing slightly ajar. I nodded my thanks and followed him.

The room was almost oppressively warm. A fire roared in an enormous stone hearth that dominated the far wall. Bookshelves lined the walls, with leather-bound volumes crammed together. Two high-backed chairs sat angled before the fire. The occupant of one chair was turned away from me, revealing only his silhouette.

I knew who he was.

"I can smell you from here," a low, dry voice murmured. Without turning, the man in the chair added, "Jordan, you smell like a corpse that's been rotting in the sun too long."

Despite everything, the corner of my mouth twitched. I walked toward him, halting when I reached the side of his chair. Slowly, the man turned his head.

Lucien was tall, even seated. His face was gaunt, almost skeletal. He was all sharp angles and hollows, with cheekbones like blades. His snow-white hair hung in waves to his shoulders. He probably hadn't been to a barber in decades. Hell, he probably hadn't left this *house* in that long. His eyes were such a pale gray that they almost shone silver, as sharp and calculating as I remembered.

He looked every inch the ancient vampire he was.

He scanned me from head to toe, not bothering to hide the same disdain his butler had shown me. "I thought I taught you to dress better. You look a bloody mess." He didn't give me a chance to explain myself before turning to the butler. "Please find something for Mr. Davenport to wear, and bring us something to drink."

The butler dipped his head, hands locked behind his back. "Straight away, sir." He disappeared the way he'd come.

Lucien wasn't through berating me. "It has been nearly two centuries since you last bothered to visit me. You must be in deep shit to do so now." His voice carried a faint French accent.

Despite my dirty clothes and Lucien's glowering stare, I settled into the chair opposite him. "You look ghastly," he went on. "I don't mean your clothes, though that shirt is an abomination. When did you last feed properly?"

"Weeks," I admitted. I'd run out of my synthetic stores soon after rescuing Elias. I had given him most of what I'd had. The boy had been through horrors that made me feel sick, and my priority had been to see him recover.

After the synthetic was gone, I'd killed the occasional rabbit, fox, or deer. None of it came close to satisfying me. I had considered reaching out to my blood dealer, but that would have been too risky, both for her and for us.

Lucien shook his head. "You will be no good to anyone if you collapse from malnutrition."

My gaze drifted to a small painting above the mantel. It was the only thing decorating this particular wall. The woman in the painting wore a soft smile, her eyes lively. Waves of auburn hair flowed past her shoulders.

My heart twisted. *Isabella.*

It had been nearly three centuries since I last saw her. Her face had only shown in my dreams. In the painting, she seemed as real as ever.

"She was beautiful," Lucien murmured. "And kind. Too kind for this world, certainly too kind for *our* world."

On that, we agreed. The emotion I had vowed to keep from showing welled up. My eyes misted, and I blinked hard.

The door opened, and the butler shuffled in, carrying a tray. The scent of fresh, warm blood hit me. Properly prepared. My mouth watered instantly, and my gums ached as my fangs threatened to extend.

"Thank you," Lucien told the man.

The butler turned to me. "I have fresh clothes and a bath drawing when you are ready, Mr. Davenport."

I nodded my gratitude as the butler left.

Lucien took one cup, nodding for me to take the other. I tried to control myself, to drink it like tea, but I couldn't do it. I gulped it down. It was human blood, heated to body temperature. The constant edge of hunger dulled slightly. I drained the cup in seconds.

Lucien chuckled. "Please, help yourself to more."

I spent long minutes drinking, and when I no longer felt insatiable, I sat back.

"Now then, tell me why you have come," Lucien invited. "Don't leave anything out. I have lived too long to appreciate abbreviated versions of stories."

I did not have long, especially if I planned to bathe before leaving, but Lucien needed to know the full truth in order to help me, if he would. I'd decided to come here before going to D.C. the moment I passed the New York border. Simply ensuring that Tatiana was okay would not help. Jessamine would know I would try it. She'd have a trap waiting for me.

Tatiana could handle herself. I had to trust that.

I had only one way to end this, and I needed Lucien to get me there.

I told him everything, starting with Victor Hume and the Conclave's fury at my "flashy heroics." I explained how I discovered Callum's plans and rescued Elias. I talked about our running, Tatiana finding me, the fights that had followed, and Beck's getaway.

Lucien listened, his expression neutral. When I finished, he sat in stoic silence for a moment before he remarked, "Deep shit, indeed."

I laughed, despite everything. It was an exhausted, harsh sound.

Lucien's eyes narrowed. "You're in love with her. This Tatiana."

It wasn't a question, but I answered anyway. "Yes."

"That didn't go so well for you last time."

It would have hurt less if Lucien had slapped me across the face.

I looked back at Isabella's portrait, at that gentle smile, and tears burned my eyes. "Lucien, I should have come sooner. I should have been here, should have seen how you were, after... We shouldn't have lost her. It was my fault."

"No." Lucien's voice was sharp.

I dragged my gaze from the painting to meet his eyes.

"The Conclave sent human hunters after my daughter as punishment for me leaving them. You were merely caught in the crosshairs." As a former Conclave elder, Lucien had seen the dangerous path his companions were going down. Too authoritarian, he'd said.

"It was my fault for not protecting her better. For underestimating how far they would go." Sorrow and regret tinged Lucien's voice.

I nodded, not trusting myself to speak for a moment. Eventually, I admitted, "I don't know if I can keep Tatiana safe. The Conclave is hunting Elias and me. As far as I know, Callum is still out there. Senator Ellwood's task force is hunting anyone connected to the magical community."

"You already know what you're going to do," Lucien observed.

I nodded. "I intend to offer myself to the Conclave. To distract them long enough for Elias to get away for good, and to ensure Tatiana's safety."

Lucien shook his head. "They won't agree to it. You can be convincing, Jordan, but it takes more than charm and good looks to sway the Conclave. Even the North American seat."

Who were known to be more lenient than the High Council in Europe. Slightly.

"I know."

"What is your *real* plan, then? What do you want me to do?" Lucien demanded.

I drew a steadying breath. "You're not going to like it."

CHAPTER TWENTY-FOUR

TATIANA

Brandon whistled as he climbed from the SUV. He looked from JD's house to me. "Is this yours? If I had a house this nice, I would be inviting people over all the time."

"Not mine," I replied absently, already scanning the perimeter for possible danger. The house sat far enough back that not much of it was visible from the street. Jake was already moving around the side of the house, weapon drawn, checking for signs of forced entry.

I followed his lead, circling the property while Margo, Duncan, and Brandon waited out front.

"Clear," Jake called after a few minutes.

"Clear," I echoed, returning to the front.

Brandon murmured something about his grandmother once living in a house like this. "Shame her and my dad had a falling out. She might have left it to us!"

I pulled out the key I still had. My hand shook slightly as I unlocked the door. Two break-ins in two weeks. JD wouldn't be happy. Especially since I had my team in tow, running from both the government and a vampire council, with no idea where JD was or if he was safe.

The interior appeared untouched, the furniture still covered in sheets. Dust motes danced in the early evening light streaming through the windows.

"Everyone inside." I ushered them in and locked the door behind us. "Jake, with me."

I led him to the kitchen, out of the others' earshot. He set down his laptop bag and immediately started checking his equipment.

"Those operatives will go back to their boss and report what happened," I told him quietly. "Ellwood knows we exposed Pike as a vampire, but if we release the footage—"

"We seal Pike's fate," Jake finished. "And probably start a war between Ellwood and the vampire community."

"Can you access the footage remotely? Upload it to a secure server before anyone realizes we still have it?"

Jake searched his bag, then his expression darkened. "Shit."

My heart tumbled. "What?"

"The hard drive. I can't find it."

I popped like a balloon stuck with a needle. "What do you mean you don't have it?"

"I thought I grabbed it before the fight broke out, but…" He searched his laptop bag again. "Someone must have taken it."

"Who? Pike? The Conclave vampires?"

"Does it matter?" Jake was already pulling up a remote connection to our office network. "I had everything backing up to the office server in real-time. If I can access—" His fingers stopped, and the color drained from his face.

"Jake?"

"It's gone. Everything. Even the backup to the cloud." He turned the laptop toward me, showing a blank directory where terabytes of data should have been. "Someone wiped it. Professional job, too, overwritten multiple times. This data is unrecoverable."

I wanted to scream. I closed my eyes and inhaled deeply, then pushed out a hard breath. "Jessamine. It had to be her, cleaning up. Pike betrayed the vampire community by working with Ellwood, but she's still one of them. If we expose her, we expose all of them." I laughed bitterly. "Jessamine probably did us a favor. If we had released that footage, every vampire in the country would be hunting us."

Jake looked crestfallen, and it killed me. "What do we do now?" he asked.

"We regroup. Figure out our next move." I squeezed his shoulder. "You did good today. We're alive because of you."

Though he nodded, he didn't look comforted. He remained where he was, saying he wanted to look into some other things that might help. "Go see to your crew. They'll want answers."

I followed my staff's voices to a downstairs half-bath. Brandon leaned against a marble sink as Margo tended to the cut on his head. "Oh, it doesn't even need stitches, Brando. Stop whining like a baby," Margo admonished.

"I got thrown into a wall by a supernatural creature," Brando protested. "I think I've earned the right to whine."

I poked my head in. "You okay, Brando? I know the acting job wasn't supposed to include..."

"Fleeing from whatever those were? Yeah, no shit." His features softened. "Sorry, boss. I know you didn't expect them to show up." He gestured at the bathroom. "This is all your boyfriend's? You really know how to pick them."

Despite it all, my lips tugged into a smile. "After you're patched up, let's meet in the living room to talk things over."

Margo's mild look told me everything I needed to know. *I trust you, boss, but there's a lot you need to explain.*

I reached the living room first and began uncovering furniture. By the time Margo, Brandon, and Duncan joined me, enough space was exposed for them to sit. I stood with my back to an empty, cold hearth, took a moment to gather my thoughts, then began. "I owe you all an explanation about what happened today and who we're up against."

"Vampires," Brandon filled in. "I got that part, what with the fangs and all. I'm beginning to think I got a concussion."

"You probably *did* get a concussion," Margo inserted.

"Vampires is correct. Believe me, I was as baffled as you when I first learned the truth."

"Which was when, exactly?" Duncan asked.

"December."

"And Marcus is one of them," Margo concluded.

I nodded.

"I always thought a few things about him were odd," she murmured.

"We're going up against not only vampires, but also Senator Malcolm Ellwood, who is running a task force targeting enhanced individuals. That is, people with abilities beyond normal human capacities. His chief of staff, Adeline Pike, is a vampire who has been feeding him intelligence on the magical community in exchange for protection."

"The magical community," Duncan repeated slowly. "So...not only vampires?"

"Shifters, witches, and other things I probably don't even know about yet." I took a breath. "Marcus' real name is Davenport. He's a vampire, has been for centuries."

The room fell silent.

"So there is no Marcus Smith?" Brandon finally asked, as if that was my entire point.

Margo elbowed him. "Really, Brando? Catch up."

"Ow! I think I have a broken rib or two."

"There is. Was. It's complicated," I explained. "JD has lived under dozens of identities over the years. Marcus Smith was his latest."

I met their gazes. "I'm sorry I didn't tell any of you sooner. I was trying to protect JD as well as you. The magical world has remained hidden for centuries, and now it's threatening to come into the light in the worst possible way."

"Because of this Ellwood guy," Duncan stated.

"And because of the Conclave. They're the vampire council who oversees their affairs. They have a lot of authority, and they're not happy that JD has been drawing attention to himself. They want him back under their control." I didn't tell them anything about Elias or the mess with Callum.

"The Conclave is what, exactly?" Brando asked. "A cult?"

"More like a government for vampires, as far as I can tell." It was better to be sparse with details. The less they knew, the safer they were. "Right now, we have two major threats. Senator Ellwood and his task force, and Jessamine Lane, the Conclave's liaison."

Brandon snorted. "Do vampire messengers usually throw people around like that?"

"We're going to lie low here until we figure out next steps," I responded, not sure how to answer the question. "My priority right now is keeping Linda and my mom safe." I explained that I'd already assigned Marc to watch my mom.

Duncan stood. "I can go watch Linda."

I nodded. "Thank you. She'll probably be with Harry, but I'll send you both addresses."

After he left, the adrenaline that had carried me through the day finally started to ebb. I was exhausted and covered in plaster dust and dried blood. I wasn't sure how much was mine. Though nothing was broken or cut enough to bleed, I had plenty of bruises. "If there are no more questions, I'm going to take a shower."

Margo and Brandon looked like they had plenty to ask, but they could see how exhausted I was. "Long and hot," Margo told me, not as my employee but my friend. The friend who'd been boxing with me for years and always made sure I was drinking enough water and taking care of my muscles afterward. I gave her an appreciative smile.

The first-floor bathrooms didn't have showers, so I climbed to the second. I aimed for two double doors at the end of the hallway and entered a bedroom grand enough to tell me who it belonged to. A king-sized bed, with an enormous velvet headboard and silk sheets I could roll in for hours, dominated one wall.

I headed for the bathroom, not surprised to encounter marble floors and a soaking tub that could easily fit three people. The shower had multiple heads and more controls than a spaceship. I stripped off my ruined clothes and stood under the hot spray, watching plaster dust, dirt, and blood swirl down the drain.

I stayed there for a long time, letting the heat work through my sore muscles. I tried not to think of everything that had gone wrong today. The trap had failed. We'd lost the footage.

My thoughts drifted to JD. Where was he? Was he safe?

When I felt I might pass out from the heat, I turned off the water. I found the fluffiest towel I'd ever seen in a linen closet and wrapped myself in it. My clothes couldn't be saved even if I washed them, so I padded back into JD's bedroom.

I opened a tall dresser across from the bed and found a T-shirt and sweatpants that were too big but sufficient. As I dressed, I let myself imagine what it would be like to live here. To share this space with JD, to wake up beside him. To build a life that was quiet and peaceful and *normal*.

Tears pricked my eyes. God, I was tired. I didn't let myself linger long, so the emotions wouldn't overcome me.

Downstairs, I checked on Jake. He glanced up from his laptop. "Good, I was about to come and find you. Considering how everything went today, I've been monitoring chatter. Ellwood is convening an emergency closed-door session with the Intelligence Committee tomorrow evening."

I slid onto the island stool across from Jake. "For what?"

"To propose legislation. He's calling it the Enhanced Individual Registration and Containment Act." Jake pulled up a document on his screen, showing me leaked talking points. "If it passes, every magical person in the country will be required to register with the government. Those who refuse or who are deemed 'threats to national security' can be detained indefinitely without trial."

My blood ran cold as I read through the bullet points. "This won't be good, Jake."

"With what happened today, his operatives seeing actual vampires in action, he probably has the votes."

"When is the vote?"

"Forty-eight hours after the meeting ends."

"Shit." What the hell were we supposed to do?

Before I had a chance to get my bearings, a massive commotion erupted from the front hall. Jake and I rushed out to find that the door had burst open.

I heard a shout. Brandon sailed toward the figure in the doorway, fire poker in hand. He swung it, and the person in the doorway moved with a shout of alarm. The poker shattered a vase on an entry table.

"Brandon, stop!" I called.

I hurried forward with Jake directly behind me. The cowering man at the door straightened, shaking.

"Vinny?"

His eyes widened. The warlock was disheveled and dirty. He looked like he had been through hell.

"What the hell happened to you?" I asked.

After he overcame the surprise of Brandon trying to bash his skull in, relief flooded his features. "Tatiana. Thank God. I didn't know where else to go."

"Should've knocked," Brandon muttered.

"Come in," I told Vinny, hurrying to close and lock the front door. "Tell us what happened."

We moved back to the living room, and Vinny collapsed onto the couch. Margo brought him a glass of water, which he drained in one gulp.

"They took me from my home. Three days ago. Armed men showed up at two in the morning. They dragged me out in my bathrobe!" He gestured at his current outfit, a pair of faded jeans and a sweatshirt. "Obviously, I found clothes later, but still. The indignity!"

"Who took you?" I questioned.

"I don't know. They never said. They brought me to this big estate. A mansion, but I don't know where. They knocked me out for the drive, and I only came to after I'd been locked in the room. Every few hours, they came to interrogate me." His face hardened. "I didn't tell them anything, no matter what they threatened."

They had roughed him up, too. Bruises bloomed across his face.

"How did you escape?" I asked.

"A window washer came this morning. Before he got to my window, I broke the glass with a chair and climbed out. I stole his van." Vinny raised a weak smile. "I've never been so terrified in my life, and I once accidentally summoned a demon in my apartment."

"You *what?*" Brandon blurted.

"Long story," Vinny replied. "Don't worry, the demon went back. I came straight here. I figured if anywhere was safe, this would be it. But clearly…" He gestured at everyone. "I wasn't the only one who thought so." He leaned toward me. "Who are these people, anyway?"

"We could be asking you the same thing," Margo retorted.

"Vinny is JD's manager. Vinny, these people work for me. You can trust them."

My phone buzzed. I pulled it out, expecting another update

from Marc or Duncan. Instead, it was a message from an unknown number.

I'm ending this. Stay safe. I love you.

My heart stopped, and I whispered, "No."

"What?" Jake asked.

As I read the message again, my hands shook. The words were simple, final. *A goodbye.*

"He's going to surrender himself to the Conclave," I managed. "JD's going to turn himself in."

"That's good, right?" Brandon asked. "If he gives them what they want—"

"They'll kill him," Vinny finished quietly. "Or lock him away forever. The Conclave won't be forgiving after what's happened, and they don't negotiate. Jordan knows that."

"So…not good?" Brandon asked, wincing.

Margo shot him a look.

I was already moving, grabbing my jacket, checking my weapon. "Jake, track that number. Find out where it came from."

"Tatiana, what are you doing?" he asked.

"What do you think? I need to find him before he finds the Conclave."

"You don't even know where he is!"

"Then I'll figure it out!" I whirled to face them, my voice rising. "I am not letting him sacrifice himself. Not for me, not for anyone. We've already lost too much today."

The room fell silent. Margo and Brandon exchanged glances. Vinny looked like he wanted to object but couldn't find the words.

Jake finally stated, "Okay, let me trace the message. Give me ten minutes."

I nodded, trying to control my breathing, trying to think. JD had survived for centuries by being smart, by staying one step ahead. He wouldn't walk into the Conclave's hands without a plan. Would he?

"Jake, I also need everything you can find on Conclave meeting locations, safe houses, anywhere they might take JD if he turns himself in."

I looked at my team. They were exhausted, battered, but still standing. Still willing to fight. I didn't need to ask before Margo offered, "Whatever you need, boss, we're here."

Brandon nodded. "I second that, but please, no more acting."

"Can we really pull this off?" Margo asked. No doubt in her voice. She was urging me to think it over.

"We have to. Because I really don't want to explain to Linda why her favorite employee isn't coming back," I insisted.

Brandon laughed, slightly hysterical. Even Margo smiled.

"Who's Linda?" Vinny asked.

Margo answered his question as my gaze moved to the window. Outside, the sun was setting, painting the sky in shades of orange and red. Somewhere out there, JD was walking into danger. Somewhere else, Senator Ellwood was preparing to wage war on people he didn't understand. No telling where Adeline Pike and Jessamine Lane had gone.

I stared at the JD's message again. An ache bloomed inside me at those last three words.

I love you.

CHAPTER TWENTY-FIVE

TATIANA

"I might have an idea," Vinny told me after he had showered and changed his clothes.

I stopped mid-pace. "I'm listening."

"From time to time, Jordan's mentioned an old friend. Another vampire who used to be an elder on the Conclave's council. Lucien lives somewhere in northern Virginia, I believe. If Jordan is planning something big, he may have reached out to him first."

The name tugged at my memory. JD had mentioned a former Conclave elder, the only person he could stand among them.

"Can we get in touch with him?" I asked.

Vinny's jaw tightened. "I can try. Vampires aren't exactly listed in the phone book, and we warlocks aren't on great terms with them. Lucien's been off-grid a long time. At least from what Jordan has told me. It might take a while."

We didn't have a while. "How long?"

Vinny didn't answer directly. "I will have to reach out through some…unconventional channels." He pulled out his phone and scrolled through his contacts. "Witch network. Someone may know someone who knows how to reach him."

In other words, it sounded like a long shot.

I nodded. "Do it."

Vinny wandered out into the hall, phone pressed to his ear. I resumed pacing. Jake had his laptop open on the dust-covered coffee table, fingers flying across the keyboard as he pulled up maps and satellite imagery. Brandon sprawled across the sofa, an arm thrown over his eyes.

Margo appeared at my elbow. "I'm going to make a supply run. We need food. Most of us haven't eaten since breakfast."

As much as I didn't like the idea of Margo going out, she was right.

She added, "I'll be careful. Nearest store is two miles from here, and I'll take a back road, making sure I'm not followed."

My stomach knotted with anxiety, but my body needed fuel. "Don't be long," I told her.

Duncan had taken the SUV, so Margo remarked, "I'll need the keys for the window-washing van from…what's his name again?"

"Vinny, and you don't need to take a stolen van. I have a better idea."

Margo simply lifted a brow as I walked past her. I led her through the side kitchen door and along a path that curved down to JD's enormous garage. I used the key JD gave me when he left the note for me to take his Mercedes.

We stepped inside, and Margo whistled at his expansive collection. "Don't let Brando see this. He'll drool all over everything."

"Take your pick," I told her. "All the keys are hanging up over there."

Margo ambled between the cars. "It's only a two-mile drive." She selected a sleek, black Mustang, one of JD's less conspicuous models.

I found the keys on the wall and tossed them to her. "See you soon."

She echoed the words, and the car rumbled to life. I waited

until she was out on the road before returning to the house. Back in the living room, Jake was still clacking away, and Vinny paced in the hallway, muttering into his phone. His expression grew increasingly frustrated.

Time crawled. Each minute stretched like an hour. I checked my phone, hoping for a new message from JD with some clue about where he was headed or what he was planning. Nothing.

Brandon's soft snores filled the silence. I shook my head. How could he be sleeping?

Within half an hour of her departure, Margo returned, arms loaded with paper grocery bags. "No tail," she reported. "I took a route that would've made it obvious if anyone was following."

She headed into the kitchen, and soon, the sounds of cooking drifted out. Water filling a pot, a knife against a cutting board. I was about to join Margo, if only to give my hands something to do, when Vinny finally lowered his phone. "I got him."

I waited, breath held. In the living room, Jake's hands paused, and he looked up.

"Lucien confirmed that Jordan contacted him. Came to visit him, actually. He left an hour ago." Vinny swallowed as if preparing to dump bad news on me. "He's going to the Conclave's North American seat."

"What does that mean?" Jake asked. He'd stood and come into the hallway.

Vinny turned his phone around, showing us a set of coordinates. "The Conclave is split up across the world. The High Council oversees a multitude of smaller councils. It's the North American seat that's making all this trouble for Jordan."

And by extension, all of us.

Jake took Vinny's phone and returned to his laptop to look up the coordinates. Vinny and I followed, peering over his shoulder at the screen. A satellite image loaded, revealing a sprawling countryside estate.

"Hour and a half from here." Jake pulled up closer images

showing a Gothic manor surrounded by dense woods. A single access road wound through the trees.

Vinny leaned closer, his face going as white as the sheets we'd bundled and tossed onto the floor. "This is the place Jordan is going to?"

"Assuming the coordinates you gave me are correct," Jake replied.

"This is where they took me."

I turned to him. "You're sure? That would mean the Conclave got you, not Ellwood's men."

"I'd recognize those spires anywhere." He pointed at the distinctive turrets on the north side of the building. "I was in a room on the third floor, that tower there. I stared at the next tower for over three days." Vinny sank jerkily onto the arm of the couch. "They were looking for Jordan. They thought I knew where he was."

"And now he's going to them voluntarily." I pressed my palms against my eyes, trying to consider the implications. "Why would he do that? What's his play?"

"Maybe he doesn't have one," Jake suggested. "Maybe he's only trying to end this before anyone else gets hurt."

I shook my head and resumed pacing. "JD doesn't give up. He has survived for centuries by being smart, by always having a backup plan. If he's walking into the Conclave's headquarters, he has a reason."

Vinny nodded, agreeing, but said nothing.

"Or he's in love," Jake replied, not looking up from his laptop. "Love makes people do stupid things."

I couldn't argue with that. I was probably being stupid by dragging my whole team into this. "We're going after him. We need to start planning an infiltration. There must be a way in."

Brandon had woken up at some point during the conversation and was now sitting upright, rubbing his eyes. "We're breaking into vampire headquarters? Cool. That's totally normal."

"Vinny, you got out through a window. Tell me everything you remember about the interior layout."

"I was only in one room…"

"Tell me everything you can anyway."

Vinny recalled guards in the hallway beyond, and he'd listened long enough to learn their rotations. Jake pulled up building permits and historical records, giving us something to go by, though plenty of gaps remained. The estate was built in the 1700s, expanded multiple times over the centuries, and now sprawled across the landscape like a stone labyrinth.

"We can use the window-washing van I stole. It's still parked a few blocks from here. We have to make sure no one has reported it as missing yet," Vinny offered.

"I can set up a mobile surveillance system inside it. Everyone will wear comms, and I can monitor from the van, help navigate after you're inside," Jake inserted.

That left me, Margo, and Brandon to infiltrate.

"When do we leave?" Brandon asked.

I checked my phone. Based on the timing of JD's message and knowing when he'd left Lucien's, he wouldn't reach the estate for another few hours.

"You should eat and rest," Jake told me. "I need time to set up the van anyway."

My stomach growled in response, and I remembered the blueberry scones Linda had brought to the office. They were probably buried under overturned furniture and plaster by now.

Margo walked into the room, carrying two bowls of soup. She handed one to me. "You won't be any use to anyone if you pass out halfway through the mission. Eat. Sleep. We'll wake you when it's time." She handed the other bowl to Vinny before going back for more.

The soup smelled heavenly. It was vegetable with rice, simple but warm and filling. I ate mechanically, savoring the flavor for only a few bites. My mind was already at the Conclave's estate, planning, worrying.

When the bowl was empty, Margo steered me upstairs. I didn't realize she was ushering me into JD's room until we reached the doors. "It will be quietest in here. No one will bother you."

I thought about protesting but didn't say a word as she folded down the silk sheets. I slid between them and sighed. The sheets smelled like him. I pressed my face into the pillow and allowed myself one moment of weakness. One moment where I admitted how terrified I felt at the thought of losing him.

Margo was already gone. I closed my eyes and fell asleep.

A hand on my shoulder shook me awake. I blinked, disoriented. "How long did I sleep for?"

"About an hour and a half," Margo answered. I glanced at my watch. It was almost ten at night. "Brandon went out while you were sleeping. He just got back with supplies."

I followed Margo downstairs, still groggy. My nap didn't feel like enough, but it would have to do.

Brandon stood in the living room, surrounded by his booty and looking pleased with himself. "I may have gone a little overboard. I figured we couldn't break into vampire headquarters dressed like refugees."

He produced tactical clothing. Dark, flexible, nothing that would snag. He'd brought Kevlar vests, which would probably do nothing against vampires but might stop a stray bullet. He had good boots, too. He held up what looked like a modified taser. "I got us some specialty weapons in a discreet shop that didn't ask questions."

"Where did you get the money for all this?" I asked.

"Company card. I figured if we don't survive the night, you won't need to pay it off anyway."

I couldn't argue with that. "Show me everything."

He'd done well. The clothing was high-quality but unmarked, the kind of thing that wouldn't immediately scream commando but would give us freedom of movement. The Kevlar was light-weight, designed for concealment. In addition to the modified tasers, he'd gotten silver-plated ammunition, UV flashlights, and something that looked like a small grenade.

"Magnesium flare," Brandon informed me when I picked it up. "Burns at three thousand degrees. It probably won't kill a vampire, but it'll sure as hell slow one down." He grinned like a kid on Christmas morning. "The guy at the shop had some interesting theories about supernatural combat."

I picked through the supplies, selecting what I would need. I was glad Brandon had thought of the clothes. I couldn't exactly go into combat in sweatpants so big I had to roll the waist three times and a T-shirt I was practically swimming in. I stripped to change, modesty be damned. Margo and Brando did the same. Within ten minutes, we looked like a professional extraction team.

I strapped weapons to my thighs, belt, and concealed beneath my vest. Two handguns, three knives, a modified taser, and two magazines of silver ammunition that I hoped I wouldn't need. The weight was comforting, familiar.

"Where are Jake and Vinny?" I asked.

"Out back with the van. They should be about done," Margo replied.

I moved to the living room window overlooking the back of the property and spotted the van. I didn't see Jake and assumed he was inside it. Vinny stood at the open side door, peering in with his hands on his hips.

For a moment, I imagined JD standing behind me, looking at the same scene. He'd had my back countless times. In every case, every close call, his impossible strength and speed had been the difference between success and failure.

"Now it's my turn to help you," I whispered to my reflection in the window.

We filed out of the house and locked it behind us. Clearly, Vinny had incurred a few dents in the stolen van during his escape. *Willie's Window Washing* was painted on the side in fading blue letters. Poor Willie was probably wondering what happened to his van. Jake climbed into the driver's seat while the rest of us loaded into the back.

Inside, Jake had transformed it into a mobile command center. Monitors lined one wall, showing feeds from cameras that could be deployed remotely. The communications array looked like it belonged in a spy movie. Weapon racks held additional equipment.

Brandon whistled appreciatively. "Damn, Jake. When did you have time for all this?"

"While you were sleeping. I don't need as much rest as you soft civilians." He smiled as he said it.

I closed my eyes and thought of JD's last message. *I love you.*

I'd be damned if he didn't let me have a chance to say it back—and more importantly, to prove it.

CHAPTER TWENTY-SIX

JORDAN

The manor house was all spires and weathered stone, the windows gleaming like watchful eyes in the moonlight. Without Lucien's help, I wouldn't have found the place.

When the Conclave summoned me after I escaped Victor Hume, I'd met them in Switzerland. In one of their older, more established strongholds. By vampire standards, this place was newer, probably a mere three hundred years old.

I parked the car I'd stolen from the vampires who'd chased us down the road from the estate. I continued on foot, sucking in deep breaths of cool air to steady myself until I reached the long, twisting gravel drive and the wrought iron gate surrounding the property.

It was here I sensed the wards. They were strong, but they would not prevent me from entering. They'd only tip off those inside that I was coming.

I didn't bother with stealth. I walked through the gate like I was taking a stroll in the park and approached the massive front doors. I didn't need to knock, because by the time I reached them, they swung open.

A thin creature stood against the warm light of torches lining the hallway beyond. They might have once been human, but that was decades, perhaps centuries, ago.

A thrall. A lesser vampire, a servant who had been turned but never given enough blood to complete the transformation. They existed in a twilight state, neither fully human nor fully vampire. Always, the thrall would be bound to serve their master.

It had been over a century since I last saw one of their kind. There were rules against a half-turn.

This one was female with papery skin and milky eyes. She wore a simple black dress with a low collar, exposing snow-white skin and jutting collarbones. When she smiled, small fangs peeked out. "We have been waiting for you," she crooned.

"I'm sure you have," I replied dully.

She stepped aside, gesturing me into the entrance hall. I crossed the threshold and stopped, taking in the space.

The front hall was vast and cold. The black marble floor was polished to a mirror shine. The walls were stone, bare except for where the torches clung. This was a far cry from Lucien's home. Though the place seemed just as old, it lacked warmth and comfort. Not a place where Conclave vampires lived, but where they convened.

The thrall shuffled ahead of me without a word, and I followed. Our footsteps echoed in the emptiness of a corridor that seemed to stretch forever. At last, we reached a set of carved wooden double doors, twice my height. With surprising strength, the thrall pushed them inward, then moved aside.

I stepped into the council chamber and instantly felt the attention of a room full of venerable vampires shift to me.

The circular room had a domed ceiling and seven arched windows spaced evenly around the circumference. A massive round table dominated the center, with seven high-backed chairs arranged around it. In each of those chairs sat a vampire, watching me with varying expressions. Some merely looked interested, as if I was a guest they had not expected to see. Others' faces held contempt or cold calculation.

Directly across from me sat the eldest, a vampire who appeared no older than sixty but had me by a few centuries. His iron-gray hair framed a face carved from granite. Valdovinos, if memory served. Ancient, powerful, and utterly without mercy. He was the head of the Conclave's North American seat.

To his right sat a woman with pale blonde hair and porcelain skin, her crimson dress a splash of color in the austere room. Beside her was a younger vampire, at least in appearance, with dark skin and sharp, intelligent eyes. The others I didn't know, but they all radiated the same aura of age and authority.

Standing behind Valdovinos' chair, like a favored pet, was Jessamine.

She looked no different than she had the last time I saw her in Switzerland. Her posture was perfect, her expression carefully neutral. She wore all black, severe and elegant, and her lips curved in a smile that promised pain.

It wasn't her who spoke first.

"Jordan Davenport," Valdovinos greeted, his voice filling the chamber without needing to raise it. "You have caused us quite a bit of trouble as of late."

I stepped to the table and stood between two chairs, their occupants angling their heads to survey me. "I'm here to end that trouble."

"Are you now?" The blonde woman leaned forward. "And how do you propose to do that?"

"I have come to offer myself," I replied simply. "Whatever punishment you want to give me, whatever penance you require, I will accept it. In exchange, you let Elias go. Leave him alone. He has done nothing wrong except exist. And leave Tatiana Sterling alone, too. She's human, and not a threat to you. She deserves to live her life without looking over her shoulder."

Silence filled the chamber, broken when Jessamine laughed, a sharp, brittle sound. "You think you can simply trade yourself for your mistakes? After all the trouble you have caused me, all the attention you have drawn to our kind."

She moved around the table, circling closer. "Your heroics made headlines, *Marcus Smith*. I've spent months cleaning up your mess, and you think I will simply let that go? Not to mention your little human lover. She has proved herself to be equally as difficult."

It didn't surprise me to hear that Jessamine had gone after Tatiana again. I only hoped Tatiana's retaliation hadn't gotten her killed. I kept my fears hidden.

"Consort Jessamine raises a valid point," Valdovinos spoke up.

The title made me blink. Consort? She must have recently earned official status within the Conclave hierarchy. No longer a mere messenger, though not yet elevated enough for a seat at this table. This could only happen when one of the seven passed the mantle or died.

Valdovinos continued. "You have violated our most sacred rule. Do not draw attention. You played the hero repeatedly, and each time, you risked exposing us all."

The dark-skinned vampire spoke next in an accented voice. "And what of the boy? If we release him, Callum will take him within days. We all know this. The boy's condition makes him too valuable to leave unprotected."

"Or unstudied," added another council member, this one elderly even by vampire standards. His voice wheezed out, and he coughed. "The boy represents a biological anomaly. We could learn from him, perhaps even replicate his condition. Imagine it! Vampires who age slower, who require less blood, who might even one day walk in sunlight. To waste that opportunity would be foolish."

My hands clenched at my sides. They weren't even trying to hide their plans. "Elias isn't a laboratory experiment."

"Elias is a vampire, and as such, he falls under our jurisdiction. You had no right to take him, to withhold him from us," the blonde woman corrected coldly, as if she was discussing a piece of cargo, not a person.

Jessamine had moved close enough that I could smell her perfume, something floral and cloying. "And then there's your human," she added, practically purring the word. "Ms. Sterling. She knows too much, Jordan. About you, about us, our world. You were a fool to involve yourself with her."

"She is a security risk," Valdovinos spoke up before I could tear into Jessamine.

Rage boiled in my chest, but I forced it down. I'd come into this knowing it wouldn't be easy. I knew they would push back.

And for that reason, I had not come alone.

Behind me, the chamber doors opened again. The thrall entered first, wearing a blank expression, followed by the man she'd led down the hall. The slightest smile of satisfaction tugged at my lips when the council members gasped.

Lucien walked in. He wore a long coat that looked like it belonged in another century, his white hair loose around his shoulders. His pale eyes surveyed the room with the air of a king returning to court after long years on a battlefield.

Murmurs passed around the table. Most of them had not heard about or seen Lucien in nearly two hundred years.

"It has been a long time, hasn't it?" he greeted the room. "Too long since I last graced these halls."

"You are not welcome here," Valdovinos insisted, though his voice had lost some of its certainty. "You abandoned the Conclave. You have no authority and therefore no reason to be here."

"No authority?" Lucien stopped beside me, and I felt the weight of his presence like a shield. "I was a council member when most of you were still human. I helped write the laws you now hide behind. Don't lecture me about *authority*."

The blonde woman stood. "Lucien, why are you here?"

"To save you from yourselves." The former elder's gaze swept the table, meeting each vampire's eyes in turn. "Look at you. Huddled in the darkness, terrified of the modern world, clinging to traditions that stopped serving us centuries ago. You punish Jordan for being flashy, for drawing attention, but the truth is you're terrified because the world is changing and you don't know how to change with it."

"We have maintained our secrecy for millennia," the elderly vampire wheezed.

"Has it served you?" Lucien challenged. "How many of our kind have we lost because they couldn't adapt? How many were hunted down during the witch trials, the Inquisition, the wars? We survive not because of our traditions, but in spite of them."

"This is ridiculous," Jessamine interjected. "You can't walk in here after two centuries and think your speeches will change anything."

"I can, and I am." Lucien's voice was mild, but his gaze on her was alert and steady. "I know your kind, Ms. Lane. Young, fierce, ambitious. Reminds me of a young woman I once held very dear."

My heart twisted. Jessamine and Isabella were nothing alike.

"The world has changed," Lucien reiterated. "Humans have cameras in their pockets, satellites in the sky, DNA databases that could expose us within days if they knew what to look for. Our old methods don't work anymore. Hiding in the shadows, punishing anyone who steps into the light, is not protection."

I watched the council members' faces. Valdovinos looked furious, his hands gripping the armrests of his chair. The blonde woman looked thoughtful as her fingers drummed the table. The dark-skinned vampire nodded slowly, and the elderly one appeared torn between outrage and consideration. The others didn't know what to make of the situation.

Lucien was swaying them. Not all of them, but enough.

"Jordan made a mistake," he continued. "But his mistake was

one of compassion. He saved lives. He protected the innocent. Are those not values we claim to uphold? Or have we become so consumed with self-preservation that we've forgotten what it means to have principles?"

"Pretty words, but they don't change the facts. Jordan drew attention. The boy is valuable. The human knows too much," Jessamine retorted bitterly.

"The boy." Lucien's voice softened. "Whatever his biological peculiarities, he deserves protection, not imprisonment or experimentation. As for the human, Ms. Sterling has proven herself trustworthy. She has kept our secrets even when it would have benefited her to expose them. She has earned consideration, not elimination."

Jessamine snorted. "Is that what you call what she did yesterday? Trustworthy? When she set a trap that one of our own, Adeline Pike, walked right into?"

I blinked, not knowing what she was talking about.

Jessamine whirled to face the thrall. "Bring them in."

A moment later, two male vampires entered. One was tall and dark-haired, the other shorter with red hair. "Matthias and Angel can tell you all about how Ms. Sterling and her team left them battered and injured. They can tell you Ms. Sterling set a trap with the intent of exposing Ms. Pike to human operatives. If not for my quick thinking, she would have leaked footage of Pike to the whole city, perhaps the world."

My thoughts raced. Was Jessamine telling the truth?

"Where is Pike now?" I demanded.

Jessamine's dark eyes met mine. "In my custody, awaiting trial for her own traitorous deeds. As you will soon do yourself."

Valdovinos cut in. "What do you propose I do with Mr. Davenport?" This question was directed at Lucien.

"Punish him for stepping out of line, according to our customs, but do as he has asked today. Leave the boy and the human alone. Send a message that we value courage and compassion over blind obedience. Show the younger generation we're capable of evolution, not just enforcement."

The chamber fell silent. I felt the tension, the weight of centuries-old politics and power struggles playing out between heartbeats. Before anyone had a chance to respond to Lucien's proposal, a woman sitting near me perked up. Her eyes widened.

"What is it, Estenia?" Valdovinos asked.

"Someone has crossed the wards."

My stomach dropped. I already knew who it was. I could feel it in my bones.

I had not wanted her to come. I wanted her to trust me, stay where she was, and remain safe. Of course, she hadn't listened. Because she was Tatiana Sterling, and she didn't know how to leave someone behind. It was why I loved her, but also why dread curdled in my stomach.

A slow smile spread Jessamine's lips as she realized the same thing. "Shall we greet our new guests?"

I stepped forward. "Wait. They're not a threat. Please, let me handle this. I'll send her away."

Valdovinos studied me for a long moment, then smiled. It was not a kind expression. He seemed almost gleeful. "No, I don't think so. I am quite interested to see why this Ms. Sterling is so important to you." His calculating gaze lingered on me. "If she is important enough to make you panic, Mr. Davenport, she is important enough for us to meet."

I stood frozen, then turned to Lucien. He stood there, mild and calm. "You knew this. You somehow told her where I was."

"Vinny called," Lucien replied simply. "Your manager, correct?"

"Your traitorous bastard," I whispered.

Lucien looked angered. "I would never betray you. I did this for your own good. Did you think you were getting out of this alone?"

His words silenced me, but my thoughts were far from quiet. Inside, I was screaming.

Valdovinos turned to Jessamine and her two servants, the ones she'd called Matthias and Angel. "Fetch the girl and bring her before us. We have much to hear from her."

CHAPTER TWENTY-SEVEN

TATIANA

Half a mile from the estate, the van slowed to a crawl. As Jake scanned the perimeter ahead, Vinny put a hand on his shoulder. "Stop the van."

Jake obliged.

"Wards," Vinny murmured, staring out the windshield at empty air.

"Wards?" I echoed.

He turned to me, his expression grim. "Magical barriers, invisible to the human eye. Usually, even I can't sense them, but these are stronger than witch wards usually are. If we cross them, whoever set them will know immediately."

I leaned forward. "Can we get through them?"

"These wards are not meant to keep people in or out. Otherwise, I wouldn't have been able to escape. It works more like an alarm system. The moment you step past the line, every vampire in that house will know you're coming."

"Lovely," Brandon grumbled from behind me. Margo's face was grim and focused.

"How far are the wards from the house?" Jake asked.

"Maybe a quarter-mile? Hard to say exactly. Wards can be

tricky." Vinny was working from his memory of his escape. No doubt he'd been more focused on getting the hell out of there than how far the wards extended.

I thought for a moment. "Jake, find somewhere to park the van where they won't see it. We'll go the rest of the way on foot."

Jake didn't look happy, but he didn't object. He got moving again.

"If the van is spotted, we lose our escape route and our surveillance hub," I added. "You should stay here, monitor our comms, and be ready to roll if things go sideways."

"When things go sideways," Margo corrected.

Jake found a service road about a hundred yards back and pulled the van behind a cluster of trees that would hide it from casual observation. He immediately started powering up the surveillance equipment. Monitors flickered to life.

"Comms check," he stated.

I touched the device in my ear. "Copy."

"Loud and clear," Margo returned.

"Ready to not die horribly," Brandon added.

Vinny looked between us. "I should stay here with Jake as an extra lookout, and I can help monitor for magical activity."

"Good idea," I agreed. I checked my weapons one more time. Handguns were secure, knives in place, the modified taser on my belt. Margo and Brandon did the same.

"Remember, these are vampires," Jake cautioned as we prepared to leave. "If they decide they want you dead, all the weapons in the world won't save you. Your weapons are distractions, and your best chance is to talk your way out of this."

"Noted." I pulled the van door open. "Keep the engine running, and stay safe out here."

Jake saluted. Vinny watched us leave with a somber expression.

We slipped from the van into the quiet darkness. The moon hung high and bright, casting silver light through the trees. Our boots were quiet on the forest floor, years of training making our movements nearly silent.

The estate came into view in pieces. First were the spires rising above the tree line, then the full Gothic monstrosity of it. Lights burned in a few windows, but most were dark. The grounds were extensive, manicured lawns giving way to wild forest at the edges.

We crossed what I assumed was the ward line. The spot Vinny had pointed out, anyway. I felt nothing, but the warlock's warning echoed in my mind.

"Jake," I murmured into the comm. "See anything?"

"I'm seeing increased electromagnetic activity from the building. They know you're there," he confirmed.

"Any movement?"

"Not yet, but...wait. Three figures appeared at the main entrance. They're coming out to meet you."

I motioned for my team to move into position. Margo flanked my left, Brandon to my right. We advanced in formation, weapons ready but not raised.

The three figures emerging from the house were unmistakable even at a distance. Jessamine stood at the center, flanked by the two vampires we had fought at the office, Matthias and the red-haired man. Both had recovered from their injuries.

My body went into fight-or-flight mode, but neither would do us any good. We had come too far to hightail it to the van and get away. If we went out to fight them, we could not hope to win. We were on their territory, with no telling how many other vampires awaited us inside.

I straightened and emerged from concealment with Margo and Brandon following. We met the vampires about fifty yards from the house. Everyone stopped at an unspoken mutual distance.

"Ms. Sterling," Jessamine drawled. Was that amusement or hunger dancing in her eyes? Probably both. She'd spent so much time fighting Adeline at the office that she hadn't satisfied herself with me. "I told Jordan you would come for him."

"We don't want trouble. I'm here to take him home," I replied evenly.

Jessamine surveyed me, then my two companions. "You certainly came prepared. Dressed for a fight. Are those silver bullets on you?"

How the hell had she sensed that?

"You crossed our wards. You trespassed on Conclave property. You speak of removing Mr. Davenport from our custody." Jessamine tilted her head. "That spells trouble to me."

Brandon shifted beside me. "Great, these two again." He nodded at Jessamine's dogs. "I thought we buried you under plaster."

The red-haired vampire smiled, showing fangs. "It takes more than a building collapse to stop us, human." He spoke the word with enough disdain to transmit exactly what he wanted to do to Brandon.

"Noted for next time," Brandon muttered.

"There won't be a next time." Matthias' voice was flat and emotionless, but ire shone in his eyes. "You're outmatched and surrounded. Surrender now, and perhaps the council will show mercy."

I met Jessamine's gaze. "I'm not surrendering, and I'm not leaving without Jordan."

"Then I suppose you will be joining him in whatever punishment the council decides." Jessamine gestured toward the house. "Come. They're waiting for you."

We had no choice but to follow.

The male vampires fell in behind us, cutting off any retreat. Jessamine led the way. The house loomed larger as we approached, its windows like dead eyes watching. The front door stood open, spilling warm light across the steps.

A small, frail person stood between the doors. She shuffled away when Jessamine motioned toward her.

We crossed the threshold, and I gaped at the interior. The entrance hall was massive, with black marble floors, stone walls, and torches providing the only light. It felt like stepping into a tomb.

"This way." Jessamine led us down a long corridor.

Behind me, Brandon's breathing quickened. Margo's hand hovered near her weapon as she scanned for threats.

"Jake," I whispered into my comm. "We're inside. Moving deeper."

"Copy. I'm losing signal strength. Stone walls are interfering. If you go much deeper, I might lose you entirely."

Jessamine stopped before massive double doors and pushed them open with one hand. The heavy wood swung soundlessly inward. "The council will see you now."

We entered the chamber, and my breath caught.

The room was circular and vast, with a domed ceiling that disappeared into shadows overhead. Seven arched windows lined the walls, curtains drawn. And in the center, around a table so dark it seemed to drink in light, sat seven vampires.

I barely registered their faces, because standing beside the table, looking both relieved and terrified, was Jordan.

Our eyes met across the room. His expression conveyed conflicting emotions. Fear, but also something that might have been resignation. He knew I would come. He probably hoped I wouldn't, but he would have known.

An older vampire at the head of the table spoke, drawing my attention from JD. "Ms. Sterling, how bold of you to visit us here tonight. Much has been made of you."

I faced the speaker. He appeared to be in his sixties, though he was probably far older. Power radiated from him like heat from a fire.

"I came for Jordan," I responded, keeping my voice steady.

"Whatever you think he's done wrong, punishing him won't solve your real problems."

"And what, pray tell, are our real problems?" a regal-looking blonde woman sitting beside the first speaker asked.

I stepped forward, painfully aware that I was surrounded by creatures who could kill me before I could blink. But I had come this far. I sure as hell wasn't backing down now.

"Your real problem is that you're trying to hide in a world that doesn't allow for hiding anymore," I insisted. "You punish anyone who draws attention, but all you're doing is creating vulnerabilities that people like Victor Hume and Senator Ellwood can exploit."

A vampire with wispy white hair wheezed out a laugh. "The human lectures us on survival. How novel."

"She's right," another voice stated, and I turned to see an elderly vampire I hadn't noticed before, standing in the shadows. He was gaunt and white-haired, with pale eyes that seemed to pierce me. "I have said as much to you tonight. The magical community's secrecy and infighting have created the very weaknesses our enemies exploit."

This man was not part of the council, but he seemed to hold some sway over them. As if he might have once been one of them. *Lucien,* I realized. I caught JD's eye, and his slight nod confirmed it.

"You can't hide forever," I continued, building on Lucien's point. "The world is changing. Either you adapt, or you will be exposed on someone else's terms. You will be hunted, cataloged, and destroyed. Not because you are monsters, but because you were too afraid to engage with the world on better terms."

"And what terms do you propose?" the blonde woman asked. She sounded genuinely curious.

I swallowed, gathering my words and my courage. "Transparency within limits. Cooperation between magical factions, instead of everyone operating in isolation. Alliances with trustworthy humans who can protect your secrets while helping you navigate a world that is changing faster than you can keep up with."

The vampire who was clearly this council's head leaned back in his chair. "You want us to trust humans, after millennia of hiding from them."

"I want you to survive, and you won't do that by punishing Jordan for showing compassion or hunting a child because he represents change you don't understand." I spoke bluntly, seeing no need to evade the truth with pretty words or flattery.

JD moved to stand beside me, and I felt the warmth of his presence like an anchor. "Elias represents the future of vampires. Adaptation, evolution, survival. If you punish him for being different, you're no better than the humans you fear. You become exactly what you claim to be fighting against."

The room lapsed into silence.

The blonde woman stood after what felt like an eternity. "I propose we put this to a vote. Accept Lucien and Ms. Sterling's counsel, modernize our approach, and release both Jordan and the boy. Or reject it and proceed with traditional punishment."

The gray-haired leader nodded slowly. "Very well. A vote."

A dark-skinned vampire with intelligent eyes raised his hand. "In favor. Our current methods are unsustainable. We must adapt."

"Céline?" The leader looked at the blonde woman.

"In favor. For my grandchildren's sake, if nothing else."

The ancient vampire wheezed. "Against. We have survived this long by maintaining our traditions. To abandon them now would be folly."

Another vampire, middle-aged in appearance with cold eyes, spoke next. "Against. The human proposes cooperation, but cooperation requires trust, and trust requires vulnerability. We cannot afford to be vulnerable."

A younger vampire, at least compared to the others, nodded.

"Against. The boy is too valuable to simply release. Callum will take him, and we will have lost a strategic asset."

The last of the council, other than their leader, was a venerable-looking woman with gray curls falling to her shoulders. "In favor. Ms. Sterling makes fair points."

Three to three.

The leader steepled his fingers. He would be the deciding vote. Beside me, I felt JD deflate. Did he believe the leader would vote against? I reached for him, and our fingers brushed. He squeezed my hand gently. I squeezed back, hardly daring to breathe.

Jake's voice crackled in my ear, distant and breaking up, "Sterling, incoming… Multiple vampires…approaching fast—"

My blood turned to ice.

Before I could warn anyone, the chamber doors exploded inward.

Six vampires poured through the opening, moving with predatory grace. At their center was a vampire I would have been happy never to see again. His head was shaved, his clothes torn and dirty. I would have recognized those tattooed knuckles anywhere.

"Callum," JD spat, rage and resignation in his voice.

Callum surveyed the room and smiled. "What a delightful gathering."

The council members rose as one with varying degrees of shock and fury.

Jessamine moved to stand between Callum and the council, her posture defensive. "You've got fucking balls, Callum."

He gave her a roguish smile but didn't respond. His gaze slid over her, landing on the council leader. "Valdovinos. Still clinging to power after all these centuries. Don't you ever get tired?"

"Callum," Valdovinos replied, his voice hard as stone. "You are not welcome here. Leave at once."

Callum *tsked.* "You always had a problem with hospitality." He gestured to his companions. Rogues, I assumed. Vampires who had abandoned or been cast out of the Conclave structure, according to what JD had told me. "I've come to make an offer. Let me have the boy, and I will leave peacefully. Refuse, and I will take him anyway. Along with this outdated council's power."

"The boy isn't here," Jessamine snarled.

"Are you declaring war on the Conclave?" the blonde woman —Céline—asked sharply.

"I'm declaring that the Conclave is dead." Callum's smile widened, showing wicked fangs. "It just doesn't know it yet. Your old ways, your hiding and skulking…over. The future belongs to those of us who aren't afraid to take what they want. And I want that boy."

Was Elias truly not here? I didn't have time to ask JD. I could only hope he was somewhere safe, far away from this madness.

JD stepped forward, putting himself between Callum and the council. Between Callum and me. "I should have killed you when I had the chance."

"Yes, you should have. You were always too soft, too human, even when we were young and could have had anything we wanted," Callum purred.

The tension in the room was suffocating. Brandon and Margo moved to flank me, weapons drawn, as if they would do anything. The council members were spreading out, preparing for a fight. Jessamine and her vampires had positioned themselves defensively.

JD and Callum faced each other like storm fronts about to collide over an ocean.

Valdovinos's voice rang out. "The Conclave does not negotiate with rogues, and it does not cower before threats. If you want war, Callum, you will have it."

Callum's smile turned feral. "As you wish, old man."

He lunged for JD, and the chamber erupted into chaos.

CHAPTER TWENTY-EIGHT

JORDAN

Callum moved like lightning, closing the distance between us before most humans would have even registered his movement. I'd been ready for this since the moment he walked into the council chamber. It had been a miracle he had wasted time with speech.

I met him halfway, and our collision made the floor tremble. We grappled, neither giving ground. His face twisted with rage, his eyes turning completely black.

"You were always a fool, Jordan," he snarled, trying to get his hands around my throat. "Wasting your immortality by playing the hero. It's made you *weak.*" His thumbs pressed against my esophagus for emphasis.

I drove my knee into his stomach, breaking his grip, and followed with a punch that snapped his head back. "Better a fool than a beast."

Around us, pandemonium erupted. Callum's rogues were not the kind to sit back and watch a fight. He had only been able to recruit them because they were equally bloodthirsty. It only took seconds after Callum and I clashed for the rogues to lunge for the council members.

They might have had more bloodthirst, but the Conclave members had a few centuries of experience on the rogues. Valdovinos moved like death incarnate, his strikes precise and devastating. Céline was a blur of crimson and violence, her strike like a dance but deadly.

Jessamine, Matthias, and Angel hesitated. I could see it in the way they positioned themselves, covering the exits but not fully committing to either side. They were loyal to the Conclave, but they also wanted me captured and punished.

My mind didn't stay on them long. As the rogues battled the council, I thought of Tatiana.

I glimpsed her across the chamber, pressed against the wall with Margo and the young man who accompanied her.

Callum took advantage of my distraction, his fist slamming into my jaw hard enough to send me stumbling. I tasted blood, and my fangs fully extended, responding to the threat.

"That's it," Callum crooned, circling me. "Show them what you really are. Show your precious human the monster beneath the mask."

I launched myself at him again, and we tumbled across the stone table. The chairs surrounding it had been overturned in the fighting. I grabbed Callum's shirt, and we flew through one of the curtained windows. Glass shattered, and moonlight streamed in.

We rolled across the ground, each trying to gain the upper hand, trading blows that would have killed any human. Callum had me turned and cornered before I knew it, slamming my back against the rough bark of a tree. From here, I could see what was unfolding in the council chamber.

One of the rogues, a female with wild eyes and matted hair, lunged at Tatiana. Brandon stepped between them, firing something I couldn't quite make out. An electrical charge hit the vampire in the chest, and she screamed, convulsing. It wouldn't stop her for long, but it bought Tatiana a few seconds that otherwise could have meant her death.

Margo used those seconds to aim her weapon, a handgun I thought would do nothing at first. She fired three shots, hitting the rogue in the shoulder twice and the chest once. They weren't killing blows, but enough to send her reeling with smoke puffing from the wounds. Silver ammunition.

"Nice shot!" Brandon shouted.

Another rogue turned toward them, sensing easy prey. Matthias intercepted him, his conflicted loyalties apparently resolving in favor of protecting the chamber from complete chaos. The two vampires collided with bone-crushing force.

I registered these things in seconds while Callum had me pinned against the tree, his hand wrapped around my throat, squeezing. "Where's the boy?" His face was close enough for me to smell the blood on his breath. "Tell me where you've hidden him, and I'll make your death quick."

It was complete bullshit, and we both knew it. "Never," I choked out.

He slammed my head against the tree. Pain exploded through my skull, and something dark rose inside me. Something primal and violent and wrong. *The blood rage.*

It hit like a tidal wave, drowning rational thought beneath an ocean of hunger. My vision went red. My gums ached, my fangs demanding blood.

I roared, an inhuman sound that made several vampires stop mid-fight to look as I threw Callum off me with renewed strength. He crashed back through the window, hitting an overturned chair on his way to the stone surface of the table.

Then I was on him, my hands turned claws, my teeth seeking his throat. Somewhere in the back of my mind, a small voice screamed that this was wrong. I was losing control, becoming exactly what Callum claimed I was.

The rage didn't care.

I barely registered the hands trying to pull me off Callum,

scarcely heard the shouts. The world was blood and violence and the overwhelming need to destroy.

"Jordan."

The voice was female, familiar.

"Jordan, stop. I need you."

I felt hands on my face. They were small and warm, not the icy touch of another vampire. The scent of her, leather and gunpowder and something uniquely Tatiana, sliced through the red haze. "Look at me, please."

I forced my eyes to focus. Tatiana stood before me, cupping my face, her expression fierce. "Come back," she murmured. "Elias needs you. I need you. Come back to me."

The rage faltered, then cracked and crumbled. It was like water thrown onto flames. "That's it," she whispered. My breathing slowed, and the red receded from my vision. My fangs retracted slightly, the ache in my gums subsiding.

Around me, the chamber had fallen silent. Everyone had stopped fighting to watch—the council, the rogues, even Callum, who lay bleeding at my feet. They all stared in amazement, some with horror and others with mere fascination.

Tatiana's voice returned my attention to her. "You're back now." She looked past me at Callum. "You can finish this the right way."

She was right. I could feel the rage lurking at the edges, waiting to consume me again, but I had to control it.

I hauled Callum up by his shirtfront, his face a bloody mess, his expression still defiant despite his obvious defeat. "It's over. Your rogues are beaten."

Callum spat blood. "There will be others. The Conclave is dying. When it finally falls, vampires like me will inherit the future."

"You might be right, but not today." I looked at Valdovinos, whose features were grim. "He's yours. Do with him as you see fit."

Part of me wanted to ensure Callum never breathed a word again, but that would have made us the same. I had come too close to becoming the beast he accused me of having deep down.

Callum laughed, shrill and bitter. "Mercy? You *are* weak."

Matthias and a council vampire moved in to restrain him. Callum added, "How disappointingly predictable."

He could say all the mocking things he wanted to while he was locked in silver chains, behind bars that a weakened vampire could not bend. He could taunt all he wanted to until they brought him to trial. The Conclave would not be forgiving. That, he could predict with certainty.

I stepped back and watched as the remaining rogues, those who were not dead or incapacitated, fled. They had witnessed their leader's defeat and could not hope for better circumstances if they lingered.

Tense silence settled around us. I registered the broken chairs, the shattered glass, and the blood splattering the walls, floor, and table. I righted one of the chairs, not caring if it was only intended for a Conclave member, and slumped into it. "Sorry about the window."

No one responded, but a few shoulders relaxed. A hand gripped my shoulder. Tatiana.

Valdovinos stepped forward, his clothing torn but otherwise uninjured. He surveyed the damage, then turned his gaze to me. "You fought well." His gaze flicked to Tatiana. "The human especially. I've never seen one stand against a vampire in blood rage and survive."

"She's exceptional," I pointed out, as if I needed to.

Valdovinos looked around at his fellow council members. Several were injured but healing. A gash across Céline's face was already closing. The ancient vampire was breathing heavily, looking every one of his thousands of years.

Jessamine hunched over Angel, who was glowering at an ugly gash in his thigh. Her gaze lifted from his leg to meet mine. Ire still glimmered there, but she didn't look ready to tear out my throat. In the end, she had chosen to side with the Conclave.

"I believe we were in the middle of a vote before we were so rudely interrupted," Valdovinos pronounced.

Lucien stepped forward from where he had been defending the chamber's perimeter. "I believe the question was whether to modernize our approach and release Jordan and the boy."

"The boy is at the center of this conflict. Callum came here for him. Others will follow. We cannot simply release him to the world without protection or guidance," Valdovinos insisted. He set another chair upright, dragged it to the table, and sat with a casual air that belied the blood splattered across it. Only the weariness in his eyes attested to the fight he'd put up.

"Jordan has proven himself today. He fought beside us against a common enemy. He showed restraint when he could have killed. He demonstrated something I didn't think vampires of his generation still possessed. Honor."

I didn't dare hope. Not yet.

"I propose a compromise," Valdovinos continued. "Jordan will be pardoned for his previous indiscretions. His actions today count as payment for his missteps. The boy, Elias, will be released from Conclave custody."

As if they already had him. I almost laughed. But I was on thin ice here with the hopes of being pulled off, so I said nothing. Tatiana's hand tightening on my shoulder told me she felt the same way.

"But only under Jordan's guardianship," Valdovinos added. His gaze moved from the council members to me. "You will be responsible for the boy's safety, his education in our ways, and ensuring he does not break our laws. If Elias becomes a problem, you will answer for it."

I nodded immediately. "I accept your terms."

Beside me, Tatiana released a slow breath.

"As do I," Céline echoed. "Enough of our kind have died today. Let us not add more to the tally."

The dark-skinned vampire, whose name I still didn't know, nodded. "The boy deserves a chance, and Jordan has proven trustworthy with that responsibility."

Even the ancient vampire wheezed his assent. "Fine, but if this goes wrong, it's on your head, Valdovinos."

I turned as Jessamine stood and strode to the table. Her dark eyes flashed. "This is a mistake. You're letting them go? After everything? And what about the human?"

"Oh, please," Tatiana muttered.

"Our own rigidity caused this chaos." It was Lucien who spoke up. "Our refusal to adapt. Jordan and Ms. Sterling have shown us a better path forward, whether we like it or not."

"I vote in favor," Valdovinos pronounced before further argument arose. He looked at Jessamine. "Consort Lane, I expect your cooperation in this matter. You may have your way with the traitor Adeline Pike, and even with Callum, if you wish. Heap your vengeance on them."

Jessamine's jaw tightened, but she did not object.

Voldovinos' gaze slid back to me. "Jordan Davenport, you and your companions are free to go. Return to the boy and protect him. And for all our sakes, try to stay out of trouble."

"I will do my best," I promised, though we both knew trouble had a way of finding me.

"One mistake, one slip, and I'll be there to bring you back in chains," Jessamine inserted.

I stood and replied evenly, "I'll keep that in mind. I have no desire to cross you, Jessamine."

Something flickered in her eyes—it was almost satisfaction. She gave me the barest nod.

Tatiana tugged on my hand. "Come. Let's get out of here before they change their minds."

We moved toward the exit where Margo and the human male

waited. They both had several cuts and bruises, but nothing to be too concerned about. They could wear this as a badge of honor. They had entered a room full of fighting vampires and walked out alive. Based on what Jessamine mentioned earlier, it sounded like it wasn't the first time in the last twenty-four hours.

The council members watched us go, some with approval, others with suspicion. Matthias and Angel stood by the door, and for a moment I thought they might try to stop us. Matthias simply stepped aside, his expression neutral. "We'll meet again, Davenport."

"I'm sure we will."

The moment we were clear of the building, Tatiana touched her comm piece. "We're fine, Jake. We're coming to you now."

He must have asked about me, because Tatiana cast me a look, then smiled and added, "Yeah, we got him."

She led us through the woods, following the path they must have taken in. The night was edging toward dawn, the air still cool. Behind us, the Conclave would be dealing with Callum and his rogues, cleaning up a mess I did not envy.

"Jordan."

I halted at the voice. All four of us—myself, Tatiana, Margo, and the man I didn't know—turned.

Lucien stood several yards behind us. I stilled as he drifted closer, hard lines etched in his face. "Forgive me for bringing her here." He nodded at Tatiana. "We could not have done it alone. We needed her word."

I was ashamed now for thinking Lucien had betrayed me. His gray eyes pooled with tears, making his irises look like molten silver. "You fought well today. I knew you wouldn't give up." His gaze slid to Tatiana. "And you have proven yourself a worthy companion for Jordan."

She nodded, swallowing. "Thank you."

I would tell her more later. About everything Lucien was to me, and the loss of Isabella. For now, I had only relief and gratitude to share. I stepped away from Tatiana and her crew, clasping Lucien's hand. "I owe you for tonight. We would not have turned the council without you."

Lucien held my gaze. "You do not owe me. It was I who paid a debt tonight. I feel as though I can finally rest. Isabella would have been proud of you for what you did in there."

My voice was husky with emotion when I replied, "She would be proud of both of us."

Lucien smirked. "It was time I got out of the house, anyway." He bid us goodbye and vanished down the road toward the gate.

I let silence wash over me before turning to Tatiana. She tilted her head toward the path leading out of the woods. "Shall we?"

Moments later, we were approaching a van with a window-washing company logo on it. I didn't ask how they had acquired the vehicle, especially when the door slid open, and a familiar face appeared. Vinny practically fell out, his face pale and anxious. "Jordan…"

"Vinny, how are you here?"

"Vinny is the reason we were able to find you and save you from self-sacrifice," Tatiana explained with a hint of amusement. Her eyes promised she would tell me exactly how she felt about my attempt at nobility and honor later.

Vinny stepped toward me, clasping my hand and bringing me in for an embrace. "I'm glad you're okay, Jordan."

"Me too, man. Me too."

We piled in and slid the van door shut. Jake already had the engine running. He pulled away from the trees, heading down a service road and toward civilization. As the Conclave's estate disappeared behind us, I felt something I hadn't felt in months. *Hope.*

It wasn't over. It never would be, really. There would always be threats, both human and vampire. Senator Ellwood was still out there with his task force. The magical world was still teetering on the edge of exposure. But for now, we had won.

Tatiana leaned against me, her head on my shoulder, and I wrapped my arm around her, holding her close.

"Thank you," I murmured into her hair. For what, exactly, I couldn't say.

She pulled back to look at me, her expression serious. "I wasn't going to let you sacrifice yourself. Not for me, not for anyone. We're a team, Jordan. That means we face things together."

I kissed her, not caring that we had an audience.

When we finally pulled apart, the man across from us was grinning. "You two are disgustingly cute, you know that?"

"Jordan, this is Brandon. Brandon—"

Brandon leaned over and shook my hand heartily. "*Not* Marcus Smith. Got it. Let's get a beer sometime."

I chuckled. "I don't care for beer, but sure."

Margo rolled her eyes, and Tatiana chuckled. Brandon leaned back, crossing his arms. "You know, I think I did a pretty good job pretending to be you earlier."

My brows furrowed. "What are you talking about?"

"Long story. I'll tell you everything later," Tatiana assured me.

"So what now?" Brandon asked, his attention back on his boss. "As far as we know, Ellwood will still be holding his vote in forty-eight hours."

They had a lot to catch me up on.

Tatiana replied, "We stop a senator from destroying the magical world." She said it so matter-of-factly, like stopping a U.S. senator was simply another item on her to-do list. Knowing her, it might as well be. She looked at me. "As a team."

CHAPTER TWENTY-NINE

TATIANA

"Ready to play Marcus Smith one more time?" I asked as JD's Aston Martin purred to a stop in front of a stately Virginia Colonial, all white columns and manicured hedges. JD killed the engine, and I turned to him. He looked like himself again now that he was back to wearing his suits.

He grinned. "Vinny will be disappointed that I've agreed to this without a higher charge. He wants me to up my acting rate after everything that's happened."

I leaned over and kissed his cheek. "He'll be more disappointed that you've vowed never to act again after this."

JD chuckled, then stepped out of the car. He moved to my side before I could open the door. Ever the gentleman, he offered his hand and helped me out. I smoothed my hands over the front of my charcoal-gray slacks, which I had paired with a cream blouse.

JD offered his arm. "Shall we?"

I smiled before settling my hand in the crook of his arm.

We walked up the flagstone path to the front door. When we reached the porch, I heard voices inside. We had arrived in time.

Ellwood was holding his emergency meeting, trying to rally support for his crusade against the magical community.

JD rang the doorbell, and the voices inside quieted. The door opened, revealing a man in his forties. Security, according to the bulge under his jacket

"Tatiana Sterling and Marcus Smith. We're here to see Senator Ellwood," I greeted pleasantly.

"I don't have you on the list."

JD's fluid grace and unmatched charisma swooped in. "We wouldn't be on the list, but Senator Ellwood will want to see us when he learns we have arrived."

The security guard's jaw tightened, but he stepped aside, speaking quietly into a radio. A moment later, he nodded. "This way."

We followed him through an opulent foyer with marble floors, a crystal chandelier, and an array of artwork that probably cost more than my business made in a year. Our walk through a hallway lined with family photos and political memorabilia ended at a set of double doors, already open. The room beyond was full of people—men and women in expensive suits, drinks in hand, expressions ranging from curious to hostile.

Malcolm Ellwood stood at the center of them all. "I apologize, ladies and gentlemen. I will need to speak with our new guests. Give me one moment." He stepped out of the room as necks craned behind him and several voices asked who we were. Ellwood strode to another room, an office.

He moved to stand behind a desk, keeping himself composed. No one had a chance to speak before a female figure appeared in the doorway. "Malcolm, what's going on? They said you paused the meeting." Her expression faltered as she took us in.

Emily Ellwood. I recognized her from the cover of Adeline Pike's magazine. She was in her mid-forties, blonde, and elegant in a way that spoke of old money and expensive taste. She wore a lilac silk blouse with a statement necklace—silver and emeralds.

Pike's issue displaying Emily would probably never see publication now that Adeline was in Conclave custody. A shame, since Mrs. Ellwood was quite beautiful. "Who are these people, Malcolm?" she asked, looking between us and her husband.

Ellwood's gaze fixed on JD in recognition. "Ms. Sterling and… Mr. Smith, is it? Or should I call you by your real name?"

JD's smile was all teeth. "Marcus is fine. We're keeping things professional."

"Emily, I will be finished in a moment. Why don't you go and rejoin our guests?"

Emily hesitated. She looked like she might do as he asked, but instead she turned and closed the study door. "This is my home, too, and you're clearly upset."

Ellwood looked like he wanted to argue but thought better of it. He faced us once more. "What do you want?"

"To make you an offer." I pulled a tablet from my bag and placed it on his desk. "We have been gathering information on your illegal task force. The one you have been funding with misappropriated federal resources. The surveillance operations on citizens without warrants, the detainment facilities you have been preparing for people you deem 'enhanced individuals.'"

Emily's face paled. "Malcolm, what is this woman talking about?"

Ellwood stammered, then his face hardened. "That is not how it is."

"Then how is it?" I asked.

JD spoke, his voice smooth and professional. "We also have testimony from Ms. Adeline Pike, your former chief of staff, detailing her role in your operations." He didn't mention that her cooperation was only the result of Conclave pressure. "She has been quite forthcoming about the nature of your arrangement."

Ellwood's cheeks reddened. He might have said we were bluffing, except he hadn't heard from Pike in days. All he knew was what his operatives had come back with, a story no one wanted leaking to the public.

I pulled up documents on the tablet. Jake had outdone himself, and I owed him a burger every day for the rest of the year. "We have sources at three separate government agencies willing to corroborate our findings. We have paper trails showing fund transfers and recordings of conversations between you and your operatives."

Ellwood's face went from red to ashen. "You can't prove any of this. It's all circumstantial…"

"We can prove all of it, and we will, if necessary. We are hoping that won't be the case," I told him.

"What do you want?" Ellwood demanded.

"We want you to kill your bill," JD returned. "The Enhanced Individual Registration and Containment Act. You go back to your colleagues and tell them that you've reconsidered. You will tell them that you've realized the legislation is too broad, invasive, and dangerous."

I continued. "In exchange, we keep this information to ourselves. We won't go to the press or the Justice Department. Your career survives."

"We will be watching you," JD added. "Make another move against the people we're protecting, and everything we have shown you goes public."

Ellwood's hands clenched into fists on his desk. "Are you blackmailing me?"

"Not blackmailing," JD replied. "We don't want your money. We only want to be left alone."

"We're offering you a choice. Comply or face consequences," I added.

Ellwood directed his heated stare at me. "And what if I refuse?"

"Then you will end up like Adeline Pike." I let him imagine what that meant. "Your choice."

The room fell silent. Emily placed a hand over her mouth as tears gathered in her eyes. Ellwood looked like he had aged ten years in the last five minutes. It was Emily who broke the silence, her voice shaking. "Malcolm, do what they say, please. I can't go through a scandal. Think of the children."

Ellwood's shoulders slumped. "Fine. I'll kill the bill and disband the task force."

"I knew you were smart." I picked up the tablet. "We'll be in touch if we need to remind you of our agreement."

JD and I started to leave, but at the office door, I turned. "Senator, if it helps you sleep at night, you should know that the people you were hunting are not the monsters you thought they were. They're trying to survive in a world that doesn't understand them. Same as everyone else."

Emily moved to her husband's side, her expression a mix of confusion and relief. Ellwood didn't respond. He should count himself lucky to still have his career and reputation. As we walked into the hallway, I heard Emily ask, "Malcolm, who are those people?"

His muttered reply made me grin. "Private security firm. That bitch doesn't know who she's messing with."

JD took my hand, and his lips tugged into a smile. "He's wrong. Ellwood doesn't know who *he's* messing with."

We let ourselves out into the cool evening air, and I drew in a deep breath.

"What now?" JD asked as he opened the passenger side door.

I slid into the seat but waited for him to enter the other side before I answered. "Are you asking as Jordan Davenport or Marcus Smith?"

JD started the car. "I'm asking as the man who loves you very much."

I hummed. "First, I want you to take me on a proper date, then back to your house. I went to spend a long time in your bed."

He chuckled, his eyes growing darker. "Trust me, Tatiana, I have very detailed plans for what we are doing tonight."

I grinned. I couldn't help myself.

"And after?" he asked as we pulled through the gate of the Ellwood estate.

I knew my answer. "We rebuild."

CHAPTER THIRTY

TATIANA

Two days later, I stood in JD's living room, now serving as our temporary office, and surveyed the organized chaos.

Linda had commandeered the dining table as her desk, her laptop surrounded by sticky notes and gel pens. Margo and Duncan were setting up a secure server in the corner of the living room. Brandon and Marc sat on the sofa, feet up, chowing down on bagels while they reviewed case files.

The space was cramped and messy and completely unprofessional.

It was perfect.

JD hadn't hesitated to offer his home as our office until we had a more permanent situation. The old office would be under renovation for months, if we were lucky, and it would take a miracle for Harry to let us back in to rent, even after Linda's begging.

I was kicking around the idea of looking for a new space altogether. Linda had already found some good property options with the help of a real estate friend. We now had the funds, and the idea of owning my office and not being subject to a landlord who wouldn't fix leaky pipes sounded nothing short of heaven.

The night before, I'd had Linda and my mom over to my apartment. Both had been surprised but delighted to see JD standing in my living room. They had greeted him as Marcus, and he'd smiled. "I'm glad you both could join us tonight. There's a lot to tell you."

They knew the truth now, though JD had left out most of his life story. They'd been shocked, of course, but everything made more sense to them. "We're just happy that you and Marcus… Sorry, Jordan, are okay now," my mom had commented.

Linda was less concerned with Jordan's enhanced abilities and background and more with our relationship status. "So what are you two now?"

"Dating," I'd replied simply, though "boyfriend" felt too small a word to apply to JD. We were busy enough with getting the security firm on stable footing. We could discuss our relationship further at another time.

JD had folded his hand over mine. "I love her, and I intend to love her as long as she allows me."

I'd ended the conversation before my mother and Linda could get weepy with gratitude.

JD emerged from his study after I asked Brandon and Marc to please clean up their bagel mess. My heart fluttered at the sight of him. He had changed out of his usual suit and into a Henley, looking more relaxed.

He hugged me and smiled. "I just got off the phone with Lucien. He told me all about the Conclave's reform committee. You know, for being as ancient as he is, he still has a strong diplomat in him."

"We should visit him. He sounds lonely," I suggested.

JD nodded, putting an arm around me. "We will do that."

"Everyone," I called, raising my voice. "Meeting in five minutes. Living room."

Brandon and Marc moved over to make room for Linda and Margo. Duncan remained standing behind the sofa, arms folded.

Jordan perched on the end of the couch, an eager listener, and I stood before them, my back to the fireplace.

"First things first, I want to thank you all for everything you've done over the past few weeks. You have gone above and beyond, faced dangers you never signed up for, and kept this company running despite…well, despite everything," I began.

"You're not firing us, are you?" Brandon asked.

"What? No. Why would I fire you?"

"I don't know. You had that serious tone."

"I'm always serious."

"True," Marco agreed.

I rolled my eyes. "As I was saying, we're going to be making some changes. Finding a new office space, for one, but I also want to talk about the future of Sterling and Smith."

"About that," Duncan mentioned. "Are we keeping the name? I mean, there's no actual Marcus Smith."

"'Sterling and Davenport' doesn't have the same ring," Margo pointed out.

JD chuckled. "I appreciate the consideration, but I think we should keep Sterling and Smith. It's already established, recognizable, and frankly, I'm happy to stay in the background."

"We will workshop some options, but for now, we'll keep the name as-is," I confirmed.

"If we're rebranding, I have some ideas for the fonts," Marc spoke up.

Brandon rolled his eyes. "No one wants to hear about fonts for the tenth time today, Marc. For Pete's sake." He turned to me. "Do we get vampire-level contracts now? Like, protecting werewolf CEOs?"

"Absolutely not. Insurance won't cover it," Margo immediately responded.

Linda spoke up. "Actually, I've been looking into specialized insurance for supernatural incidents. It's expensive, but it exists.

Apparently, we're not the first security firm to encounter these situations."

"Wait, you're seriously considering taking on magical clients?" Marc asked.

"I'm considering being open to all clients who need our help," I clarified, glancing at JD. He returned a small, reassuring smile. "We're in a unique position now. We know about both worlds, and we have contacts in both communities."

"Assuming we don't get killed," Duncan spoke up, but there was a gleam in his eye.

"There is that risk," JD inserted. "In my experience, Tatiana is very good at keeping people alive despite impossible odds."

I smiled at him and was about to continue when the doorbell rang. Everyone tensed, old habits from weeks of being hunted. JD checked the security camera, and his expression shifted to somewhere between wariness and resignation. "It's Jessamine."

Brandon shifted. "She didn't bring those two vampires with her, did she?"

"She's alone," JD reassured him.

"I'm surprised she doesn't just blow down the door," Margo murmured.

"I'll handle it." JD walked to the living room entrance. "The rest of you take a break. We'll finish this meeting later."

The team dispersed quickly, though I noticed Margo and Duncan positioned themselves within earshot in case things went south. I went with Jordan to open the front door.

Jessamine stood on the porch, looking as polished and intimidating as ever in a tailored black suit. She carried a leather portfolio and wore a neutral expression. "Ms. Sterling, Mr. Davenport. May I come in?"

I stepped aside and gestured her into the foyer. "To what do we owe this pleasure?"

"Conclave business," Jessamine stated crisply.

We moved to JD's study, which was more private. Jessamine

settled into one of the chairs, opened her portfolio, and withdrew several documents. "First, the guardianship agreement for Elias. It needs your signature, Jordan. Standard terms—you're responsible for his care, education, and integration into vampire society. He answers to you, and you answer to the Conclave if he becomes a problem." Exactly as they had discussed.

JD read the document carefully. The paperwork was bizarre, written in both English and what looked like Latin, with symbols in the margins that probably had magical significance.

When he agreed that it looked right, he asked, "Signage?"

He did not reach for a pen but waited until Jessamine produced the inkwell and quill I'd seen her use before in the security footage. JD was signing this contract in blood.

I still had plenty to get used to.

Jessamine continued as he signed. "Second, the Conclave is forming a reform committee. As you know, Lucien is heading it up. Their mandate is to modernize our approach, develop new protocols for the modern world, and create better systems for cooperation between magical factions.

"As part of this initiative, the Conclave is looking to bring in outside perspectives. People who understand both our world and the human one." She produced another document, this one stamped with an ornate seal. "We would like to offer you the position."

JD arched a brow. "Are you sure my 'flashy heroics' won't get in the way?"

"Not you," Jessamine's gaze slid to me.

I blinked. "Are you serious?"

Jessamine's expression remained unreadable. "Quite serious. The Conclave offers you a position as a liaison. A human adviser to help us navigate modern society, provide perspective on how humans might perceive our actions, and assist in developing strategies for coexistence rather than isolation."

I stared at her. "You want me to work for the vampire council."

"With, not for. You would maintain your independence and your own business. This would be a consulting arrangement, but with official status and authority."

JD was trying not to smile. I could feel his amusement radiating from across the desk.

"I...don't know what to say. I'll need to think it over."

"Of course. Take your time." Jessamine stood, gathering the papers Jordan had signed but leaving the one with the ornate seal. "I should mention that Lucien specifically requested you. He was quite impressed by your performance. He said you had 'the spine of a vampire but the heart of a human,' which I believe he meant as a compliment."

"I'll take it as one," I replied.

"He thought you may need time to consider the job, so for now, would you be willing to consult on a case-by-case basis? As situations arise where your perspective would be valuable?"

I could agree to that. "Yes, case-by-case works."

Jessamine moved toward the door, then paused. "Ms. Sterling, I want to be clear about something. I still believe you and Jordan made things unnecessarily complicated. I still believe you took risks that could have exposed us all. But..." She drew a breath, as if the next words pained her. "You also showed courage and integrity that is rare in either world. If we're going to survive the future, we need more people like you. So...thank you."

I could hardly believe it. Had Jessamine Lane really uttered the words "thank you" to me?

Before I could respond, she was gone, the door closing quietly behind her.

JD crossed the room and pulled me into a hug. "I'm proud of you."

I laughed against his chest. "For what?"

"For standing up to the Conclave. For changing their minds.

For being exactly who you are and refusing to apologize for it." He pulled back to look at me. "You're extraordinary, Tatiana Sterling."

Happy tears pricked my eyes. "We make a good team."

He smiled and kissed my hand. "The best."

From the living room, I heard Brandon shout, "Now that the scary lady is gone, are we doing the meeting or what? I've got questions about the werewolf CEO thing!"

JD laughed. "Your team awaits."

"Our team," I corrected.

EPILOGUE

JORDAN

I adjusted my tie in the mirror and smoothed down the navy fabric, the same shade I'd worn countless times as Marcus Smith. Some habits were hard to break, and my preference for navy suits was one of them.

Behind me, the bathroom door opened, and I glanced in the mirror as Tatiana emerged. She had forgone her usual ponytail for a half-up, half-down look. The hair that was down fell in soft waves past her shoulders. Her makeup was subtle but striking, making her eyes even more alluring. Her dress was midnight blue, fitted at the waist and draping to her feet.

I turned to see her properly, and I must have been drooling, because she laughed. "Do you like it?"

I picked my jaw up off the bedroom floor and scanned her head to toe. "You look…delightful."

She stood in front of me, reaching to adjust my tie. "Delightful? That's the best you can come up with after three hundred years?"

I grinned roguishly. "What can I say? You render me speechless. Stunning. Gorgeous. Breathtaking. Beautiful beyond measure. Shall I continue?" I captured her mouth with mine, my hands finding her waist and tugging her closer until our bodies were flush.

She melted against me, her fingers tangling in my hair, and for a moment, I forgot we would have a house full of guests soon.

"We could cancel," I murmured against her neck. "Tell everyone there's been an emergency."

She laughed. "What emergency would that be?"

"The one where I need you desperately. We could stay in this room all night. This dress is beautiful on you, but it would look even better on the floor."

Tatiana pulled back, but her cheeks were flushed, and she was smiling. "Tempting, Jordan. We have been planning this party for two weeks, and Elias would be disappointed."

As if summoned, Elias appeared in the doorway, scowling at his tie. "Why do humans insist on wearing nooses around their necks?"

Tatiana slipped away from me with a laugh. "Because we're civilized, Elias. Let Jordan help you."

I nearly groaned at the loss of her warmth and gave her a look that promised what, exactly, I would be doing with her dress later, after everyone left. I moved to Elias and began working on his tie. "It won't feel like a noose if you wear it right."

He glowered but let me work. Elias had grown more comfortable in the month since coming to live with me, his initial wariness giving way to cautious trust.

The doorbell rang downstairs, and Tatiana's eyes lit up. "I'll go let them in. You two finish getting ready."

She kissed my cheek and hurried out, her heels clicking on the hardwood floor.

Elias fidgeted with his cufflinks. "Are you sure this is a good idea? Having all these people over?"

"They're friends. People who know what you are and don't care," I reminded him.

"I've never been good with people," Elias remarked quietly.

Despite his seventy years of life, he had not spent much time in group settings.

"You're safe here, Elias. With me and Tatiana, all of them. No one is going to hurt you."

He nodded, but he still looked nervous. Seventy years as a vampire, and he seemed like a scared ten-year-old about to face his first day of school. "Come on." I nudged him toward the door. "The sooner we get down there, the easier everything will be."

We descended the stairs together. Now that the makeshift office furniture was gone, the place was beginning to look like a home again. Tatiana had found a property and was gradually turning it into the new Sterling and Smith headquarters.

In the front hallway, Tatiana had opened the door to Beck and Miranda. Vinny stood on the porch, declaring, "Am I ever going to be let in?"

"Elias!" Beck called when she saw us. "Come and tell us how your first month has been."

Elias' face brightened, melting away the nerves. His two weeks in Beck and Miranda's care had been enough to make him comfortable with them.

As Vinny stepped inside, a fourth figure appeared. Jake Molina carried a bottle of Scotch and a laptop bag. Elias spotted him and grinned.

"Hey, kid. I brought that coding tutorial I was telling you about."

Jake and Elias had been introduced two weeks ago, on a day that Tatiana and Jake needed to meet in my living room. Though wary of him at first, Elias had taken an interest in Jake's work. "The one about encryption algorithms?"

Jake winked. "We can work on it after dinner if you want."

Tatiana had hardly closed the front door and ushered the first four guests, along with Elias, into the living room before the doorbell rang again. I opened it this time to greet Margo, Duncan, Brandon, and Marc. Margo leaned toward Tatiana and muttered, "Don't ever let me agree to carpool with these men again."

Tatiana's laugh was bright enough to light up the whole room.

Linda and Harry arrived next, with Whiskers in a harness. The cat ambled down the hall with the air of a king surveying his domain and selected a spot by the living room window. Harry headed directly for the table we'd arranged in the living room, laden with enough refreshments to feed an army.

Last to arrive was Amy Sterling, a bottle of wine in hand. She hugged me first. "Jordan, this is lovely. Thank you for hosting."

I smiled. "Thank you for coming."

She kissed Tatiana's cheek. "My, don't you look lovely."

Tatiana escorted her mother into the living room to join the others, and I brought up the rear. We settled in with food and drinks. I caught Tatiana's eye across the room. She nodded and moved to stand with me in front of the fireplace.

"Everyone?" I called, raising my voice enough to be heard. "Can we have your attention for a moment?"

The conversation died down as all eyes turned toward us. Linda had her phone out, ready to capture whatever moment was coming. Beck and Miranda were holding hands, smiling like they already knew what we were going to say.

"Tatiana and I have some news," I continued, my hand finding hers. "As you all know, she has found an office space that will perfectly fit the needs of the firm."

"And get us all out of your hair," Duncan added.

I smiled, and Tatiana picked up where I'd left off. "The office is an inconvenient drive from my apartment, and with my lease being up next month, Jordan and I thought, what better time than now for me to move in?"

Linda squealed, and the others broke into a smattering of applause. Amy's eyes filled with joy, and she immediately looked at Tatiana with an expression that clearly said, *Grandchildren when?*

"Don't start," Tatiana warned her mother, but she was laughing.

Amy put on an innocent air. "I'm just saying, I'm not getting any younger."

Beck raised her glass. "To Jordan and Tatiana. May you have many happy years together."

"To Jordan and Tatiana," everyone echoed, glasses raised.

Tatiana turned to me, her eyes bright, and I couldn't help myself. I kissed her in front of everyone. The kiss was met with more cheers, some good-natured catcalls from Brandon, and Vinny's dramatic sigh about young love.

"We're not young," I murmured against her lips.

She laughed. "Speak for yourself, old man."

<u>Tatiana</u>

The party had shifted into full swing by the time I headed to the kitchen for a refill on wine. The living room was full of laughter and conversation. Someone had put on music, and Marc was explaining a board game that sounded more complicated than the current tax codes. Through the windows, I glimpsed the clear night sky.

I was pouring myself a glass of the white wine my mother had brought when she joined me, her own glass in hand. "This is nice, seeing you so happy. I don't think I've ever seen you this relaxed."

"It has been a good month. Stressful in some ways with setting up the new office, making sure Elias adjusts, keeping an eye on Ellwood…" I sipped from my glass. "But good."

"Jordan makes you happy."

It wasn't a question, but I answered anyway. "He does. More than I thought possible."

"That's all I care about. And your father would be proud. He would have loved Jordan." My mom squeezed my arm, and my eyes misted. The only thing that could have made this night more perfect would have been having my dad there. "Though I do have questions about the whole sunlight thing for future family dinners," my mother added.

I laughed. "We'll figure it out. There are ways around it. Covered patios, late afternoon timing, that sort of thing."

"Good, because I refuse to have a son-in-law I can only see after dark." She paused. "He is going to be my son-in-law, right? Eventually?"

"Mom." I couldn't help but smile.

"I'm just asking!"

"Let's maybe get through the moving-in phase before we start planning weddings."

I kept smiling because the truth was, I'd thought about it. A future with JD that wasn't measured in cases, but in years.

We returned to the living room, where the party had only gotten louder. The conversation was full of laughter and friendly arguing. Brandon wanted to play pool, not the complicated strategy game Marc suggested.

I scanned the room, looking for JD, but didn't spot him. As Margo passed me to refill her plate, I asked where he had gone. "Bathroom, I think," she replied.

He wasn't in the downstairs hall restroom, so I headed upstairs. His bedroom bathroom was empty, too. Then, I noticed the balcony door was slightly ajar. I stepped through, and the balmy night air greeted me.

Jordan leaned over the railing, his hands folded idly as he looked out over the property. His expression was thoughtful.

"Hiding from your own party?" I teased, standing beside him.

"Taking a moment," he replied. "It's been a while since I've had this many people in my home. I'd forgotten what it feels like."

"Good or bad?"

"Good." He faced me, his expression serious. "Tatiana, there's something we should talk about."

My stomach clenched.

He took my hands in his. "You're human. I'm not. Which means you're going to age, and I won't. In ten years, you will look ten years older. In twenty, twenty years older. I will still look exactly like this."

He didn't finish the thought. That I would die much sooner than him, if age was the reason I went.

"I know," I replied quietly, letting my gaze fall to our joined hands.

The words hung between us, heavy with implication. I had thought about this, of course. How could I not? But hearing him say it out loud made it real in a way it hadn't been before.

"You could be turned. It isn't something to decide lightly, of course. It's permanent and painful at first, but it would mean we'd have centuries together instead of decades."

I looked up at the man who had somehow become the center of my world. "I can't do it now."

His expression flickered with something that might have been disappointment, but he nodded. "I understand."

I added quickly, "I'm not saying never. Just...not yet. Right now, I like being human. I like working for things, fighting for things, knowing my time is limited so I make it count more. I like eating food and sleeping and feeling the sun on my face. Maybe someday, that will change. Maybe I will be ready to give all that up for more time." I squeezed his hand. "Can you wait?"

He smiled. "Tatiana, I have waited hundreds of years for you. I think I can manage twenty more."

We kissed, softer this time, tender and full of promise. The future stretched out before us, uncertain in its length but certain in one crucial way.

We would face it together, for however long we had.

From downstairs, I heard the unmistakable opening notes of "Don't Stop Believin'" blasting at maximum volume.

I groaned. "I believe my mother has brought her karaoke machine."

JD laughed. "Your mother has had almost a full bottle of wine." He offered an arm. "Shall we rejoin our friends?"

We headed back inside and down to the party, where sure enough, my mother had set up a karaoke machine and was currently butchering Journey with enthusiastic abandon. Linda and Harry danced, while Whiskers watched from the back of the sofa with feline judgment.

Brandon grabbed the microphone next, launching into an off-key rendition of "Livin' on a Prayer" that had Margo covering her ears. Duncan and Marc provided backup vocals, which somehow made it worse.

Jake tried to escape to the kitchen, but Vinny dragged him back, insisting he had to sing at least one song. Beck and Miranda swayed together near the fireplace, laughing.

Elias sat on the sofa between Jake and Vinny, watching the spectacle with wide eyes. Slowly, a smile spread across his lips. It was not the polite smile he had been wearing all evening, but a real smile. He laughed. The sound was rusty, unpracticed, like he had forgotten somehow. It bubbled up from somewhere deep inside.

JD slipped an arm around my waist and pulled me close. "You did this. You gave us this. A family, a home."

"*We* did this," I told him.

I looked around the room, at my mother murdering another '80s classic, at my team singing backup and dancing, at Beck and Miranda and Vinny and Harry and Linda and even Whiskers. JD was right. We were all family. Human and vampire and shifter and warlock and cat. Bound not only by blood, but by choice, loyalty, and the simple decision to show up for each other when it mattered.

Brandon finished his song and tried to pass the microphone to me. "Your turn, boss!"

"Absolutely not."

"Come on! You have to sing at least one song!"

"I really don't."

"I'll sing with you," JD offered, his eyes gleaming with mischief.

I stared at him. "You're seriously going to make me do this?"

"Partners share everything, including public humiliation."

I couldn't help but smile. We sang "Summer Nights" off-key, forgetting some of the lyrics. The room joined in, and when we finished, a chorus of cheers, laughter, and applause broke out.

JD pulled me close and kissed me. I let the world narrow to only him and me.

Tomorrow, there would be cases to solve, enemies to face, and a whole magical world navigating its way into the modern age. There would be challenges and dangers and moments when everything hung in the balance. But tonight was for cake and terrible karaoke and the people who had become my family.

When our lips parted, I told JD, "Don't ever make me sing that again."

His eyes gleamed. "No promises, Sterling."

MICHAEL'S NOTES

DECEMBER 8, 2025

<u>**Las Vegas, NV**</u>

First, thank you for not only reading this story, but these author notes in the back as well!

<u>Honey, I Shrunk the Doctor</u>
<u>(And He's Swimming Through Your Veins)</u>

Scientists have created a remote-controlled robot **the size of a grain of sand** that can swim through your blood vessels, deliver drugs to a specific location, and then *dissolve into your body*.

Let me say that again: **A robot. In your blood. That dissolves when it's done.**

I've been writing about nanobots for years. YEARS. And now they're real. They're swimming through blood vessels. They're delivering drugs directly to tumors instead of poisoning your whole body with chemotherapy. And when they're finished? They just… disappear.

The future is here and it's smaller than a grain of sand.

***Note:** *I've done chemotherapy – I'm ready for the little machine's, please.*

Here's where my brain immediately went: Can I swallow a pill full of these little bastards and have them eat the fat around my gut? Asking for a friend. That friend is me. I am the friend.

Turns out, researchers are already exploring targeted therapies for all kinds of conditions including diabetes monitoring, cancer treatment, even delivering drugs to specific tissues that regular medicine can't reach. The nanobots can sense their environment, detect tumor cells, and release their payload based on local temperature or pH changes.

So theoretically? Fat cells. Diabetes management. Blood sugar monitoring from INSIDE your body. It's all on the table.

These things can navigate through viscous biological fluids like tiny submarines, reaching places conventional medical tools can't access. They're working on brain-targeted drug delivery. Nerve regeneration. Blood clot removal.

I write science fiction, and I'm sitting here reading actual scientific papers about microscopic robots dissolving inside people after completing their missions, thinking "I didn't make this up hard enough."

The challenges are still real which include (but not limited to…hehehe) propulsion efficiency, biocompatibility, imaging them in real-time inside the human body. But the fact that we're talking about *challenges* instead of "this is impossible fantasy nonsense from some space-opera author with more creativity than common sense" tells you everything you need to know about where we are.

We're not asking, *"can we do this?"* anymore. We're asking, *"how do we do this better?"*

The implications are staggering. Precision medicine where the treatment goes ONLY where it's needed. No more carpet-bombing your body with drugs and hoping the cancer dies before you do.

(I had 3 courses, I was willing to go a few weeks before course 4 because I really wasn't sure why life was worth living at that moment. It wasn't as ominous as I just made that sound, it was more NOTHING TASTED GOOD AND I DIDN'T WANT TO EAT ANYMORE.)

Ok, back to the earlier conversation. There would be no more systemic side effects with these little bugs because the medication never touches healthy tissue.

Just tiny robots. Swimming through your blood. Doing their job. Then vanishing.

F#$# me. I need to go update about half my books.

Ad Aeternitatem,
Michael Anderle

P.S. - If these things can eventually target fat cells, I'm first in line. I don't care if they have to swim upstream. Get in there, little guys.

P.P.S. - The fact that they dissolve is both reassuring and slightly terrifying. "Where did the robots go?" "They're part of you now." Cool. Cool cool cool.

Wait, does that mean a magnet will pull them out, and I'll have little red splotches of blood as they get yanked out?
MORE STORIES with Michael newsletter HERE: https:// michael.beehiiv.com/

BOOKS BY MICHAEL ANDERLE

Sign up for the LMBPN email list to be notified of new releases and special deals!

https://lmbpn.com/email/

For a complete list of books by Michael Anderle, please visit:

www.lmbpn.com/ma-books/

CONNECT WITH MICHAEL ANDERLE

Website: lmbpn.com

Email List: michael.beehiiv.com/

Facebook: Facebook.com/LMBPNPublishing

Twitter/X: Twitter.com/MichaelAnderle

Instagram: Instagram.com/lmbpn_publishing/

Bookbub: Bookbub.com/authors/michael-anderle